CREDO'S HONOR

ALISON NAOMI HOLT

Denabi Publishing

ACKNOWLEDGMENTS

I'd like to thank my wonderful cover artist, Kat McGee, from Covers Unbound, for creating all the covers for the Alex Wolfe Mystery Series.

CHAPTER 1

Grumpy because my sergeant, Kate Brannigan, had dragged me out of bed at an ungodly hour for someone else's case, I peered over the lip of the dumpster, "Yup."

"Yup?" Tucson Police Homicide Sergeant Jon Logan pulled the zipper on his quilted coat a little higher, then stepped up next to me and leaned towards the green metal container, carefully keeping his hands behind his back to forestall accidentally touching the several years accumulation of putrid grease, old burger meat and dried milkshakes lining the edge of the rim. Little white puffs streamed from his mouth with each breath.

The two of us stood in a dead-end alley to the side of a neighborhood greasy spoon. He was a handsome man, blonde even into his forties, with a quick wit and a sharp, questioning mind.

Midnight had come and gone and other than our flashlights, the only illumination was from the red and yellow neon sign of the Sling 'Em burger joint blinking above the opening to the alley.

Sling 'Em's claim to fame was their "world famous" Beefcake Sliders —a two-ounce beef patty slathered in an oily pink secret sauce and tucked into an unwholesome white bread bun.

Kate had come to the call-out as well, and when she walked up, I turned to her and shrugged. "He's dead."

Logan moved to stand next to her and it occurred to me they could have been the models for Mattel's Ken and Barbie dolls. Kate's ponytail perfectly matched the coloring of his hair, but now that I thought about it, she didn't have Barbie's buxom body. She was well built though and not someone you wanted to take on in a fight.

It was obvious Logan wasn't happy about being called out for the third time in three consecutive nights and the sarcasm of his next words were in direct proportion to his accumulated sleep deprivation. "He's dead? What was your first clue, Alex? Of course, he's dead, you m—." He stopped himself in the middle of the word, raised his hands in surrender before rubbing his tired eyes.

I shrugged. "I wasn't sure you'd seen the hole in his face big enough to drive a locomotive through. Why does the homicide unit need me to come to one of their scenes, anyway? The guy's dead, Sarge. It's your case, right?"

His homicide detectives had finished setting up the portable lights and the dumpster was suddenly bathed in so much light that even the rats paused to squint in blind stupefaction before scurrying out of sight.

Sgt. Logan shielded his eyes with an upraised hand. "The killing has all the earmarks of an execution. Since you've become the de facto expert on the local mafia, we thought you might know who it is."

A second set of lights switched on, illuminating the parking lot in front of the restaurant. I blinked at Kate who looked as awake and well-groomed as she usually does when she first walks into the office at nine in the morning. Confused about why they'd dragged me out of bed for a run-of-the-mill homicide, I ran a hand through my sleep-induced mohawk trying to get it to lay down. "Doesn't he have I.D?"

The muscles of Logan's jaws twitched, his growing irritation showing in the ever-tightening muscles along his shoulders and neck. "If he had I.D, *Alex*, do you think I would have called you out here?"

I didn't like his snarky tone, but when Kate crossed her arms and began tapping her pen on her forearm, I turned back to the bin and mumbled, "No, Sir. I guess not." Logan was one of the few really good sergeants on the department and I didn't want to irritate him anymore than I already had.

Truth be told, I hate dead bodies. I can compartmentalize just about everything about my job, but I have a difficult time shutting out certain images and odors whenever I sit in front of a plate of food that resembles some aspect of a mutilated corpse.

When I'd worked patrol, I'd had a call where an old man had died alone while sitting in his Barcalounger eating refried beans. The beans had nothing to do with his death, but the sight of them flowing out of his mouth had soured me on anything remotely resembling smashed Pinto beans.

Realizing I wasn't going to be able to get away with a cursory look, I, Alexandra Wolfe, a one hundred twenty-five-pound, five foot six, brown-haired, brown-eyed detective in the Tucson Police Department Special Crimes unit, steeled myself and once more peered over the green dumpster's rim.

Gunshot wounds to the head tend to follow standard patterns, one of which is unless the entire face is blown off from a shotgun blast or a large caliber weapon, the entry hole will be small and the exit large, but the end result is usually at least part of the face is left intact to make an identification.

Unfortunately, this victim, lying on his side on a bed of discarded buns and old lettuce, had been shot point blank in the back of his head, thus blowing out most of his face and rendering him unrecognizable.

Except... I moved to the side of the dumpster to get a better view of what was left of the lower part of his face. I glanced up at Logan, "Can I move the head to get a better look?"

Logan shouted to Detective Andy Montagne, who'd been working homicides for as long as I've been in special investigations, "You finished taking pics yet, Montagne?"

The too-handsome-for-his-own-good Montagne straightened after photographing something on the sidewalk leading into the restaurant. He pushed a shock of his thick black hair out of his eyes and gave Logan the thumbs up. "All good, Boss."

When Logan lifted his chin in my direction indicating I could do whatever I needed to do, I pulled a pair of latex gloves from my pocket, wrestled them on and stepped onto a wooden box someone had set next to the dumpster. Leaning in, but still careful not to touch the rim with any part of my body, I gingerly put my fingers on the man's jaw and turned the head so it faced me straight on.

Kate and Logan moved closer and craned their necks to get a closer look at the pulpy mess that remained attached to the neck by a few strands of skin and sinew.

Most everything above the mouth had been blown apart, but a quick look at the lips confirmed what I already suspected. I'd caught a glimpse of it during my first cursory peek over the rim but turning the mouth away from a ketchup covered fry confirmed my suspicions. A v-shaped scar bisected the man's lower lip, exposing a couple of fake teeth that had been jolted loose by the blast.

Kate motioned with a gloved hand. "Pito?"

"That'd be my guess."

Logan's brows came down low. "Pito?"

Nodding, I used my thumb and forefinger to move a piece of limp lettuce off the sleeve of the man's right arm. I pushed up the overcoat, undid the button on the shirt cuff and pulled it back, exposing a line of six small, gray, amateurishly inked tattoos that vaguely resembled human skulls stair stepping the inside of the arm. "Agapito Mancini, a bodyguard for the Angelino family."

Sergeant Logan indicated the skulls, "More like a hitman than a bodyguard. Each of those skulls represent a body he's put in the ground."

Since Gianina Angelino, the head of the Angelino crime family, is a friend of mine, I bristled at his implications, regardless of the fact that he was absolutely correct. "He was a *bodyguard*," I emphasized the word, "who came to Tucson to protect Ms. Angelino after the Andrulis family killed her father."

He shrugged. "Whatever. Looks like this is your case if you want it, Kate. We're swamped right now and could use the help. Some lowlife gangster gets blown away, it's not like it's going to make the front-page news."

I started shaking my head. "No, no, Kate. That's not a good idea." I really didn't want to be the one investigating Gia or anyone else among her circle of friends...or...enemies—I never could be sure on a day-to-day basis which was which.

Pito, an obnoxious, loathsome, nasty little toad was universally disliked among the various mafia syndicates, and I wouldn't be surprised if someone in the Angelino family had decided to give the guy a final facial.

"You have something against doing your job, Detective Wolfe?" Kate's tone was one that brooked no dissent.

"No, but—"

"No? Glad to hear it." She turned back to Logan. "Can your people leave the lights in place? I'll have my guys return them when we're through." She pulled her cellphone off her belt and began composing a group callout text to the other members of our unit.

Logan nodded once. "No problem, and thanks. I owe you one." He walked out to the middle of the parking lot and motioned his people over. I heard him tell them to go home and one by one they ducked beneath the yellow crime scene tape and drove away in their sedans.

I glared down at Pito, thinking he'd been a thorn in my side ever since the day I'd met him and cursed the guy for getting his head blown off, in the middle of the night no less, just to aggravate and inconvenience me one last time.

"Start searching around the dumpster and in the parking lot while we're waiting for the others to arrive." Kate's gaze roamed over the garbage surrounding the body, expertly taking in every little detail. "You and Casey will have to dump this trash out onto tarps and go through it after the body is removed."

I held my hands out to the sides. "Kate, this is Pito. Agapito piece of shit Mancini. Do we really care who did us the favor of blowing his little peabrain all over creation?"

Kate stepped so close I could see the gold flecks in her otherwise dark brown eyes. "Sometimes I wonder whether you'd rather go back to patrol instead of being part of my investigative unit."

Sighing, I held my hands up in surrender. "Okay, okay. You're right." I buttoned the topmost buttons on my quilted winter coat and silently thanked the gods Pito hadn't carked it in the middle of summer. At least he'd saved me from the stench of rotting flesh and the irritating buzz of hungry flies.

I returned to my car, popped open the trunk and searched around for my dwindling supply of evidence bags. This was my third callout this week, and I hadn't had time to restock. I found some and while I was stuffing them into my pocket, an emaciated teenager sidled over and leaned her hip against my car.

I'd seen her a couple of times walking Miracle Mile, the local boulevard frequented by hookers and their johns, and I motioned to her skinny legs barely covered by an extremely short miniskirt and her light blue sweater, the ends of which she held pulled in close around her chest. "You should be inside the Sling 'Em. Where're the rest of your clothes? You'll freeze to death dressed like that."

When her lips pulled back in a fake semblance of a smile, a smile that probably hadn't reached her eyes in a very long time, the gaping holes and rotted black teeth told me everything I needed to know. She lifted one shoulder and spoke with a timid, childlike voice. "Don't let folks in if ya got no scratch. If ya can't buy no burger, they kick ya out." She pulled the sweater tighter and lifted her chin toward the dumpster. "I'm th' one foun' 'im. I was lookin' fer slops they throwed in th' trash."

"Did you tell that to the other detectives who were here first?"

"Nope." She shook her head back and forth. "Dempsey..." She raised her chin off her chest and squinted at me. "You know Dempsey?"

I nodded and tried to keep the derision I felt for the man off my face.

"So, Dempsey spit on my shoes when I walked up t' tell him. He used t' wanna give me a bam in th' ham when he wore th' blues, but now he won't even look at me." We both looked down at her tattered secondhand Nikes. I could see the wet spot on the toe where the spit had landed and she moved that foot behind the other to hide it.

"What's your name?"

"Cherry."

"No, I mean your real name."

She blinked a few times and slowly shook her head. "I been Cherry so long, before don't mean nothin'. I'm just Cherry, now."

I studied her a minute and had to change my first impression of her age. She had the rail thin look of an anorexic teen, but when I took the time to really look at her, the signs of age became apparent. Small wrinkles fanned out from the edges of her eyes and her cheeks hung looser than they would on a teenager. Despite the fact that a heavy meth addiction had robbed her of several teeth, a young woman's skin should have been a bit tighter and have a lot less stretch. I'd say mid to late twenties, maybe? Thirty? It was hard to know.

"Let's go inside, Cherry. I'll buy you a burger and you can warm up and tell me about finding the body."

Cherry looked behind her and then over at Kate, suspicious of any kindness coming her way.

I grabbed my recorder out of the car and walked toward the restaurant, hoping she'd follow.

Kate called over to me, "Alex?"

"I need to do a quick interview, Boss."

Kate sized up Cherry and must have realized if I didn't get the woman's story now we'd likely never get it. She nodded and waved her notepad at me before stepping off some measurement or another. We'd get precise measurements when the rest of the unit arrived, but I'd been with her long enough to know she was working out a possible scenario and would enlighten us when she thought the time was right.

I held the door open for Cherry, who looked like a dog about to get a beating as she lightly stepped over the threshold.

The night manager, a clean-shaven man in his forties, started our way, ready to cut Cherry off at the pass.

I wrestled my badge out from under my heavy jacket and held it up. "She's with me." To make sure he understood we were paying customers, I turned to Cherry and asked, "What would you like? You can have anything on the menu."

She studied the menu board high on the wall behind an elderly woman manning the cash register.

The plumpish, gray-haired woman had a kind smile and gave Cherry an encouraging nod. "Can you read okay, Sweetie Pie? I'm happy to help if..." She spoke with a slight southern drawl as her deep green eyes took in Cherry's thin sweater and bare legs. Her gaze flicked to me and pity poured off her in waves.

Closing her lips and lifting her hand to her mouth to hide her ruined teeth, Cherry gave the woman a small nod. "Yes, Ma'am, I kin read."

There were no other customers in the place at this time of night and the woman, whose name tag read, Annalee, nodded her approval. "Take your time, then. There's a lot to choose from."

Cherry glanced at me. "I don't eat much. I get full real easy."

I pulled my wallet out of my coat pocket. "That's okay. Order what you want and you can take what you don't eat with you. Save it for later, if you like."

That decided her and she moved closer to the counter. "Could I please have a cup of hot coffee, a batter fried fish sandwich, some french fries..."

Her cheeks flushed a faint shade of pink when she turned to me. "Do you mind if I get an apple fritter? My momma used to buy me fritters whenever she had a few extra dollars. They always remind me of her."

"Sure. Get whatever you want."

"And one of them apple fritters, please."

The woman looked at me and I held up two fingers. She nodded and added an extra fritter to the order. "And for you?"

"Just a hot chocolate, please."

"Oh...they have hot chocolate?"

"Make that two hot chocolates and another coffee for my sergeant outside."

The woman smiled. "That'll be on the house since you're law enforcement."

I quickly shook my head. "No Ma'am, I always pay for what I get, but I appreciate the offer." Annalee quickly filled the order and after I'd paid and had Cherry safely ensconced in a corner booth where I could watch her through the huge plate glass window, I grabbed the extra coffee and took it out to Kate. "Here you go, Boss. This should help warm you up."

Pulling off her glove, she gingerly took the hot cup and nodded her thanks. "Who's the girl?"

I glanced back to make sure Cherry was still inside. "She says she's the one who found the body."

"Didn't she give a statement to the homicide dicks?"

I thought about how to answer that. Even though Dempsey is a waste of a good badge, it went against my grain to rat on the guy.

Kate must have seen my hesitation because after she took a sip, she said, "Never mind. I get it. Go get her statement and then come back out and search around that dumpster."

"Yes, Ma'am." I returned to the lovely warmth of the seating area and sat facing the front door instead of the one that read "Employees only" that opened onto the crime scene, since Kate was in the alley and would cover my back if need be.

Cherry had bypassed the fish sandwich and had gone directly to the fritters. She nibbled on the last bite of the second one as I took the cap off my hot chocolate to let it cool.

I'd had Sling 'Em's hot drinks before and knew they'd scald the hair off a gorilla's knuckles if you didn't let them cool before taking a sip. "Do you mind if I ask you questions while you eat? My sergeant's anxious for me to get back out to help." It didn't matter if she minded or not, but I figured it didn't hurt to be courteous to someone to whom the idea of getting respect from another person was a foreign concept.

"No, I don't mind." She unwrapped the fish sandwich and took a tiny bite, setting the remainder neatly on the wax paper she'd laid out in front of her.

While she moved the food around in her mouth, probably trying to find a tooth that actually worked, I brought out my notepad and the recorder and set it on the table in front of us. "This is Detective Alexandra Wolfe..." I went on to give the date and time before introducing Cherry. "You told me your name is Cherry. Can you give me your last name?"

She glanced down at the recorder. "Don't remember it."

"People usually remember their name."

She lifted her shoulder. "I don't."

"Can you tell me why you don't?"

She chuckled half-heartedly, "Too many drugs, I s'pose."

"Do you remember your birthdate?"

"January fourth."

"What year?"

She lifted a shoulder. "Nineteen-ninety probably. That's what my Momma thought, but she wasn't too good on rememberin' neither."

I wrote down 1/4/90, added a question mark and tapped the pen on the pad. I doubted we'd ever be able to find her again, let alone use her as a witness, but I decided she might accidentally give me something I could follow up on. I reluctantly continued with my questions. "Where do you live?"

"In the tunnels under Fourth Avenue."

"Cherry, you told me you were the one to find the man in the dumpster. Can you tell me some more about what you saw?"

"Well, around eleven-thirty, I know it was around then 'cuz they usually dump whatever burgers 'n such they don't sell out there in the dumpster. When I got here I—"

"How did you get here?"

"I walked. I don't own no car. Anyways..." She took another small bite of her battered fish and carefully set it down again. "I went to see what they'd left and when I looked in, I saw that man."

"How did you know it was a man?"

"Jus' the way he was dressed. Couldn't tell by his face or nothin'."

"Did you see anyone else around?"

"Not really. Jus' Tom Handy."

Tom is a seventy-something Vietnam vet who panhandles more money in a month than I earn from the department. He lives in an RV parked out in the desert with his dog, a lurcher named Max. "Where did you see Tom?"

"He was leanin' over the edge of the dumpster when I walked up. I thought he was gettin' all the burgers so I yelled out, 'Leave some fer me, Tom!'"

I nodded, waiting for her to continue.

"So, Tom jumps back real quick like, an' it looks like he's got somethin' in his hand."

"Food?"

"Don't know. Don't think so. He had a small knife in one hand an' he jammed somethin' inta his pocket with th' other."

"What did he jam into his pocket? Which pocket?"

"Don't know what he stuffed in there, but it was his coat pocket."

"That old green World War II field jacket he wears?"

"Nuh uh. He got a warmer one for when it gets cold like this. It's..." Her brow crinkled while she tried to figure out a way to describe it. "Well, ya ever seen the book called Moby Dick?"

"Yes." I smiled, curious as to where her meth addled brain might be taking me.

"It reminds me of Captain Ahab's coat. Kinda black or maybe dark blue." She shrugged. "I dunno, somthin' like that."

I tilted my head trying to picture Ahab on the cover of the book. "You mean like a peacoat?"

"Dunno what it's called, but my momma read me that book over an' over an' over again. I used t' love the pictures an' such."

"Where's your momma now?"

"Dead. Long time ago."

"Where did you live with your Momma when she was still alive?"

"A little town called Artesia Wells."

"Where's that?"

"Texas."

"And your Dad?"

"Went to prison for killin' Momma."

I felt like I was in the middle of a bad western. Papa kills Momma and ends up in the hoosegow. Children left to fend for themselves, oldest daughter turns to prostitution and gets hooked on meth. Only I knew there wouldn't be any happy ending to this one. My guess was Cherry would last another month at best and we'd probably find her frozen in a fetal position down in the tunnels. "Can you give me any idea what Tom had in his hand?"

"Nuh uh."

"Paper? Hamburger, money?"

"Well, it kinda looked like part of a chain hangin' down before he stuffed it in his pocket, but I can't say fer sure." The fritters and the few bites she'd taken of the fish had apparently filled her up because she wrapped the rest in the red and yellow checked wrapper and put it back into the bag with the fries.

Headlights lit up the interior of the restaurant before suddenly winking out. I twisted around and saw my partner, Casey Bowman, getting out of her sedan. She walked over to talk to Kate and I turned back to Cherry. "What kind of chain? A bike chain? A dog chain?"

"A chain, you know." She put her fingers around her neck.

"A necklace?"

Nodding, she let her hand drop back into the bag and pulled out a french fry. "Maybe." Nibbling the fry, she nodded slightly. "Maybe."

"Cherry. This is important. Can you describe what little of the chain you saw? Anything."

Her forehead wrinkled again while she tried to concentrate on what she'd seen. "Kinda black."

I blinked and sat back. "Black? The chain was black?"

She shook her head. "Not really the chain. I mean, it dangled like a chain, but it weren't no chain."

Okay, the lack of synapses in her meth damaged brain was beginning to give me a headache.

"I mean..." She paused to allow the tiny protein dude in her brain to jump the chasm between synapse and receptor. "Maybe there were baubles or somethin' on a chain. Black baubles."

Sighing, I dutifully wrote down 'black baubles.'

"It was dark. I just seen it for a second."

I didn't want to discourage her cooperation, so I said, "That's okay. Which hand was the knife in?"

She blinked in confusion and then turned around in the booth so her back was to me. Presumably she now faced the same way Tom had faced when he looked at her. "This one." She held up her right hand and wiggled her fingers and then turned back around.

"What did Tom do when you called out to him?"

"He took off, kinda runnin', you know, th' way he kinda hops and then runs and then hops again?"

The bell above the door sounded and I looked back to find Casey striding toward us. "Kate wants to know how much longer you're gonna be." She lifted her chin in Cherry's direction. "Hey, Cherry. How ya doin'?" Apparently she and Cherry were acquainted, which didn't surprise me because she had a soft spot for the down and out.

I held up a finger asking Casey to wait a second.

She dipped her chin once before moving to the register and ordering something from Annabel.

"Anything else you think I should know about?"

"You mean besides the man's face bein' blowed off?"

"Yeah, besides that."

"No, Ma'am."

I suddenly remembered one last question. "Oh, did you take anything out of the dumpster?"

She shook her head. "No, Ma'am. Them burgers didn't look so good no more."

Stomach a little queasy at that last tidbit, I turned off the recorder and stood. "Wait here a minute." I went out to my car and pulled my workout bag from the trunk. I took my sweatshirt and sweatpants out and rezipped the bag before returning to where Cherry waited obediently in the corner booth. "Here. Put these on. They're clean." Right after I added that last part, I realized how stupid I sounded. Clean to her meant they'd been washed in the last two months.

She stared at my offering before lowering her head. "No, thank you. You done fed me an' all and I can't take your clothes, too."

I set them on the table. "Yes, you can." I knelt beside her. "Listen, Cherry. You know we can get you into a program, right? You don't have to live like this."

She stood and carefully folded over the top of the bag a couple of times.

Knowing she'd never go into a program where she couldn't get her fix, I straightened and picked up the sweatshirt. "Look, these are workout clothes. I'm allergic to gyms, so you'd actually be doing me a favor by taking them." I held open the bottom of the sweatshirt until she relented and set the bag back on the table. She pushed her stick arms into the sleeves and pulled it over her head. The sweatshirt hung off her like a father's t-shirt engulfs his six-year-old son. The bottom almost dropped to below her miniskirt and I knew there was no way the sweatpants would stay around her emaciated waist.

Annabel must have realized the same thing because she pulled her belt out of the loops of her pants, making a zipping sound in the process, and came over to us. "You go on and pull on those pants, Child. We'll tie 'em on with this."

Cherry did as she was told and after she'd doubled over the waistband, Annabel slipped the belt around her waist and cinched it tight. I must have had a surprised look on my face because Annabel smiled and recited from memory, "'Truly I tell you, whatever you did for one of the least of these brothers and sisters of mine, you did for me.' I try to live by those words, Detective, and I can see you do as well."

I glanced over her head at Casey, who raised her fist to her mouth and was doing her best not to scoff out loud.

I grinned at her and then motioned to the bag Cherry had reclaimed. "Enjoy the rest of your meal and if I need to find you for some reason, I'll check the tunnels."

Annabel tut-tutted. "You live in the tunnels? You poor..."

Her voice trailed off as Casey—who had just accepted a burger and coffee from the manager and paid her bill—and I made our way outside to join the rest of the detectives in our unit.

They were all huddled in a circle around Kate who was briefing them on what we knew so far, which wasn't much. I stepped between Nate Drewery, a handsome twenty-seven-year-old who stood six foot two with wide, muscular shoulders and handsome, Scots-Irish features and Allen Brodie, a forty-something sugar addict whose belly bulged over his waistband. Tony Rico stood to Allen's right with his hands tucked beneath his underarms and his chin hiding beneath his fully buttoned up coat.

Kate finished her briefing and then asked, "Did you find out anything new, Alex?"

"Yeah, Cherry says when she was walking to the dumpster to look for food, Tom Handy, a local transient, was already rooting around in there. When she yelled at him, he jumped back with a knife in one hand and he stuffed some kind of chain or necklace into his coat pocket with the other. She said she thought it was black, but she didn't get a very good look at it. Tom ran off and that's all she knows."

At the beginning of an investigation, any tiny little bit of information can either prove to be crucial or absolutely worthless. Because of this, everyone listened quietly while I told them what I'd found. Well, that and because Kate ran a tight ship and she would have bitten anyone's head off for interrupting.

Kate glanced around the circle. "Casey, you and Alex have the body and the dumpster."

Nate snorted at our misfortune until Kate gave him the stink eye. He shut up after that.

"You'll have to use blue evidence tarps and after the M.E. comes to get the body I want you to dump everything out onto the tarps and go through it." This elicited chuckles around the group and Kate allowed a slight smile to tug at her lips. "Okay, okay. They get the dirty job today, tomorrow it'll be one of you jokers."

Brodie stage whispered behind his hand loud enough for everyone to hear, "Unless Alex pisses her off for some reason, then we're in the clear."

There was a general nodding of heads around the group, which in all fairness I had to join because pissing Kate off was my secondary job description. "Glad I could be of assistance to you guys." When I glanced from Brodie to Kate, her smile had been replaced with a warning glare in my direction.

After I shrugged and mumbled, "Sorry Boss," she turned her attention to Nate. "Nate, you have the parking lot and surrounding area, let's say a good twenty-five-yard radius around the whole restaurant, and include the entire alley back here. Go over it with a fine-tooth comb. Tony, I want you doing interviews. Restaurant employees, any witnesses if you can find them. Knock on doors and wake people up if you have to."

Tony Rico, whose black hair clumsily hung across his forehead and ended abruptly just above his ears, nodded. He'd done a stint in the navy and his hair was a combination messy chic and military regulation cut. He walked around in a perpetual good mood and was always quick with a smile or joke.

"Brodie see if you can find this Tom Handy. Bring him in if you have to, but I want to know what he took away from my crime scene."

"You got it, Boss."

I didn't know if he knew where to find him, so I added my two cents. "Cherry says he's wearing something resembling a peacoat now instead of his usual military fatigues, black or maybe dark blue. And the last time I saw him, he was living in his RV in that desert lot near 22nd and the freeway."

He'd pulled out his notebook and was taking everything down. "What kinda RV?"

"It's one of those that have the front that looks like a truck. You know, like the RV is sitting on the truck chassis." I didn't know much about motorhomes and I could tell by the slight tilt of his head he didn't either. I added helpfully, "They have the bed part sticking out over the cab."

Casey stepped next to him and showed him a picture on her phone. "They're called Class C's. His is pretty small and looks like this."

Everyone gathered around and Casey held up the phone so they could get a better look.

Pointing at the picture, Brodie asked, "What d'ya mean he's livin' in one of those? I thought you said he was a bum?"

Kate, always ready to give vets the benefit of the doubt, corrected him. "Homeless. Not necessarily a bum."

Brodie shrugged, "Yeah, sorry Boss." He looked back at me. "So, he's homeless but he lives in an RV?"

"Well, yeah. People pour money into his hands because his limp suddenly gets worse when he works a corner. He has the pitiful look down pat. He made enough last year to buy an old RV." I shrugged, "More power to him I say if he can get in out of this cold..." I pulled my coat tighter around my chest.

There were shrugs of acknowledgement all around as everyone shuffled their feet back and forth in the freezing night air trying to get warm.

"Got it. Anything else I should know?" When I shook my head, he said, "Thanks. That'll at least give me a starting point."

At Kate's, "Let's get busy then," we all scattered like football players leaving a huddle.

Casey and I retreated to the dumpster. When I squatted to get a better look beneath it, the smell of putrefied oil hit me. There was a drain in the back left of the enclosure and I assumed that was where the restaurant dumped their used frying oil.

The employees apparently weren't particular when it came time to dump, and a line of white grease ran from the drain to the left rear wheel of the dumpster where it parted and flowed to either side and then congealed in a dip directly beneath the center of the waste bin.

The portable lights illuminated the inside of the enclosure, but I had to pull out my mini Maglite to get a clear picture underneath. I wondered if the Health Department ever came back here to check because the rotten food, discarded wrappers and the skeleton of a dead rat all combined to be the perfect breeding ground for the plague.

I glanced up at Casey, relieved she hadn't brought her burger to munch on before we got started. I assumed she'd dumped it in her car before joining the group. "Uh, Case. You might want to rethink the burger you bought in there."

She squatted, took one look at the rat and turned her head to the side. "That's disgusting."

"Yup. My guess is the poor little bugger ate a slider and that was all she wrote."

We both stood and Casey stepped onto the wooden box. After quickly checking in the bin, she retrieved a shovel from her trunk and began systematically shifting trash around to get a better idea about what was inside.

Kate came over with a pair of rubber wellingtons and a packet containing a paper Tyvek suit and handed them to me.

Tyveks are disposable bodysuits made from a fairly dense polyethylene and I had no idea why she thought I needed one. "What am I supposed to do with these?"

"Pull 'em on before you climb in there."

"I'm not..." At the tilt of her head I knew it was useless to argue, so I pointed at the bin and then at a stack of tarps she'd dropped near the dumpster. "I thought you wanted us to dump it out onto the blue tarps."

"Dump it out? You mean tilt it over onto its side?" She smiled at my naivete and with a gloved hand pulled on the dumpster's lip. "Do you know how much these weigh?"

Casey piped up. "About eight-hundred-pounds empty." She poked around a little more with her shovel. "I think it's safe for you to get in over here, Alex."

I gave her my best stink eye before donning the body suit and rubber boots and gingerly climbing into the bin with Pito. Kate handed me two paper bags to place over his hands, which I did before taking the proffered zip ties and zipping them in place.

She held out a third bag and used it to motion toward his head. "Bag his head, too."

My lip curled in disgust and I was grateful when she pulled on some gloves and pulled over an old wooden pallet, which she stepped on in order to lean in to hold up what was left of the head so I could slide the bag over and secure it. Not many sergeants actually get their hands dirty, but Kate had always been the exception to the rule—one of the reasons there was always a long waiting list to get in whatever unit she was in charge of.

That accomplished, I finished rolling Pito to the side so we could see beneath his shoulders and butt. The movement released the odor of crap that had been hiding in his pants. He must have eliminated when they shot him and that combined with the grease and rotting food nearly did me in. I tried my best not to gag and mentally reminded myself exactly why I would never, ever transfer to the homicide unit.

Kate stepped back, blinking her eyes rapidly and obviously trying not to show her disgust. "Looks like he was killed somewhere else. There's hardly any blood beneath him, or anywhere around for that matter."

I knew Gia paid her people well, but the overcoat seemed much too nice for a goon like him. When I opened his camel brown coat and slipped my fingers into his inside pocket, I felt a small, rectangular piece of cardboard. I pulled it out and realized I'd found the price tag for the coat. Bruno Cuccinelli was embossed in raised gold lettering and the price, $7,200, had been done in shiny silver numbers. I whistled and then handed the tag to Kate.

When she read it, she kept her head down but raised her gaze to meet mine. I knew what she was thinking and I didn't like it. If Pito was on the take behind Gia's back and Gia found out...I pursed my lips and felt in the pocket on the other side.

Kate said, "You need to stay impartial, Alex. It's part of the job."

I angrily threw the lapel back down on his chest. "This is why I didn't want you to take the case, Kate. I knew, and *you* knew, we might end up investigating Gia and her people for offing the douche bag and..."

She stepped close and lowered her voice, "And which would you prefer, Alex? To have me in charge of the case with you involved in the investigation or Jon Logan and Dempsey investigating? Logan would be fine, but do you honestly think Dempsey would give the Angelinos a fair shake when all he ever talks about is how the department should take Gia down?"

That cooled my temper. I honestly hadn't thought of it that way and although I knew Kate didn't like my friendship with Gia, she'd always do right by an investigation.

She glanced around to make sure we were alone and then continued in an even quieter tone, "Why do you think Jon called me? Because his guys are too busy? They are, but they've worked multiple cases before with no problems. Or did you buy that b.s. about you being the..." She held two fingers up on each hand like quotation marks," "resident expert on the local mafia?"

That hurt my ego a bit, but she was right. The homicide detail wouldn't give up a case simply because the mafia was involved. Just the contrary, normally they'd love a case like this. And my friend Chuck had forgotten more about the mafia and local gangs than I'd ever know.

She continued, "Remember, Sgt. Logan inherited Dempsey from the previous sergeant and he's well aware what kind of investigation would happen if Dempsey knew Pito was one of the Angelino family. I need you to keep an open mind and investigate this to the best of your ability and I'll do the same."

Realizing Kate had actually done me a favor, I nodded my thanks, and then grimaced as I felt in his back pocket for a wallet. Logan had already said there was no identification on the body, but I always double-checked details like that. It felt squishy beneath the pants material and I could only imagine what lay beneath. The rest of his pockets were empty.

The back-up beeper on the M.E. van filled the air and I looked up to see them backing it close to our scene. Jayne, with her big-toothed smile and Kendra, the younger one who always wore her dark brown hair pulled into a bun, got out and began pulling out their equipment. Jayne stepped over to Kate. "What you got, Sarge? Dispatch didn't give us much."

As Kate motioned for me to get out so they could retrieve the body, she escorted Jayne to the lip of the dumpster. "GSW to the back of the head. We bagged the hands and head but go easy on the head as there's not much left and I don't want you accidentally decapitating him from the jaw up."

At Jayne's "Got it." I put one boot on the dumpster's rim, swung my leg over and hopped down onto the box. As I stepped off, my foot slipped in a coagulated puddle of grease.

Jayne grabbed my arm before I fell into the muck, a small favor for which I will be eternally in her debt. She and Kendra made quick work of getting Pito zipped into the body bag and off to the morgue. One body was the same as the next as far as they were concerned.

That is, they headed off once they'd gotten their stubborn engine to turn over. It had taken three tries and I'd begun to wonder whether they'd have to bring a second M.E. van to the scene. In the meantime, I helped Casey cover the ground in front of the crime scene with the blue tarps. That accomplished, I watched as she, too, donned the protective overclothing and boots.

We both climbed into the bin and began tossing old buns, meat patties, and discarded paper plates over the side. A lot of the trash was already tied up in thick black garbage bags, so it was fairly easy to toss them onto the furthest the tarp to search once we were back on solid ground.

Anything we found that looked like it didn't belong we set onto a small portion of the tarp we'd designated for that purpose. Even little things, like a small ballpoint pen, a single cowboy boot and the broken bottom of a blue and white flowered lamp went into that area. We tried to keep all the food items on a single space so it would be a simple task to pick up all four corners of the tarp and toss them back in with one fell swoop.

Both of us heaved a sigh of relief when we finally began seeing the bottom of the container. A half of something round and black poking out from under a dill pickle caught my eye. On top of the pickle, a shiny white maggot had apparently ingested too much brine because he lay in an immovable stupor.

Kate had been splitting her time between running the crime scene and acting as our photographer since we couldn't exactly handle the camera with the same slimy gloves we were using to sort through the trash. "Hey, Kate. Can you come take a picture of this?"

Casey leaned over my shoulder. "Whaddya got?"

"Maybe nothing, except Cherry said the chain Tom Handy tried to hide from her was black. But then she said the *chain* wasn't black. What if she was trying to describe a chain with a bunch of beads on it?" I pointed to my find. "Well, here's a black bead..."

A camera flashed off to my side and Kate said, "Good find. Now let's hope Allen finds the necklace to go with it."

I gingerly moved aside the pickle, maggot and all, to expose a small black bead.

The camera flashed again and then Kate pulled out a small evidence envelope and a pair of tweezers from her pocket, saw my greasy gloves and pulled out two clean ones. "Here."

I dropped my used gloves over the side onto the tarp and pulled on the fresh ones. Only then did Kate hand me the tweezers, which I used to carefully pick up the bead and drop it into the proffered bag.

Kate closed the bag and then motioned to Casey. "From here on out, you toss and let Alex collect anymore beads with the tweezers and clean gloves."

Usually an amiable teammate, Casey's lips were clenched tightly shut. Even she was feeling queasy about rooting through all this greasy trash. Her jaw set with determination, she nodded slowly, "Yes, Ma'am."

Kate chuckled, "Maybe this will convince you to take that sergeant's test that's coming up."

My head shot up and I stared at Casey. The little green gremlin of envy reared his ugly head because Kate hadn't ever suggested to me that I should take the sergeant's test.

Casey chuckled and shook her head. "No, I'm right where I want to be, Sarge. I have no intention of ever taking anymore promotional tests. Getting to detective was hard enough."

My head swiveled between Casey and Kate, who raised her eyebrows at Casey's refusal and shrugged. When she glanced at me, I quickly stood and began moving trash around with the toe of my boot. I'd be damned if I'd let her see I was even a tiny bit affected by her words. Truth be told, I'd be thrilled for Casey to become a sergeant and I'd even be happy to work for her. It just stung that Kate thought she was ready for it and I wasn't.

Actually, I knew I wasn't, but that didn't make it any easier. I glanced over my shoulder and saw that Kate had gone to see whatever had caught Nate's attention as he was kneeling down poking an object on the ground with his pen.

Casey reached out to companionably punch me in the arm but remembered her dirty gloves at the last minute. "We're partners, Alex. Maybe someday, when you become sergeant, I'll come work for you, but right now, you're stuck with me."

I sighed dramatically, "Well, if I'm stuck with you, I'm stuck with you. Somebody has to keep an eye on your work or God only knows what you'd get up to."

Smiling her assent, Casey went back to chucking the last few buns and bags while I carefully looked around for any more baubles. I picked up a silver colored back that slips onto the post of a pierced earing, slipped it into a bag and set it on the top of the lip of the bin. "Keep your eyes out for a pierced earring."

By the time we finished, it had been more than a couple hours since the sun had peeked over the top of A-Mountain. The "mountain" was more of a hill than an actual mountain, situated on the west side of Tucson. Nate had turned off the extra lighting a while ago and was currently packing the tripods away in order to return them to the homicide unit.

As I climbed out of the bin, I noticed the only detective cars remaining in the lot were mine, Casey's, Kate's and Nate's older blue clunker, which always went to the newest member of the unit. Apparently the Sling 'Em did a good midmorning business because the lot had begun to fill up with Ford F-250's, Toyota Tundras and the occasional SUV or older model sedan.

The trucks made me realize the rodeo had returned to our not so sleepy town and I was sure my best friend Megan would be standing at the main gates of the rodeo grounds with her protest sign scoping out the herd and hoping to find her newest cowboy du jour.

Casey and I had begun taking off the Tyvek suits when Kate called out to us. "Hold it." She pointed at the evidence van backing in our direction.

We both slumped and dutifully rezipped and for the next hour we helped load every black garbage bag and bagged and tagged anything we had separated out as possible evidence.

When we finished, Kate told us to throw our old gloves and the paper body suits into a bag as well. People tend to get cranky when they find possibly contaminated crime scene clothing and gloves at their place of business, even if the clothes are cleaner than their dirty, stinking, maggot infested garbage bin.

Since today was Sunday and a usual day off, I was looking forward to a hot shower followed by a hotter bath and then a long day of sleep on the new memory foam mattress that had arrived two days ago.

Kate quickly disabused me of that notion. "Casey, I know you have animals to tend to, so I want you to accompany the evidence back to the garage and get it checked in. That shouldn't take too long and then you can get home and feed your critters."

Casey was the proud mother to several children, including but not limited to five goats, three pigs, two donkeys, a horse and I'm not sure how many dogs, cats and birds. She ran her hand through her short-cropped, dirty-blonde hair. "I'll run home after I get the evidence sorted, but if you and Alex are going to keep working, I'll feed and then head back into work."

Kate picked up the bag of our dirty coveralls and tossed it into the evidence truck. "No, if I need you, I'll give you a call. I sent everyone else home. Alex and I just need to pay a visit to either Pito's family or to Ms. Angelino if he has none and let her know Pito is dead."

I appreciated her acting like this was a normal death notification and not an interrogation of a suspect. The muscles in my neck had begun to ache and I massaged the area where my shoulders met my neck with stiff fingers. "Pito's father worked for Gia's dad. He's dead now and Dante told me his mother was never in the picture. I guess she ran off with some stable hand at the Angelino's barn right after he was born—can't blame her there—and hasn't been heard from since."

Kate's brows puckered in confusion. "Who's Dante? I've never heard you mention him."

"Dante Corsetti. You've seen him. Not super muscular, about five-foot-nine, medium build."

Casey piped up, "You mean the guy with the nose that's too wide for his super thin face? Only has four fingers on his left hand?"

"Yup."

Kate muttered, "Oh yeah," as she turned and headed for her car. "Let's go, Alex. You're with me."

I called after her. "I'm gonna run into the Sling 'Em and wash my hands first, Boss. I'll meet you there."

She waved a hand over her shoulder and by her quick pace I knew I didn't have long before she'd either be impatiently tapping her fingers on her steering wheel while she waited for me in front of Gia's home or heading inside to give the notification herself.

It turned out to be neither because as I came out of the restaurant, she was standing at the back of her car with the trunk lid up squirting anti-bacterial sanitizer on her hands. "Here." She held out the container and pumped some of the green goo into my hands.

I finished rubbing the stuff up and down my arms just as Kate pushed the trunk lid down. When I headed toward my car, Kate stopped me. "Get in, we'll ride together."

"But..."

She'd already gotten behind the wheel and I reluctantly slid in on the passenger's side. By the time we arrived at Gia's home, my stress level had ratcheted up several notches. Kate hadn't had much to say and I felt strange just sitting next to her in complete silence. There wasn't exactly a friendly camaraderie between us and I had no clue how to start any kind of interesting conversation.

Relief washed over me when we were finally in front of the door with Kate pushing the doorbell. Gia's distinctive gong echoed throughout the house and we waited in silence for someone to open the door. To my surprise, it was Gabe who did the honors.

Gabe, Gia's major domo, had been shot by a rival gang several months earlier and had nearly died. I'd known he was on the mend but hadn't realized he was back as Gia's head man. "Gabe! Good to see you back. You look as grumpy as ever."

He tilted his head slightly to one side. "What do you need, Alex?" He raised his gaze to look behind me and nodded respectfully to Kate. "Sergeant Brannigan."

Classical music rose and fell in the background and I knew Gia was home. "We'd like to talk to Gia."

"It's Sunday. She's busy."

"It's not exactly a request."

"Sorry, Alex."

He stepped back as though about to close the door and Kate put her foot out to block it. "Please tell Ms. Angelino we're here. *Now*." Apparently even a bodybuilder with meaty fists and biceps that strained his coat sleeves understood that tone of voice.

His lips thinned as he nodded once. "Wait here."

He hadn't invited us inside but since I came here often I stepped into the foyer to watch him rumble down the hall. Unfortunately, the piano concerto still played in the background and I couldn't hear anything being said in the living room.

Kate hummed some of the parts and then said, "Rachmaninov's 2nd Piano Concerto. They played that at the symphony Friday night. Ornella Detti was the guest pianist and the Symphony accompanied her." She smiled at my look of consternation. "What?"

"Well, I didn't think you did stuff like that. You know, cultured stuff."

"Do you think Thom and I just sit around the house eating popcorn and watching Netflix?"

I blushed since that was pretty much what I did most nights. I was saved from having to answer by Gabe's return.

"Ms. A. says since it's you, you can come back, but you gotta be quiet for a while."

Kate and I looked at each other and shrugged as we followed Gabe down the hall. I noticed several oil paintings hanging on the walls and was happy to see Gia had begun the process of redecorating after the Andrulis mafia had shot up the interior of her house and murdered her father. She hadn't wanted to put up any paintings or clean up the bullet holes in the walls until her war with them was over, one way or the other. Too much of a possibility they'd come back and destroy everything a second time.

When we entered, I saw Gia sitting on the leather sofa in the center of the room. Her back was to us and she held a snifter resting on the arm of the sofa in one hand while the other rested along the sofa's curved back with a Cuban cigar held relaxed between her fingers. A thin wisp of smoke rose toward the ceiling and I recognized the spicy aroma of a partagas mini, one of her favorites. I'd become something of a cigar smell connoisseur since meeting her.

Speaking of becoming a connoisseur, the ubiquitous bottle of Glenlivet sat on the glass coffee table and my salivary glands fired up as I stared at the label.

That, however, wasn't what stopped Kate, and by extension, me, in our tracks. What did that trick was the elegantly appointed woman with the flowing black hair sitting with her back to us playing Gia's piano.

Actually, I'd learned several visits earlier not to call it a piano. I guess that was too plebian for the type of instrument it was. I'd had to look up the word 'plebian', too, after Gia had teasingly called me that during the same conversation.

To be accurate, the woman sat in front of a super expensive Steinway, apparently one of only two in the world. La De Da. I could feel my envious plebian roots rushing to the fore and I made an effort to tamp them down. I glanced over at Kate and did a double take.

She stood open-mouthed with her hands turned up at her waist as though caught midmovement. If I had walked into the room and found her in that position, I'd say she'd walked through a door and had been surprised by either a friend or foe holding a gun pointed at her with her brain trying to figure out which was which. Within moments, her hands and shoulders relaxed and her face brightened in delighted surprise.

The music increased in both volume and tempo, and I turned my attention on the woman whose fingers were flying from one end of the keyboard to the other at an impossible speed. Her skill was truly remarkable and the change in the music had my heart racing in a matter of moments.

And then suddenly, to my disappointment—something I'd keep to myself as I had no intention of letting Gia or Kate know I'd enjoyed something cultured—the song ended and the pianist rose from the bench and turned with a jubilant smile aimed at Gia, who had risen to her feet and was now walking toward her with arms outstretched, inviting her to fall into them, which she did.

I glanced at Kate who pulled in a deep breath as though only now remembering to breathe. She, too, was smiling and shaking her head in obvious admiration or disbelief, I couldn't be sure which.

Gia led the woman to us and introduced her. "Sergeant Kate Brannigan and Detective Alexandra Wolfe, may I introduce..."

"Ornella Detti." Kate interrupted to supply the answer, something that showed me exactly how excited she truly was. "I saw you two nights ago when you and the symphony gave an outstanding performance." She held out her hand, which Ornella graciously took into her own two hands. I'd never witnessed Kate as enthusiastic as she was in meeting Ms. Detti.

"I'm happy you enjoyed the concert." Ornella smiled at Gia. "Aunt Gianina couldn't rearrange her plans in order to attend so I offered to give her a private recital here at home. Who could resist playing on the Alma-Tadema Steinway?" She turned and gave the Steinway an adoring look.

Gia smiled. "The Alma-Tadema will be yours one day, my dear. You of all people have earned the right to own such a wonderful instrument." She smiled at me and raised her eyebrows. "Something bothering you, Alex?"

I closed my mouth, which I'd unwittingly let drop open. "I'm still stuck on 'Aunt Gianina.'" I knew Gia had only had one brother, and he'd only had one child, Shelley Greer.

Ornella laughed and prettily took the snifter from Gia's fingers. "Aunt Gia is really my godmother, but it's so much simpler calling her my aunt than trying to explain the wonderful relationship we've had my entire life." She tipped the snifter to her lips and closed her eyes in seeming ecstasy as the golden whiskey flowed across her tongue. "Mmmmm. No one has better whiskey than you, either, Auntie." She handed the snifter back and then stepped over to the Steinway. "Would your guests like to join us for the next movement?"

Gia raised an eyebrow in Kate's direction but Kate, after hesitating a moment, reluctantly shook her head. "As much as I hate to say no, we did come here with a specific purpose in mind. Could we speak to you in private, Ms. Angelino?"

Gia turned to Ornella who immediately took the hint. "I'll pop off to the kitchen to get us some snacks."

Once she'd left the room, Gia resumed her place on the sofa. "Please, have a seat. Can I offer you something to eat or drink?"

Always the perfect hostess, I thought, as I sat down hoping Kate would accept some Glenlivet so I could as well. I'd never tasted better whiskey than what Gia kept at her house, and since I couldn't afford the price of the stuff she bought, the only time I could have any was when I came to visit.

Unfortunately, Kate again declined. "Thank you, but this isn't a personal visit."

Gia turned laughing eyes on me and I hoped to hell she wasn't going to say that hadn't stopped me before. Although, truth be told, I'd always refused her offers whenever I was actually at her house during on-duty hours. Relief washed over me when she said, "Perhaps later, then, when you're officially off-duty."

Kate looked from Gia to me, and I innocently raised my eyebrows. "What?"

Shaking her head, Kate moved to the wing chair facing Gia and I moved to the small refrigerator behind the bar. "Could I have a diet coke, please?"

"You don't need to ask, Alex. Please help yourself. And you, Kate, would you like a soda or perhaps some tea?"

Kate surprised me when she said, "Actually..." and walked to the small bar sink and washed her hands. "Yes, a coke would go down well right now. Thank you." It must have just occurred to her that although she'd worn gloves and had minimal contact with the corpse and had used hand sanitizer, she hadn't yet washed her hands. Or at least, I hadn't seen her do so. My guess was she'd used the Sling 'Em's restrooms during the night and felt the urge to wash off the memories of Pito's disgusting corpse and the equally nauseating trash bin before eating or drinking anything.

I pulled two glasses off the shelf, filled them with ice, and then poured our respective drinks into each glass. I handed Kate hers, picked up mine and followed her back to the center of the room where we each made ourselves as comfortable as possible given the situation.

Kate took a sip and then jumped right in. "I'm afraid we have some unsettling news. One of your employees was found murdered this morning. Pito..." Since she hadn't yet taken out her notebook, she looked to me to supply his full name.

"Agapito asshole Mancini."

"Alex!" Kate bit off my name.

I shrugged. "It's not like it's a secret or anything."

As I suspected, Gia's eyes held a hint of amusement before she turned back to Kate.

When she didn't comment, Kate's eyes narrowed, "You don't look surprised."

Gia took a sip and set her snifter on the coffee table next to the whiskey bottle. "Chief Sepe phoned me earlier this morning to give me the news."

A spark of anger ignited in Kate's eyes. The chief had no business involving himself in her case and could have seriously compromised the investigation by doing so. At the very least he should have let Kate know. The first impression of a suspect's reaction to hearing of the loss of a loved one, or of an employee in this case, can be a vital clue as far as their guilt or innocence was concerned.

That being said, any sociopath can be bathed in the person's blood and still pull off a perfectly convincing portrait of surprise, grief, and innocence upon hearing the news. They'd say, "Of course, their blood is on me! I must have found them and then my mind must have gone into shock when I realized they were dead. Oh, I don't remember anything of the last few hours, Detective. My God, is she really gone?" Or some such drivel. Luckily, Gia was far from being a sociopath.

Kate continued as though she hadn't just been punched in the gut. "Does Mr. Mancini have any relatives we should notify?"

"No. His parents are both dead, along with his two brothers who were killed in Chicago."

Probably during a mob hit, I thought, but didn't say out loud. Usually, when Casey and I deliver this type of news to someone who may or may not be a suspect, we play off each other, each one asking questions and moving in one conversational direction or another based on the answer.

With Kate, I always let her take the lead and only jump in when she wants me to or when I think she's forgotten something, which, now that I think about it, never actually happens.

Ornella must have popped some bread in the toaster because the scent of freshly buttered toast came wafting down the hallway and into the living room. I hadn't wanted to eat anything at the Sling 'Em and aside from a Granola bar Casey had given me, my last meal had been at five-thirty the night before. I glanced down at my stomach when it roared out its displeasure at not partaking of the aforementioned toast and hoped no one else had heard the rumble.

They had, of course, and they both turned to stare at my stomach.

Gia leaned forward and picked up her cigar from the ashtray. "There are always snacks in the drawers, Alex."

I raised my eyebrows at Kate who shook her head but then waved at the bar with an open hand. Conflicting messages. I chose to disregard the first and wandered behind the bar and pulled out a few drawers. Apparently Gia's idea of snacks and mine were two totally different things. I'd been expecting Corn Nuts and potato skins and maybe a few skittles.

Noticing my perplexity, Gia asked, "Problems?"

"Yeah. How do I eat sardines? And for that matter, *why* would I eat sardines? And saltless wafers? Who eats saltless wafers? And this?" I held up an unopened can of tuna in one hand and a package of seaweed in the other.

When I looked up and saw her incredible gray eyes laughing at me, my heart skipped a beat. The woman really was absolutely stunning.

"Try the third drawer down. Shelley used to stock it with other snacks before she went to the Regency Academy. She's loving it there by the way. Thank you for suggesting it."

"No problem." Shelley is Gia's a great niece, whom she only learned about upon the death of Tancredo Angelino Jr.'s wife. Tancredo, or Credo as they affectionately called him, was Gia's twin brother who was killed by a rival mafia family when they were still in their teens.

I found a package of Granola bars—it seemed they were going to be my sustenance for the day—and some packages of lightly salted pistachios. I grabbed both and returned to the sofa.

Kate's pen tap-tap-tapped on her thigh and I noticed the muscle in her jaw getting a good amount of exercise. I held out the Granola. "Want one?"

Her eyes narrowed before she turned back to address Gia. "You don't seem upset that one of your employees has been murdered."

Gia looked at me when she answered. "Even though Alex has a definite lack of finesse when speaking in polite company..."

"Hey." I sat up and glared at her, the effect of my insulted glare marred by the crunching of the large bite of the Granola bar I'd just stuffed in my mouth.

"Despite a lack of finesse, which is always a breath of fresh air for me, by the way, Alex has a way of cutting out the bullshit and coming straight to the point." Gia, who'd turned her attention back to Kate, didn't usually swear, and I was surprised she used the word bullshit in front of Kate. "Pito was not a nice man. He was universally disliked and if I were to be perfectly honest, I have wondered why he hasn't insulted the wrong person before now. He was, however, an excellent bodyguard. Not on the level of Gabriel, but very protective of me. In that aspect, he will be missed."

"Do you have any idea whom he might have insulted enough to get himself killed?"

"I don't generally know what my people are doing during their off time, Sergeant."

"Could it possibly have been someone in your employ?"

Gia remained silent long enough that I looked up from the pistachio I'd just cracked open. When she finally answered, she bit off the word. "No."

"You just said he was universally disliked. I assume that means people in your organization disliked him as well."

Gia's gray eyes turned to ice. Not a good sign. "No one who works for me would dare murder anyone." She stopped short of saying 'without my express permission.' "I assume there are police officers who are disliked among their fellow officers. What stops someone on the police force from murdering them?"

Kate raised her eyebrows and had to concede the point. "That is an excellent point and I apologize if I wrongly insinuated people in your organization routinely dispatch people who insult or irritate them. That wasn't my intention."

That most certainly was her intention and everyone in the room knew it.

Kate continued, "Is there a possibility that Pito was an unfortunate byproduct of someone who is targeting you or trying to send you a message?"

Bringing her cigar to her lips, Gia pulled in a deep breath. She glanced into the distance with her eyes slightly unfocused. Smoke drifted out of her mouth as she spoke. "There is always that possibility. Although, things in my world are very quiet right now. My business dealings are all running smoothly and as far as I know, all is well. I do intend to have Gabe make some inquiries, however."

Kate's eyes narrowed at that. "While I appreciate the offer, this is a police investigation and your people need to steer clear."

Gia gave her a mirthless smile that didn't reach her eyes. "Of course." Which translated into 'I'll do exactly what I intend to do whether you approve or not.'

I thought I was doing pretty well catching all the behind the scenes nuances and wished I had a bowl of salted, buttered popcorn so I could sit back and watch my two favorite power women engage in their verbal sparring.

Kate set her coke on the coffee table and pulled out her notebook.

Gia watched her and then said, "Has this become an interrogation, then? If so, you'll have to speak with my attorney, William Silverton."

Kate shook her head. "Not at all. I need to refer to my notes at times so I don't end up forgetting to ask you something and then need to bother you at some other point." She flipped to a clean page and tapped her pen on the open pad. "Do you know what time Mr. Mancini left last night?"

"The only employee who stays with me at this house overnight is Gabe. He is on duty twenty-four seven. The other bodyguards patrol the grounds outside my home on a rotating basis and then go home to their families. I do know Pito had Friday and Saturday off, and was scheduled to report for duty this morning."

"Do you know where he lives or what type of car he drives?"

"You'll have to ask Gabe."

I'd done a thorough background check on Pito the first time I'd met him because he was hands down the meanest looking man I'd ever seen. From his slicked-back hair, pockmarked face and left eyebrow that had been rearranged by a pair of brass knuckles, to his eagle-beaked nose and the v-shaped scar that bisected his lower lip, I knew from the start he was trouble with a capital T. "He drove a 1969 Pontiac GTO, bluish gray, spoke rims, RAM air hood with a V8 engine. And he lives on E. 2nd street. I'll get you the exact address."

Both women looked at me with amazement and I shrugged, "Hey, I'm not just a pretty face you know."

"You investigate my people?" The chill in the words coming from those flawless lips didn't escape me.

"Only when they're as mean as vipers and I want to make sure my community will continue to be safe with them living here as law abiding citizens. Don't forget, he came here after your father was murdered. I'd never met him before and he stuck a knife in my face the first couple times we met."

Kate sat forward. "He *what?*"

I waved her off. "It was nothing and I took care of it. The point is, he was a dangerous man and I needed to know all I could about him since I'm your friend and I come here and visit you at your home from time to time."

I could tell that mollified Gia's sense of righteous indignation. I was a little worried about the scowl Kate had turned on me at the mention of the knife and in retrospect I wished I'd left that little gem out of my explanation.

She tapped her pen again and once more turned her attention to Gia who retrieved her snifter from the table and settled back into the soft cushions of the sofa. "You must pay your people well for him to afford a classic muscle car like a GTO."

Gia lifted a shoulder and took a sip, obviously not intending to tell us how much she paid her employees.

"I realize your payroll is none of my business, but I have a reason for asking. Mr. Mancini was wearing what I consider to be a very expensive overcoat. One that even my husband and I couldn't easily afford."

"Pito was a single man with no ex-wives or children to support. I'm sure it wasn't too difficult for him to save up for a nice car and coat."

"Have you ever seen him wearing a Bruno Cuccinelli overcoat? Alex found a tag in the pocket that said it sold for $7200."

Gia stilled at the mention of the brand.

Kate had been looking at her notes to make sure she had the brand and price correct and hadn't caught the tension her words engendered.

Gia set her drink down and stood. "Excuse me a moment." I watched her walk to the door, her perfectly tailored dress fitting her curves to perfection with the sleeves a tight but comfortable fit. A large belt accentuated her waist and the dress reached to just above her knees. I admired the curve of her legs as she stopped at the door and called for Gabe.

Gia always captured my imagination. She's elegant, poised, powerful, well-bred and well-spoken. Everything, I suppose, I'm not. As she returned to the sofa, I admired the square neckline that flowed into a tight fit around the curves of her breasts. On most women, the effect might look tacky, but on Gia...

I felt her looking at me and when I raised my gaze to meet hers I knew I'd been caught out. Blushing, I turned back to Kate who watched me with lowered lids. Her eyes seemed to be saying 'get a room' while at the same time screaming 'don't you dare.'

Gia retook her seat and when Kate opened her mouth to speak, Gia raised a finger. "One moment, please. I'm checking on something. In fact, I have a question of my own. Chief Sepe didn't know many details when he called this morning. How was Pito murdered?"

"I'm not at liberty to give out details at this time." She thought about her words a moment, and then added, "Suffice to say, it looked like an execution to me."

I nodded my agreement but since Kate had withheld a ton of information, I decided to follow her lead and not add any specific details. Not that I would have dared do anything else—with her in the room, anyway.

Gabe came in and whispered in Gia's ear. When he finished, he straightened and waited to see if there was anything else.

With a flick of her finger, she said, "Thank you, Gabe."

At that, he left the way he'd come.

Kate and I waited in silence, something which every competent investigator is very comfortable with. There are times when silence elicits a ton of information you wouldn't have gotten otherwise simply because suspects become nervous and come down with a bad case of verbal diarrhea.

In Gia's case, we were simply giving her time to process whatever Gabe had told her. In the years I've know her, I can't say I've ever seen her nervous, in any situation she's been in. Grief stricken and numb, yes. Angrier than hell, again, yes, but barely showing it. Nervous? Not gonna happen.

After a few sips of Glenlivet and a puff on the second cigar of our visit, she finally looked up at Kate. "I think its best that I lay my cards on the table and allow you to do with the information as you will. My father often wore Bruno Cuccinelli. In fact, as far as overcoats go, that was the only designer he would purchase them from. I've not been able to bring myself to empty his things out of his room, and Gabe tells me one of father's overcoats is missing."

Kate nodded as though she'd known this information all along. I'm sure she may have guessed it, as had I, but as Gia spoke, Kate kept her expression neutral. I wanted to grab Kate and drag her out of there for the simple reason that if Pito really was stealing from Gia, and if she knew about it, his lifespan would have rivaled that of a mayfly, which *may* live anywhere from thirty minutes to a full day.

Kate asked, "Do you know the color of the missing overcoat?"

"His camel brown coat. And the color of the one Pito was wearing?"

Flicking a quick glance at me, I knew Kate was running various scenarios through her head. I guess she decided it would be better to give a little in the hopes of getting more. "Camel Brown. Do you know whether anything else is missing?"

"Such as?"

"That I can't help you with. I really don't know."

"I'll ask Gabe to go through my father's belongings. He was my father's personal valet for several years and is well acquainted with what should be in his rooms."

"I appreciate that." Kate stood and I followed suit. "I need to ask one more time. Can you think of any reason *anyone* might want to harm you by killing one of your employees?"

"None. As I said, recently my life has been very ordered and balanced." Her eyes finally lit with the amused smile I'd come to love. "No burnt barns at the racetrack, no one has riddled my home or my cars with bullets, and Leonis Andrulis has been a man of his word."

Gia and the Andrulis mafia had been involved in an all-out war several months earlier. In fact, it had been a member of the Andrulis family who had shot and nearly killed Gabe. Thank God Gabe had survived because if he had died, nothing would have stopped Gia from wiping out the entire Andrulis family. Or die in the attempt.

Yes, they'd killed her father, but she'd said she'd rather see her father go out with his Tommy Gun in his hands than slowly lose himself to the Alzheimer's that held him in its insidious grip. I think in her own way, she was thankful his death happened the way it did and therefore didn't feel the need to wipe out an entire family empire because of his murder. But if Gabe had died...

She walked us to her door where Kate had one last question. "Do you have a key to his..." She looked at me for clarification. "Home? Apartment?"

"Apartment."

Gia shook her head. "No, I'm sorry. As I said, my employees live their own lives when not on duty."

That was the second time she'd said, 'on duty' instead of 'at work' and it reminded me that her people were soldiers first rather than your run of the mill employees.

Gabe stood holding the door and I asked Gia, "Does Jerry Dhotis still work for you now that Gabe's back?" Jerry was ex-special forces who'd stepped in for Gabe when he was out of commission.

Gia crossed one arm over her midsection and held the cigar close to her cheek. The wisps of smoke curling around her head created a mysterious, ethereal effect. "Get some sleep, Alex." Without another word, she turned and made her way back to her inner sanctum.

Ornella stepped from the kitchen holding a plate full of nuts, an assortment of cheese and several varieties of crackers—all of them salted, I noted with amusement.

So, Gia wasn't going to answer me. I wasn't all that surprised. Her business was none of mine. She kept her nose, usually, out of my work and I kept mine, usually, out of hers. I followed Kate to the car and waved at one of the guards I recognized making his rounds.

He lifted his chin in a friendly hello before turning the corner and patrolling the near side of the house.

I climbed into the passenger seat and buckled my seatbelt. "We done for the day?"

"No, you're going to show me Pito's apartment and we're going to go through it, hopefully before any of Gia's men do."

My shoulder's slumped and I asked, "Can we at least go through a drive thru? I'm starved."

Twenty minutes later I happily washed down a bite of

Whataburger with a diet coke. What made it taste even better was that Kate had paid for the entire order and it hadn't cost me a dime.

Kate liked to keep the heater in the car at full blast and I ended up taking my coat off and throwing it onto the back seat. We were sitting in Pito's parking lot and Kate had just put a fry in her mouth when a tall man wearing a baseball hat, Arizona Cardinals jacket and blue jeans knocked on Pito's door.

When no one answered, he glanced to the right and left and then took a small, oblong box out of his pocket. He pulled out a set of lockpicks and within seconds had the door open.

Kate shoved my shoulder and said, "Go!" before opening her own door and jumping out.

Without thinking, I automatically did as ordered and the box of fries in my lap went flying. I sprinted through the gate of the four-foot chain-link fence that surrounded the apartments and managed to shove my foot in the front door before it fully closed. I rammed my shoulder against the wood and heard a thunk when the edge of the door hit the guy in the back of the head.

He grabbed his head and bent over at the waist. "What the fuck!" He pulled his hand away and stared at the blood covering his fingers. When he turned, looked down his nose and focused on my face—he was a good six-inches taller than me—his eyes were filled with such rage I involuntarily shifted my weight onto my back foot to brace myself if he decided to throw a punch. He balled up his fist and pulled his arm back, fully intending to punch my lights out.

That is until Kate's .40 caliber Glock snaked over my shoulder and into his face. She spoke with a menacing growl. "Back up, Asshole."

He raised his hands in surrender and took two steps back. Then suddenly deciding going to jail wasn't in his best interest, he growled, turned on his heel and ran through the kitchen, smashing out the window of the backdoor with his fist, clearing out the rest of the glass with the heavy sleeve of his coat and diving through.

"Hey!" I ran after him knowing that if I took the time to unlock and then open the door I'd lose him, so I did what any self-respecting cop would do; I dove through the hole he'd made. He'd pretty much cleared out most of the glass and the only cut I got was on my forearm when I landed on a piece of glass that had fallen to the back stoop.

By the time I picked myself up, I saw his ass disappearing over the back fence. I couldn't reach as high as he could, so I jumped onto a short weight bench stored up against the fence, hit the top of the slats with both hands and swung my feet over to land on the other side. I chased him another three blocks before he began to stumble. A half block later he went to his knees, and then finally, fell on his face.

When I pulled his arms back and cuffed him, I realized why he'd suddenly gone down. Bright red blood had soaked through the sleeve of his jacket and when I pulled the coat off his shoulders and down around the cuffs, I could see where a piece of glass had sliced through the jacket and into his upper arm.

Kate ran up, took one look at the amount of blood and got on her handheld radio to order meds. "Stay here with him, Alex. I need to get back to secure the apartment. This isn't the best of neighborhoods and we left everything, including my car, wide open."

She threw a set of gloves at me and then jogged back the way we'd come.

I pulled on the gloves and then wrapped his wound as best I could with strips I tore from his shirt. Luckily for him, we were in the center of town and it wasn't long before I heard sirens and then saw two beefy paramedics running down the alley carrying their equipment. Two others followed at a slower pace rolling a wheeled stretcher through the dirt in the alley.

At the request of the lead paramedic, I uncuffed the suspect and once they lifted him onto the gurney, re-cuffed him to that.

"You gonna follow us to Banner?" Banner Hospital was only a few miles away and it wouldn't take long for them to get there.

I unclipped my radio from the back of my pants and called Kate. "9David72 to 9David70."

"Go ahead."

"Do you want me to go with them to Banner?"

"Negative, I already have a patrol unit on the way. He'll be here at the apartment by the time they get back to their truck and he'll follow them to the hospital."

I nodded, and without keying the mic, said quietly, "Of course you do."

Apparently the medic heard me because he smiled and said, "Is that Kate?" A lot of the firemen and paramedics get to know the officers because after meeting at scenes like this for several years, you develop a kind of rapport.

"Yup."

"Tell her Max says hello."

"Will do. Well, actually, she's at the scene so you can tell her yourself." I pulled off my gloves and he held open a garbage bag they use for such things. I threw them in and he took hold of my hand and turned my forearm so he could see the cut.

"Not too bad, but it needs some attention. Come back to the truck with me and I'll have one of the guys clean that up and bandage it."

I nodded my thanks and fell into step alongside the stretcher. I reached into the bad guys back pocket and pulled out his wallet. Since he had a couple forms of ID, I grabbed the driver's license and handed Max the rest. "Here, could you give that to whatever patrol officer follows you to the hospital?"

"Sure thing." When we were back on the street, Max motioned to one of the firefighters and after a quick consultation, the guy brought over a bottle of sterile water and a first aid kit and bandaged my arm. Cute didn't even begin to describe him. I could picture him barechested wearing only his turnout pants, suspenders pulled up over his massive pecs and holding a kitten while he posed for one of those firefighter calendars.

By the time he'd finished, a couple of the guys from our unit had arrived. I walked up to Tony and nudged him with my elbow. "I thought you'd be home tucked into bed by now."

His grin always cheered me. I'd spent too much time with officers who never see anything but the glum side of life. Tony saw the world from the eyes of a permanent optimist. "Hey! It's Sunday. Can you say overtime?" He pumped his fist in the air. "Cha Ching!"

His girlfriend also worked for the department and I knew they were hoping to start a family soon. As far as Tony was concerned, overtime was just one more golden brick in the highway to fatherhood.

Nate strode up to us yawning and my answering yawn joined his. He shook his head and blinked rapidly as though trying to keep himself awake. "Sorry. I'd just pulled into my driveway when Kate texted. I got called out two nights ago, and then last night too, and I haven't had a chance to catch up on my sleep. Anyway, Kate said for you to go finish your burger and then help her search the apartment."

The medics pulled away with siren blasting and we all waited in silence until they were far enough away that we could hear again. A breeze blew Nate's bangs down into his eyes and he brushed it away as he turned to Tony. "Since you did all the interviews at the scene, she wants you to talk to all the neighbors around here and see what they know."

Tony nodded amiably. "Will do. What about you? You gonna get to sleep anytime soon?"

Nate indicated the direction the medic truck had taken. "She wants me to follow up with numbnuts at the hospital." He sent me an apologetic look before continuing. "She wants to know if he works for Ms. Angelino and what he was doing breaking into Mancini's apartment."

The look irritated me and I said a little too sharply, "Look, if someone from the Angelino family offed Pito, I'll be the first to step up and arrest them. You don't need to worry about me playing favorites, you got it?"

Both men nodded emphatically and Tony said, "We know that, Alex. You're like a bulldog with a bone when you catch a case." He glanced at Nate before continuing, "And if you catch shit from anybody about, well, you know, the Angelinos and all, we...well every-body in the unit...we all got your six."

That actually surprised me. It shouldn't have really. Kate had molded her detectives into a close knit, highly respected unit and the fact that they'd take the time to reassure me they had my back was icing on my cake. Blushing, I glanced back at the apartment, back to where I knew Kate was working, and said quietly, "Thanks, guys. That means a lot."

Nate punched me in the arm. "And if you screw up, I promise to be the first one to rub your nose in it." He shot me a huge grin before heading to his car.

Tony folded his fingers into the shape of a pistol and made a clicking sound before grinning and turning to grab his recorder out of his briefcase.

I returned to Kate's sedan, lamented the fries that were strewn all over the pavement, but then sat down and enjoyed one of the best burgers I'd had in a very long time. The guys' support had lifted my mood and I felt like I was walking on the top of the world.

That is until Kate opened the driver's side door and swung in behind the steering wheel. She grabbed her burger off the dashboard and reached into her Whataburger bag to pull out a fry. She'd had the presence of mind to set the bag to the side before leaping from the car and I shrugged, happy for her good fortune.

We ate in silence until she swallowed a bite of burger and said, "Pito held a knife to your throat."

It was a statement of fact, not a question.

The bite I'd just swallowed stuck halfway down and I had to move it along with a big gulp of diet Coke. "Just the second time I met him, but I dislocated his thumb that time by using a throw Mr. Myung taught me." I grinned over at her. "He forgot to mention I was supposed to let go when the guy came crashing back down to earth."

I got a chuckle out of her for that and then she asked, "Why didn't you arrest him?"

My reasons had seemed sound at the time, but now that I was getting ready to share them with my sergeant, they didn't have the same, je ne sais quoi. "Um."

She turned toward me and raised her eyebrows, not needing to verbalize what she thought about my answer.

"Well, Gia's father had just been killed and at the time, I thought she needed all the goons she could get because, well, even you said we were looking at an all-out war breaking out between the Angelinos and the Andrulis families."

She took a bite of her burger and said, "And the other time?"

"The other time?" I tried for innocent confusion in an effort to muddy the waters.

"Back with Ms. Angelino, you said he'd done it a couple times. What happened on the other occasions?" I forgot Kate has a near-perfect, laser-sharp recall when it comes to work related matters.

"Um..." I really didn't want to tell her about the second time.

She'd been about to take another bite but ended up pounding the steering wheel with the side of the fist holding the burger instead. "Alex. Just out with it, would you? I shouldn't have to drag this out of you. Agapito Asshole Mancini held a knife to your throat and I should have heard about it when it happened, not months after the fact."

"Okay, okay. It was nothing, really. I'd heard that the doctor told him that if they'd been twisted any further he would've been in danger of something called 'genital torsion.' Whatever that is..." I added the last part hoping she'd assume it was no big deal and move on.

She'd just taken a sip from her soda and I actually saw little droplets of Coke spitting out of her nose as she tried to hold in her choking cough. She managed to swallow and turned her head toward the window, but not before I noticed a slight crinkling at the sides of her eyes. She jerked her car door open and got out, coughing her way down the sidewalk before regaining control and finally returning with a serious expression plastered across her face.

I popped the last bit of burger into my mouth as she once more took her seat.

Without saying a word, she finished hers as well. "Let's go. Farbers should be here soon with the plywood to board up the window."

Farbers, a residential construction company, has a contract with the city to secure any buildings we believe need to be boarded up. Since the window was broken on our watch, Farbers had been called to clean up our mess.

We gathered the few remaining evidence bags from her trunk and went in to begin our search. For an asshole, Pito kept an unusually clean and organized apartment. I guess I just assumed a moron would have old pizza boxes laying around, old underwear scattered across the floor and beer bottles littering every surface or countertop.

Not so, Pito. No dirty dishes filled his sink, the dishwasher had dishes in it but the little "clean" light meant he had recently done a load. Some laundry remained on his kitchen table, but the shirts, along with his pants and underwear, were neatly folded and stacked according to color or type. Who knew a guy like him would have a cornucopia of tighty whities, a couple of package-holding jock straps, and a c-string that covered his manly dongles with nothing more than a red mesh jock pack?

I picked up a jock strap with two fingers and examined it. It was a red number with yellow straps that ran around his waist and left no need for the imagination as far as butt hair was concerned. "No way."

Kate called from the other room. "What did you find?"

"He must have a roommate or something. Do you think he was gay?"

Kate stepped partially out of the bedroom to see what I'd found.

"I mean look at the size of this. There's no way they're Pito's."

"Put it back, Alex, and do your job."

"No, I'm not kidding, Sarge. Believe me, I *know* how much of his junk fit into the palm of my hand when we had our little, uh, altercation and this is for something twice that size."

Sighing, Kate brought an evidence bag over and held it open for me to drop the jock strap in. She folded the top over and handed it to me. "Seal it and tag it. God knows you've worked miracles on cases with evidence that no one in their right mind would collect."

I squinted at her retreating back, unsure whether she'd just given me a compliment or an insult. I used evidence tape and sealed the opening and then wrote my name and the date across both the tape and the brown paper bag. I set it down next to the door and continued with my search.

Apparently, Pito stacked his silverware according to type, with everything nestled in columns, each column in its designated place within the tray. His pots and pans were either stacked according to size in one of the lower cupboards or hung from a rack above the immaculately clean four-burner stove.

I heard Kate's phone ring in the other room but wasn't really interested in knowing who it was. Sure, sometimes, I'd listen in if I thought I could get away with it, but this early in the investigation, no one really knew anything and I tuned out the quiet droning as she spoke to whoever had called.

I pulled out a few more drawers and opened all the cupboards and found the same obsessive organization in every single one. The last cupboard held various bottles of different types of spirits, but what I found most interesting was a bottle of Glenlivet peeking out from behind all the rest. And not just any bottle.

Over the past couple of years, Gia has been teaching me the finer points of drinking good scotch. Prior to meeting her, the most I'd ever paid for a bottle was around $10, less if I could find a good sale. Now I was learning that the more I shelled out for a bottle, the more my friends and I enjoy our movie nights. Good Scotch whiskey is, well, it's hard to describe, but let's just say even Megan and Casey have learned to tell the difference.

But the bottle nestled behind Pito's collection of, among others, a $20 Canadian Club Premium Extra Aged Whiskey, an approximately $10 bottle of Svedka mango pineapple vodka, and a bottle of something called Kimo Sabe Mezcal, was a Glenlivet 50-year-old Winchester Collection 1964 collector's addition whiskey...

...Just like the one Gia showed me when she gave me a tour of the wine cellar beneath her Sonoita mansion...

...A $23,000 bottle of Glenlivet 50-year-old Winchester Collection 1964.

I moved aside the Mezcal and growled under my breath. "Damn."

The more evidence I found that implicated Pito in stealing from Gia only added to the growing body of circumstantial evidence linking her—or more precisely one of her minions upon her orders—to his murder. Nobody steals from Gianina Angelino. Let alone one of her own people.

Kate stuck her head around the corner again. "What now? More underwear?"

My luck to have a sergeant who not only has Superman's x-ray vision but also the unbelievable hearing capabilities of Mr. Spock. For a brief moment I considered putting the Mezcal back in place and walking away, but the instant the little devil sat down on my right shoulder and began swinging his legs and whispering in my ear, his nemesis, the angel, punched him in the face.

I stood up from my crouch and faced her.

My discomfort must have been written in the tense set of my lips because Kate came to stand in front of me, hands settled firmly on her hips. Her cocked head and the slight squint in her eyes dared me to come up with something 'not quite the whole truth'. "Something you want to tell me?"

"I just want to say..." What did I want to say? That Gia hadn't ordered Pito's execution? I wasn't sure whether she had or hadn't. That I didn't want to play anymore and could I please go home and crawl onto my new memory foam mattress and pull the covers over my head?

She glanced down at the bottle of Mezcal I still held and held out her hand. "What do you have there?"

I looked down at the bottle. "This? It's nothing. It's what I found hiding behind it that has me worried." I indicated the lower cabinet with the bottom of the Mezcal bottle.

Kneeling in front of the cabinet, Kate brought out her mini mag flashlight and shone it on the remaining bottles. "So, he drinks the same whiskey as Gia. He probably saw her drinking it and like you, thought he'd try paying more than $10 a bottle for it." She looked up at me and shrugged.

"Yeah, like $22,990 more."

Her gaze returned to the cupboard. "No way."

After a few moments of staring at the bottle, she looked up at me again and I raised my eyebrows. "Way."

She pursed her lips. "Damn." Rubbing tired eyes, she pointed at the Mezcal. "Where was that?"

I knelt beside her and replaced the bottle.

She snapped a picture showing the Glen Livet hidden behind the Mezcal bottle, and then snapped another one showing the bottle in full view. "Go get one of the evidence bags from the bedroom."

I nodded, but on the way to the door, I stopped and turned. "Kate. That is a really expensive bottle of whiskey. If it's the one Gia had in a special case in her wine cellar, I'd really hate to have it get ruined in our evidence section while we're trying to solve this case or worse yet, while we're waiting for a case to go to trial."

Kate stood and took out her phone. She hit one of her speed dials and held the phone to her ear a few seconds. "Stace? Kate. How's it going? The business doing well?" She waited for a response and then said. "That's wonderful. Listen, I need some information. First, can you tell me how much a bottle of..." She knelt again and read the label, "Glenlivet 50-year-old Winchester Collection 1964 whiskey would sell for?"

Alex heard the woman's exclamation all the way over to where she was standing.

Kate's eyebrows rose and she glanced at Alex. "And let's say I maybe had one of those bottles in my possession. What temperature would it need to be kept at?" Pause. "Okay, thanks for the info. You guys still coming to dinner next week?" Pause and then a chuckle. "Yeah, you wish. Listen, I have to run. Talk soon."

She hung up and then hit another speed dial. While she waited for someone to answer, she said quietly, "You were about $12,000 too low." Someone answered and she said, "Marla? Kate Brannigan. Listen, I have an extremely expensive bottle of Scotch I need to keep in evidence, but I'm afraid if it gets mishandled and ruined, the department could be facing a lawsuit. I have a friend who's a Master Sommelier and she says it has to be stored upright and between fifty-five- and sixty-five-degrees Fahrenheit."

Another pause and then, "Awesome. That'll be perfect. Thanks. I'll keep it with me tonight and drop it off with you tomorrow when you come in. Thanks again...what's that?" Pause. "That would be great. I should be done here in another hour or so and can bring it by the station, say, fifteen minutes after that? I really appreciate you coming in on your day off." She laughed. "Yes, enough to sign your overtime slip." Smiling at their interaction, she hung up and, losing the smile, pointed at the door. "The bag?"

I retrieved one of the last bags in Kate's collection. She needed to restock sooner than later and I hoped there wouldn't be much more evidence to collect. I held it open while she carefully set the bottle inside. "Marla is going to meet me back at the station. She said they keep one of their evidence refrigerators at exactly that temperature and she'll personally contact my friend for instructions and will guarantee the bottle is stored as it should be." She caught my eye and smiled. "Good catch, by the way."

I blinked and stood a little straighter than I had been just moments before. Compliments from Kate were rare and I watched as she personally took the bottle out to her car. When she returned, we finished our search without finding anything else that might have pertained to Pito's murder. Peeling off her gloves, she slipped the camera cord over her head and absently held it close to her chest. "I need you to fingerprint the place. If you're right about Pito's small hands and feet, I want to know who else has been in his apartment."

"His hands and feet?"

She rolled her eyes and the penny dropped. "Ohhh, his *feet*. Right. So, if I see anyone walking around in size sixteens..."

"Drop it, Alex."

As she walked to her car, and I moved to get the fingerprint kit out of my trunk, the other penny dropped. "Wait! You drove me here, remember?"

Without turning, she called over her shoulder. Nate's finished at the hospital. He's on his way. He'll help you with the prints."

That must have been who she'd spoken to on the phone. I called out, "Is the guy gonna live?"

She was at her car now and as she slipped behind the wheel she yelled, "Yes."

"Does he have big feet?"

I watched her shaking her head as she drove away and I liked to imagine she had a smile on her face as well. I went back inside to wait for Nate but wasn't surprised when I saw Gabe drive up in Gia's shiny new bulletproof Land Rover. Wanting to see the inside, I walked over just as he was getting out. I knew Gia wouldn't be with him on such a mundane task, so I pulled on the passenger side door hoping to get a peek inside.

The handle wouldn't budge and I guessed locked, immovable handles were part of the security feature. I rapped on the window, "Hey. Can I see inside?"

Without answering, Gabe shut his door and walked around to my side. "Just leave it, Alex."

"C'mon. I might have to rescue you in this one day and it would really help if I knew what the inside looked like." When he started walking toward the house, I said, "Or I might have to rescue Gia if you're out of commission. Don't you think it would be a good idea if I knew my way around?" I know that sounds far-fetched, but not too long ago I'd had to do just that.

He stopped and turned. I knew I'd won when I saw a hint of a dimple form in this cheek. He slipped his hand in his pocket and I heard a click near the door.

I pulled on the handle and again nothing moved. "It's broken." I indicated the handle with a flick of my thumb.

The dimple got bigger and he came close enough that I could smell his Salvatore Ferragamo F Black cologne. How do I know the type of cologne he uses? It's not because I have this great scenting machine for a nose. I happened to see it in his toiletry bag when I used his bathroom at the hospital. I'd be willing to bet it was a midrange cologne that any self-respecting, honest mob bodyguard could afford.

Which made me think I needed to check out what kind of cologne Pito had in his medicine cabinet. Then I happened to look down. "What size shoe do you wear, anyway?"

There's the grin I know and love. Okay, for most people, it would be a slight upward motion of the sides of his mouth, but for Gabe, it was the equivalent of a hearty laugh. "11."

Probably not him, then.

He waved his hand in front of a non-existent panel and lo and behold, an actual number pad appeared. Wow. Gabe saw me staring at the pad and moved his body in front of mine to block my view.

"Ya know, I might have to get into this thing at some point. How the hell am I supposed to do that with all this fancy schmancy security?"

A click sounded and the door magically opened by itself. "I don't know what schmancy is, Alex, but you need to talk to Ms. Angelino about getting put into the system."

"You know, schmancy. I think it might be Yiddish or something. My grandfather used to say things like 'look at that fancy schmancy car Leon's driving' or 'that's some fancy schmancy outfit Frieda had on when she went to buy her bagels this morning.'"

Gabe responded by raising one eyebrow and stepping aside. He waved an invitation for me to climb in.

I rested my foot on the running board, and then turned suspicious eyes on him. "You're not gonna lock me in here while you go get whatever you're here for from Pito's apartment are you?"

He rolled his eyes and sighed, "Ya wanna see it or not? I ain't got all day, Alex."

To my probably paranoid relief, Nate drove up in the blue Taurus. I yelled through the seam between door and car. "Number three on the right. Dust everything."

His gaze was fixed solidly on the Land Rover and without even looking I could sense Gabe's absolute refusal to let him anywhere near the interior of the vehicle.

A truck with the word Farbers stenciled on the side pulled up behind the Taurus. "Take them in and show 'em the back door. You stay with them at all times and they don't touch anything except the door."

Reluctantly, he walked over to talk to the guys from Farbers, who, now that I took a closer look, were actually gals instead of guys. One of them, a redhead, with all-American good looks, whatever that means, met him half-way. Since I happened to know Nate is partial to gingers and would stick to this one whether I'd told him to or not, I breathed a sigh of relief that I wouldn't have to tell him he couldn't come over and drool on Gia's upholstery.

Everything inside seemed a little anti-climactic until I saw some kind of machine gun mounted on a swivel beneath the passenger side console. I couldn't figure out how it worked. Did they have to shove the muzzle through the windshield to fire it? Then I looked up and realized the square panel in the roof above my head wasn't for letting sun in. A long, jointed arm attached to the plate the gun was secured to and it seemed as though the gun swiveled out and up high enough so the shooter could, what? Stand on the seat and spray the area with bullets?

I stared open-mouthed at Gabe who shrugged. "I told you ya probably shouldn't look inside."

Stepping out, I moved to the side as the door automatically swung closed. "I think I'll ask for a private tour some other time, maybe, probably not." There were some things that I'd like to have plausible deniability on and this vehicle was one of them.

"It's got a permit, Alex. Ms. Angelino likes to dot her I's and cross her T's when it comes to staying legal."

My eyebrows descended as I stared at him, and then decided I'd be better off not stating the obvious; that Gia was head of the largest crime syndicate in the western United States, whose father had built up the thriving business through brutality, murder and your all around run of the mill mayhem. Gia had never been convicted of any crime, nor had she ever been a suspect in a crime, but the Angelino empire had doubled since she'd taken over the business from her father, Tancredo.

Gabe fell into step with me as I walked toward the apartment.

I moved slightly ahead until I could turn and put my hand on his chest. "Whoa. This is the personal residence of a homicide victim and as such, part of our wider crime scene. I can't let you in."

He stared down at me a moment and then nodded and turned back toward his car.

"Hey, what are you looking for, anyway?"

He shrugged and kept walking. "Stuff."

I ran after him and stepped in front of him again. "What kind of 'stuff?'"

"I dunno, Alex, I'll know it when I see it. You want me to walk through your crime scene and see if I see somethin'?"

I thought about that a moment. He definitely might see something we missed, like more of Gia's stuff laying around. On the other hand, I don't think Kate would want a potential suspect—I hope he's not a suspect—traipsing around Pito's apartment on my go ahead. I had no doubt he'd come back after we'd gone, but that'd be on him, not me.

I shook my head. "No." When he started forward, I stopped him again with my fingers on his beefy chest. "But, if you find something interesting, let me know, will ya?"

The dimple appeared again and this time I let him get in the Rover and drive away. When I walked into the house, surprise, surprise, Nate hadn't started dusting for prints yet. He was leaning against the wall near the backdoor with his arms crossed over his chest talking to the redhead who was holding a piece of plywood to the open window while her partner used a drill to screw it in place.

Nate was usually a hard worker, so I decided to let him flirt while I took the fingerprint kit into the bedroom, retrieved the fuzzy brush from its case and began scattering the black powder on every surface likely to contain a fingerprint. It's a messy process and I always feel bad for victims of property crimes who end up having to clean up the powder themselves. I didn't think Pito would mind.

The front door shut with a quiet thud and Nate hurried in to help. "Sorry about that but you said to keep an eye on them and—"

I smiled at him over my shoulder, my brush poised mid-swipe on a full-length mirror. "Don't worry about it. Grab some tape and start lifting." I swiped a couple more times, "Did you get her name?"

"Yeah, I actually know her from high school. Her name's Michaela Simone and she's doing this construction gig to put herself through the U of A."

I heard the ratcheting sound of fingerprint tape as he tore off a piece to lay over the powder and pick up the prints. Once he had the fingerprint stuck to the sticky side of the tape, he set it onto a 3x5 card and labeled the back with the location, date and time.

We repeated the process over and over until we'd gone over the entire apartment. Curious, I looked in the closet to see what kind of clothes Pito wore when he wasn't at work. At work he'd worn cheap polyester suits, usually some variation of gaudy blue and I could count on being able to guess what he'd had for breakfast based on the food stains decorating the overwide ties he preferred.

That certainly didn't jive with the expensive coat he died in, nor with the condition of his apartment. Sure enough, a line of polyester coats, slacks and shirts hung in an organized fashion across the closet, almost all of them covered in plastic bags from the cleaners. I pulled off one of the cleaning tags and wasn't surprised to see "Mancini. Angelino Account" written across it. I folded the tag in two and stuck it in my pocket intending to throw it away when I got home.

Other than the suits, there were a couple of gaudy shirts you'd expect to see on John Travolta as he danced his way through Grease and a 1980's style track suit I assume Pito wore to the gym.

Nate and I locked both doors as we left and he drove me back to my car that Kate had me leave in the Sling 'Em parking lot. For a greasy spoon, the place was hopping. All of the parking spaces were full, which made me wonder why Pito's killer or killers had dumped his body here.

I went inside hoping to find someone I could talk to about the business. The harried manager, a smallish Asian American woman, held up a finger asking me to wait after I'd flashed my badge. The woman ran a tight ship, barking orders with the zeal and volume of a drill sergeant.

Her people responded with alacrity or the woman's hot-tempered follow up was immediate. She stood no taller than five-foot-one but that didn't stop her from tearing into one of her six-foot employees who apparently wasn't moving fast enough.

The man, or boy really—he looked like a high school football or basketball player—doubled his speed, wrapping burgers and loading them into bags and nodding at everything being yelled at him. Surprising, really, since many teens hold all adults in a permanent state of derision and rarely stand still for the type of bollocking this woman was handing out.

When she had the kitchen and servers running to her satisfaction, she wiped her hands on a towel and came out from behind the counter to speak to me. "Are you here about the body someone dumped in my dumpster last night?" I had expected a heavy Asian accent, and although I could detect the slight emphasis on certain letters such as a heavy sounding D, for the most part she spoke with less of an accent than my Jersey grandmother.

"Yes, Ma'am. I need to ask some questions about your business. When I was here after midnight last night, there were very few customers. In fact, I think I saw at the most five or six people enter the business the whole time I was here. Right after the sun came up this morning the place became packed." I pointedly glanced around the room. "And it's still packed. What time in the evening would you say your business starts to slow down?"

"So, you see all these people, right?"

I nodded.

"Do you think a manager has time to give an interview in the middle of *this*?" Shaking her head, she made shooing motions with her hands. "No, I can't. All these people? They wanna eat, and if I'm out here talking to you, maybe they don't get their food as quick as they should." As though she had eyes in the back of her head, the woman yelled over her shoulder, "Don't take the fries out before the dinger, Jessie!" Turning back to me she said, "I leave tonight at seven. You come back then." Without waiting for me to acknowledge her words, the woman rushed behind the counter and began issuing orders.

I watched her for a bit, wondering what could be happening that required a non-stop harangue from the manager. Every cash register had a line in front of it at least five if not seven people deep. I sidled up next to a cowboy standing in the near line with his hands tucked under his armpits. "I don't get it. This is a burger joint. What's the big draw to the place?

He looked down on me and smiled. "Y'ever tried one?"

Remembering the dumpster, I had to consciously suppress my initial disgust at the question and settled with a simple, "No."

Another smile tugged at the corner of his mouth and he turned his attention to the controlled chaos happening behind the counter. "Must be the secret sauce. That's all I can figure."

I couldn't bring myself to try a burger, secret sauce or not. I sat in my car with the heater at full blast and watched the customers and servers through the windshield. The lady did a heck of a business, that was for sure. I didn't see anything out of the ordinary, so I backed out of my space and cruised slowly by the alley.

When I was in line with the dumpster, I stopped and looked over my shoulder. Unless someone sat in one or two specific tables in the eating area, there was no way to see the dumpster from inside the building. Realizing I'd done all I could for the day, I decided to pack it in and head for home. I had no intention of returning at seven, but I'd try to catch the manager some other time.

CHAPTER 2

I walked into the office the next day and found Casey already sitting in Kate's cubicle talking. Our offices are on the third floor of the police station. As you walk through the door, our secretary, Sharon sits on the right in a square, glassed in cubicle. On the side of the cubicle facing the walkway is a counter and sitting on that is my favorite device in the whole office. A round M & M man with his arm raised in the air. I pulled down on the arm and was rewarded with five M & M's that I promptly popped into my mouth.

Looking forward from Sharon's desk, there are three sergeant's glassed-in cubicles on the left, and behind them begins the bullpen area housing child abuse, domestic violence and on the right side of the room sits our unit, the Special Crimes Division. The top half of the wall on our side of the building is all glass and we get to look out on a lovely view of the back of the fire station and the side of St. Augustine's Cathedral.

I dropped my briefcase on my desk, which butted up against the front of Casey's work area and wandered over to Kate's cubicle to see if we had anything new on Pito's death. "You two must have come in bright and early."

Kate glanced up from her computer screen. "I sent Casey out on a possible familial kidnapping last night. She located the little girl and got her back to the custodial father."

I sat in one of the chairs and waited for Kate to finish what she was working on. When Allen Brodie walked in balancing several evidence bags on his arms, Kate stopped him. "Brodie, did you have any luck finding Tom Handy yesterday?" No one called Brodie by his first name. Apparently he'd been known as Brodie since elementary school and from what he'd told me, it became so entrenched that even his mother gave in to the inevitable and stopped calling him Allen in high school in favor of their last name.

He shifted one of the bags with his elbow. "No luck, boss. I looked everywhere for that RV Alex was talking about."

"Okay, thanks."

Brodie nodded and continued to his desk where he set the bags on the floor and then left, apparently either going back out for more or returning to retrieve his briefcase and files.

Kate swiveled around to face us. "I want you two to go find Tom Handy. Alex, since he doesn't have an official address, do you know any distinguishing characteristics of his motor home...license plate or vin maybe?"

I shook my head and she glanced at the ceiling, thinking. "I'd like to get a search warrant before you find him so we can look for whatever it was he took from that dumpster. When you find the motorhome, I want you to get close enough without being seen to get his license plate, then the two of you call in and get a warrant."

Casey and I stood but Kate motioned for us to sit back down. "I've spoken to Chief Sepe about this case. He's obviously concerned about more mafia bodies showing up. It didn't seem to me that Ms. Angelino was too concerned about finding out who killed Pito. Did you, by any chance, find that..." She pursed her lips while she thought of the correct word. "...curious, Alex? You know her better than I do. Why wasn't she concerned that one of her people had been executed? Those are the kinds of questions the chief is asking, and I need to find some answers for him."

I knew her first inclination had been to say 'suspicious' and I appreciated her last-minute change of direction. "Well, yes and no.

Gabe got to Pito's apartment shortly after we arrived, so that means one of three things." I glanced about to make sure no one was within hearing distance and held up one finger at a time to illustrate my points. "Either she's having her people investigate his death herself, probable, in which case she's not going to show her hand if some rival gang member all of a sudden shows up dead in another dumpster."

I held up a second finger and shook my head slightly. "Two, she ordered the hit herself. Even though she'd never come right out and admit to the fact, she's not the type of person to put on an act to hide the fact, but my gut is telling me that's not the case. And three, she wasn't minimizing the situation when she says Pito was universally disliked. And honestly, disliked is too nice a word. She might just be relieved someone did her a favor."

Kate pulled out her bottom desk drawer, propped her foot on it and began tapping her pen on her thigh. This quirk wasn't just confined to when she was irritated or angry at me. She also did it when she was thinking and needed to focus her thoughts. "None of which are suitable answers for the Chief."

Casey leaned forward and spoke softly. "Alex told me the chief had notified Gia about Pito's death before you were able to get there. That's almost unheard of. Since when does a chief get that involved in a case, and why is he pushing for answers less than twenty-four hours after a body turns up?"

The pen stopped tapping and Kate's gaze settled on me for just a moment before she lowered her foot and leaned forward, answering in the same hushed tones Casey had used. "What the Chief does in this case is my concern, not yours." She turned her piercing brown eyes on me to make a point, "And no one else needs to hear about his involvement in this. Understood?"

I turned my hands palm side up in my lap. "Sure. I didn't know it was a secret. Sorry."

Kate sighed and sat back with a purpose, her chair squeaking with the strain. "It's not a secret. It's just not something I want bandied about for the exact same reason that Casey asked the question. I've known Michael Sepe for my entire career and I absolutely guarantee he is not in Ms. Angelino's back pocket."

When Casey and I nodded, she continued, "That being said, he serves at the whim of the City Manager, which means he has to be very adept at playing politics. None of us are naïve enough to think that if Ms. Angelino is upset about how we're doing our jobs, people in our government won't hear about it."

All of us were aware of Gia's far reaching political connections, which had tentacles that wriggled way past our city's politicians. In politics, money talks louder than morality, and Gia has plenty of it to spread around.

Casey and I waited to see whether Kate had anything else to say. When she waived her hand at us and said, "Okay, get going." we walked back to our desks to pick up our briefcases and headed out to our cars.

Casey followed me to the desert area where I'd seen Tom's motorhome several weeks earlier. He'd apparently moved, since there was no motorhome in sight, but in its place were several old blankets draped between a mesquite bush and a palo verde tree. We parked and walked over to talk to the current occupants.

A rail-thin white woman and an equally skinny Hispanic man were going at it like bunnies when we walked up. At least he was anyway. She didn't look like she cared one way or the other. They were laying on top of a greasy sleeping bag and two other bags had been rolled up and stashed beneath an overhanging branch.

Various articles of clothing were hung from the protruding sticks of the palo verde tree, aptly named since the actual translation of the tree's name means, "green sticks."

I glanced over at Casey and rolled my eyes. It's not that we thought homeless people shouldn't have sex, but lately it seemed like every time we walked up to a homeless encampment to look for a witness or a suspect, at least one pair would be doing the nasty.

I held out my badge. "Hello? Police."

The man, whose jet black, braided ponytail hung down over his shoulder, didn't stop, and the woman just lay there with her legs spread wide letting him go at it. The knots in her thin brown hair were all jumbled up, covering her head as though she hadn't quite managed to completely duck when passing beneath the tendrils of a sticky spider's web.

I nudged the guy's leg with my toe. "Hey. We need to talk to you guys."

The man grunted. "Hang on. I paid fer th' hole an' I ain't quitin' 'till I get my money's worth." He had a light Mexican accent but definitely spoke English as his primary language.

Casey and I pulled on some gloves while his off-white, hairy butt continued to pump up and down. We both grabbed an arm and hauled the guy off the woman, who lay in a drug induced stupor and didn't even bother to close her legs.

The man, who's wanger was more like a Vienna sausage than a full-blown Kielbasa, shouted, "Hey! You can't do that!"

Casey pointed to his pants. "Pull 'em up or I'm haulin' your ass to jail."

"On what charge?"

I supplied the answers. "Let's see. Solicitation, public indecency, vagrancy..."

By now he'd pulled up his dirty jeans. "Ok, ok. I get it."

I picked up a filthy blanket between the tips of my thumb and forefinger and draped it across the woman's hips. She still hadn't moved and I bent down to get a closer look at her face. I turned to the man, "All those previous charges, plus defiling a corpse, unless I miss my guess."

The man, who appeared to be in his mid-forties, moved his head forward and squinted at the lady's face. "Naw. She's alive. Was when we started, anyway."

Casey pulled out her handcuffs, ratcheted them onto his wrists and read him his rights. Then she motioned to the body with her chin. "How'd you pay her?"

He looked scared now. "Just some crisscrossin'. Nothin' she ain't done before."

I saw the needle lying next to a small Bunsen burner. "Heroin and Cocaine?"

"Yeah, but..." The initial panic that had washed over him was slowly being replaced; first by a dawning comprehension, followed by a sickening revulsion crossing the finish line a close second. "I was pumpin' a dead body?"

Even though Casey had cuffed his hands behind his back, that didn't stop him from walking a few paces away and turning a full 360-degree circle. "That's—" He broke off abruptly and bent over as his empty stomach dry heaved the absolutely nothing he'd had for breakfast. When he regained control, he finished his sentence "—disgusting."

He continued pacing in circles, mumbling curses and kicking pebbles this way and that.

Casey took hold of his arm. "Stop. You're messing up the crime scene."

The man slipped from revulsion right back into panic mode and his voice rose several octaves. "Crime Scene? *Crime Scene?* Oh Christ, this ain't no crime scene. I didn't commit no crime! I was just..." He stopped to find the right words, "...Stace 'n me, we was just fuckin' each other. I didn't know she'd—" Another round of dry heaving ensued.

I knelt and placed my fingers on top of the woman's carotid artery, which should have been pumping furiously with a speedball running through her veins. Nothing. "Do you at least know Stace's full name?"

He absentmindedly shook his head.

Looking over her shoulder at the body, Casey said, "Stacey Lynn Beckett. Don't you recognize her? We got her into rehab a couple months back."

I tilted my head trying to look at her from a different angle. "The one who didn't want her baby? Gave him to her mother? No way." I moved the tangled hair off the face and only then did I see the half-moon shaped scar on her right temple where someone had stabbed her years ago with an apple corer. "Damn."

Stacey was only twenty-five or so, but ignoring the fact that she was dead, she looked horrible. My first impression when we'd walked up was that the woman on the ground was at least forty-five or even fifty. I stood, pulled off my rubber glove and dug my cell phone out of my pocket. "We don't have time for this."

Casey sighed. "We do now, at least until Logan sends somebody."

Kate answered on the second ring.

"Hey Boss."

"Did you find him?"

"Not the him we were hoping for. But, we did find a guy playing hide the salami, or in his case, the cocktail weenie, with a corpse. Do you want us to call Sgt. Logan?"

Her sigh came over loud and clear. "No, I'll get things started on this end. Where are you?"

I gave her directions to our car and we moved the guy away from the scene. He slumped down with his back against our front tire while we waited for a homicide dick to arrive.

After about a half-hour, our friend, Ruthanne Stahl, bumped across the desert in a cloud of dust. Thankfully she stopped far enough away that we weren't completely engulfed in a lung clogging miasma of silt and valley fever spores. When the dust settled, she pushed her door open with her foot and stepped out holding two large cups of coffee, one in each hand.

Casey had peeled off her gloves by then and we both gratefully accepted one of the cups.

"Here ya go. For Casey it's a large, filled ¼ of the way up with high-test creamer and a ton of sugar, and for you, eight little cups of hazelnut creamer and six packets of Stevia. Who knew they'd started stocking Stevia in the convenience stores, anyway? So, what do we got?" She rubbed her hands together while studying the man slumped against the front wheel with a practiced eye.

He refused to look at her, instead turning his face until the side of his forehead rested against the car's wheel well.

Ruthanne and I headed for the makeshift encampment while Casey stayed with him. I began to fill her in on the way. "We were looking for Tom Handy—"

"The vet who drives an RV?"

"Yeah, and when the RV wasn't here, we came over to see if there was anybody staying here who might know where he's moved to. We see Numbnuts back there with his pants down around his ankles humping this lady. When we pulled him off, I realized she was dead and called Kate." We ducked beneath the blanket, which was hung about a foot above head height, and surveyed the scene.

"Did you move or touch anything?"

It was pretty obvious I had since the blanket covering her private parts would have made it extremely difficult for the village idiot to bump nasties. "Just that blanket. At first we thought she was stoned, laying there with her legs spread and her twat peeking out for the whole world to see, so I covered her up, you know, to..." I shrugged not sure how to put it.

"To preserve her dignity. I get it. I wish you hadn't, but I get it. Do you know if he came? Will we find any fluids on or in her?"

"He hadn't by the time we pulled him off, but who knows how many times he'd done her by then. He said he paid her with a speedball, well, he called it 'crisscrossing' and thought she wasn't moving because she was stoned. From his reaction, I don't think he knew he was doing a corpse, but I guess that's for you to decide."

She shrugged. "At the very least, we can hold him on solicitation, supplying illicit drugs, and manslaughter if we can prove he gave her the drugs." Can I borrow your radio? I left mine in the car so I could bring your coffee out."

I unclipped my handheld from the back of my belt and she radioed dispatch and asked for a patrol unit to transport one subject back to the main station. Then she called her sergeant and told him what she had.

When she disconnected, I said, "We'll hang around long enough for patrol to get here. You got anything to snack on in your car?" We walked back to the suspect who'd decided it might be in his best interest to clarify a few things. I guessed Casey had had a little chat with him, suggesting that if he had any hope of getting out of this, that hope lay with Ruthanne.

"You the dick gonna interview me? Listen—"

Ruthanne held up a hand and walked to her car to retrieve her recorder. When she returned, the guy opened his mouth to speak and she held up her hand again, silencing him. After she gave all the preliminaries like reading him his rights, which she technically didn't need to do again since Casey had already done it, she listed the time, the place, and who was present—at this point the man told us his name was Herman Busto—and Ruthanne then set the recorder on the hood of the car. She motioned with an open hand. "Okay, Mr. Busto. Tell me what happened."

He suddenly had verbal diarrhea, speaking rapidly while staring up into Ruthanne's face. "Look, I ain't had no bacon fer like forever an' I had a chance t' score a speedball fer some work I done fer this fella. I ain't gotten m' skankie on fer weeks, an' I needed t' ball some'un real bad. I knew Stace needed a hop so I gave it to her. All I wanted was t' ball her, man. That's all!"

Ruthanne scratched her head. "Okay. I'm going to try to translate what you just said for the tape, and you tell me if I get it right."

Hank scowled but grudgingly nodded.

"You've been broke, without money, for a long time. A man paid you for some work you did for him with a syringe full of heroin and cocaine, what you referred to as a speedball. You haven't had sex in a while and wanted some. You knew Stace—" She interrupted her translation. "Do you know Stace's full name?"

He shook his head. "Nah."

I helped out. "Stacey Lynn Beckett."

She nodded and made a note in her book. "Anyway, you knew Stace was a prostitute with a habit, so you paid her for sex with the syringe full of heroin and cocaine you'd obtained from your boss. Is my translation correct so far, Mr. Busto?"

When Herman nodded, Ruthanne made rolling motions with her hand. "You need to speak your answer for the recording."

"Yeah, yeah, yeah. That's what I said without all them fancy words. An' then, these two clowns," he looked up at me and made a prissy face with his lips and scrunched up nose, "I mean *officers*, come along and—"

"For the record you mean Detective Bowman and Detective Wolfe, correct?"

"These two, yeah, and they come along and jerked me off."

I held out my hands. "Whoa, whoa, whoa. Can I clarify, or can he? One of us needs to clarify."

Ruthanne stifled a laugh so her sniggers didn't show up on the tape and Casey covered her mouth with her fingers to hide her smile.

Ruthanne swallowed and finally choked out, "Mr. Busto, what exactly did you mean by that? What did the detectives do?"

"They pulled me off 'er. I didn't know she was a stiff, I swear!"

I tuned out the rest of the interview while Ruthanne continued with her questions, getting all the details she could before Herm decided maybe he needed a lawyer after all and clammed up.

As soon as she turned off the recorder, I spoke up. "Herman, do you know a man named Tom Handy?"

"Everybody knows the asshole. Big time prick if ya ask me."

"Didn't he have his camper parked somewhere around here the last few weeks?"

"Yeah. Mr. high 'n mighty. Thinks cuz he's here nobody else kin stake a claim. That's bullshit if you ask me. That's why I put m' stuff here, cuz the asswad told me I couldn't." He leaned to his right and spat in the dirt before turning and grinning up at me. "Sumpin' scared him though. Last night he come runnin' up here, jumped in his rig an' took off. Ran a truck that was headin' this way out inta th' desert." His grin widened as he blinked up at me.

"Last night or early this morning?"

"How th' hell would I know? It was dark, that's what I know."

I didn't like his tone and told him so. "You don't need to be rude, Herm. What kind of truck?"

Acknowledging my point with a sheepish shrug, He mumbled, "Hell if I know. It was dark and ya don't see any streetlights out here do ya?"

"Big, little, dark, light, new, old?"

"Big. Probably dark, but like I said, couldn't see much. And not from th' sixties or nuthin'. Not fancy old anyway, but I couldn't see if it was new neither."

"What did the driver of the truck do?"

"Spun around and hauled ass after Tom." He put his head back and laughed. "Served th' bung hole right. Hope they caught 'im."

Casey and I exchanged glances. Both of us were hoping he hadn't gotten a new train tunnel through his forehead like Pito.

Casey knelt next to him. We usually tag team people, so I backed up a step hoping she'd get more out of him than I had. "Have you ever seen the truck before?"

"Nope."

"Would you recognize it if you saw it again?"

"Nope." He pointed a long, filthy finger in the direction we'd come in. "You can see th' donut over there, though."

"Donut?"

"Where th' tires spun out. Don't you know nothin'?"

We knew what a donut was, but it never hurt to clarify exactly what a suspect or witness was saying. Casey pushed to her feet and after grabbing our coffees off the roof of her car, we walked down the dirt path looking for tire tracks. Sure enough, off to the side, a little way into the desert, the truck's tires had etched a perfect circle in the dirt.

I pulled out my phone. "Damn it. We're never getting out of here."

A patrol car came bouncing down the dirt path toward us.

Casey held up her hand and walked forward, silently directing the officer not to come any further so he didn't mess up the tracks any more than the three of us had already done.

While she was busy doing that, I called Kate again.

"What do you need this time, Alex? Find another corpse? If you did, I don't want to know about it. Just bury it and get back to work."

"Sure thing, Boss. But the guy who was shagging the corpse said Tom came running back to his RV last night and drove out of here like a bat out of hell. He said Tom ran a truck off the dirt path and that the truck spun a donut in the sand and chased after him. That's why I'm calling. We found the tracks. Do you want the evidence techs to come out and make a cast of the prints?"

"No. Just photograph them." She didn't say anything for a while and I knew better than to interrupt when she was thinking. "Did we mention anything about Tom Handy to Gia?"

"No."

"And I haven't mentioned him to Chief Sepe yet, so why was someone chasing him? Look, while you're looking for the RV, see if you can locate that girl you were talking to at the scene."

"Girl?"

"The meth head."

"Oh, you mean Cherry. She was actually older than she looked. I'd guess early to mid-thirties."

"See whether you can find her and let me know if you do."

"Yes, Ma'am."

"I tried to find the registration for Tom's RV, but it must be under someone else's name. I want to put out an ATL, but until we get something more than 'an RV' there's no hope for that." An ATL, or attempt to locate, would go out to the Sheriff's office and the Department of Public Safety as well as our own officers. It would sure make finding Tom a lot easier.

"By the way, there's no one matching his description in the system named Tom or Thomas Handy. Are you sure that's his name?"

"That's what everybody calls him. As soon as we photograph these tire tracks we're gonna head out again and try to find him."

"Okay, and Alex?"

"Yeah?"

"If you see anyone else having intercourse, could you just leave them alone?"

The plaintive note in her voice made me smile. "Sure thing, Boss." I went to my car and pulled out a measuring tape, my notebook, and a camera and walked to where Casey stood talking to the cop. I hadn't realized at first that Terri Gentry, Casey's fiancé, was the patrol officer who'd come to pick up Herman.

The two of them hadn't tied the knot yet. They were waiting for Terri's divorce from her abusive, asshole cop husband to come through. I envied her five-foot-six-inch frame, which was well-padded with solid muscle. She had the reflexes of a mountain lion and could chase a suspect several miles if need be. She was a cop's cop, respected by most everyone on the department.

A lot of the women on the department wore their hair either in a bun or short ponytail, but Terri wore her honey-blonde hair short on the sides and spiked on top. She was someone who had sworn to remain in patrol for her entire career, and seeing as she'd already made it fifteen years, there was no reason to think otherwise.

"Hey, Alex. So, this is a new one for me. I have to admit I've never arrested someone for defiling a corpse before."

"We aim to please."

"Casey said it's Stacey Beckett. I guess we all saw that one coming. Who's the perp?"

"Herman..." I couldn't remember the guy's last name but Terri knew him from just the first name.

"Herman Busto? He won't be around much longer, either, but sometimes these guys surprise you. You think one more arm or nose full will do 'em in, and five years later you're still picking 'em up off the sidewalk in a stuporific haze."

Ruthanne was bringing Herman down the path toward us and when he saw Terri he called out. "Well if it ain't purty little Officer Gentry." His smile was friendly and I knew he wasn't trying to insult Terri. There's usually a weird dynamic between patrol officers and the criminal element in their beat. Not exactly a friendship, but an acknowledgement that they both belong there.

Terri lifted her hands out to her sides. "What's with you shaggin' a corpse, Herm? I've seen some nasty things in my day, but..." She let the rest of the sentence hang.

The blood rushed into Herman's face and he stopped in his tracks. "I wasn't shaggin' no corpse!"

I shrugged and added helpfully, "She was dead and you were—"

"It don't count if she was breathin' when ya started. How was I t' know she kacked it, anyways? Ya can't spread that nowhere. Ya can't!" His normally alto voice had risen to a tenor, maybe even a male soprano by the time he stopped talking.

Terri grinned and opened her rear door. "My lips are sealed." Once she'd put him in the car and closed the door, she said, "At least until I get him booked in for the night." She took the booking sheet from Ruthanne, waved goodbye and headed off to the jail.

Casey and I photographed the tire marks, using a tape measure to document the size and depth of the tread as best we could. I was starving by that time and we decided to grab lunch at our favorite watering hole, the Sleepytime Café before heading out to look for Tom again.

The place was empty when we walked in, which was unusual around this time of the day. I expected Maureen, our usual waitress to come take our order with her usual grumbling, "Hello and what you want?" but instead, a two-ton septuagenarian came rolling down the aisle.

Every time she took a breath, a wheezing sound like an overinflated balloon being set free to zip around the room sounded out long and loud. But worse than that, a dried booger flowed in and out of her left nostril with each breath. Sweat stains colored her waitress uniform beneath her armpits. And not just any sweat stains. There had to be three- or four-days' worth of white semi-circles of dried sweat that had been covered over again and again as each day's ooze came to the fore.

Casey and I stared at the woman while she rooted around in an oversized pocket for a pen and order pad. Scratching some dried white flakes off her nose with one hand, she moved aside a bottle of ketchup and an old drinking glass with the other before she finally found what she was looking for. She glanced at me and wheezed, "You gonna need any a dis ketchup? If ya' are, tell me now cuz I ain't makin' a special trip back to da kitchen jus' t' git yer ass sumpin' I can give ya right now."

My stomach turned over several times and when I didn't immediately answer, she scrunched up her nose, which already had the misfortune of having its end resting firmly on her upper lip and pulled out the dirty bottle. "Here, den. If ya can't make up yer mind, dat jus' means you'll 'spect me t' run 'n git it fer ya when I bring yer food. Do I look like a woman what wants t' run get yer sorry ass a bottle a ketchup?"

My mouth dropped open and for the first time in a very long time, I had no smartass comeback. Heck, I couldn't even form the word "no" so I settled with slowly shaking my head.

"So whaddya wanna eat? Ya t'ink I kin stand here all day waitin' on yer sorry ass? Look at dem swollen ankles."

We all three looked down at a couple of hairy legs that ended in two hunks of Gyro meat that belonged on the spindles you see in Greek fast food places. I almost did a Herman but was able to stave off the dry heaves before I embarrassed myself.

My handheld radio chose that time to come to life. The dispatcher asked for any unit to respond to a man complaining about a car parked in a disabled parking space.

Casey beat me to the punch and grabbed the radio seconds before I could and quickly depressed the mic. "9David72 and 73, show us en route."

As both of us slid out from behind the table, I gestured to the radio. "We gotta run. Maybe you'll see us later." Not.

The woman's nose did the unpleasant scrunch action again. "What da foock's wrong wit' you cops? You're the fifth or six bunch 'a morons wit' badges come in t' eat an' every one a ya gits a call an needs t' leave. I can't wait fer Maureen t' git back from Jersey. Doin' th' woman a favor. Never again. Ya make me walk all dis way t' get yer order an..."

Her voice trailed off to nothing as the door swung closed behind us. I had an almost pathological need to wash my hands and I hurried to the back of my car to get the bottle of hand sanitizer out of my trunk. I squirted some onto Casey's outstretched hands and then liberally doused my own. "I'm gonna start bringing my lunch. I don't think I'll ever be able to sit down at a table again without seeing those white stains under her arms and—." I almost dry heaved again thinking about that thing sticking out of her nose.

My radio chirped, "9David72, did I copy you're on the way to the illegal parking call?"

I unclipped the radio from where it hung on my belt near the small of my back. "9David72, that's negative. 9David73 thought it might be related to a suspect we're looking for, but we need to be somewhere else right now."

"9David72 copy." The dispatcher put out another call for a patrol officer to respond, and good luck with that. No one had time to take an illegal parking call. The department was short staffed as it was and barely had enough people to handle burglaries and shoplifters.

The slightly nauseous look on Casey's face probably mirrored my own as she ran a hand through her short, blonde hair. "I am so not hungry right now. Let's just go look for the RV."

I managed to nod and get in behind the wheel of my car.

Casey knocked on my window and when I rolled it down, she asked, "Where are we going?"

I thought a minute and then pointed north. "Follow me. There's another out-of-the-way spot where Tom used to park when I worked patrol in Team Two. I rousted him out of there a couple of times so maybe he's gone back there to roost."

She tapped on the roof of my car. "I'll follow you, then."

My cell phone rang from the depths of my front pocket and after a few gyrations I managed to pull it out. I didn't recognize the number and almost tossed it onto the passenger seat when I remembered I'd given my card to Cherry Saturday night and had told her to call if anything else occurred to her. I answered the unknown caller with a bit of trepidation because there's nothing worse than letting a telemarketer know they have a cop's phone number. The calls come on hot and heavy then if only because some moron thinks it funny to harass a cop in the middle of the night. With that in mind, I decided not to answer it with my rank and name. "Yeah?"

"Detective Wolfe?" The caller whispered the words so quietly I almost didn't hear the question.

"Yes."

"It's Cherry. He's after me." Her words ran together so fast I knew she was flying high on crank.

"Where are you?"

"I'm in a bank usin' some lady's phone."

"What bank?" I started up my car and pulled up next to Casey's. She had backed out and was facing me waiting to follow. We both rolled down our windows and I held up a finger silently asking her to wait.

I heard Cherry hiss to someone, presumably the woman who owned the phone. "What bank is this?" There was some murmuring in the background, then silence.

"Cherry?"

A woman's voice came on the line. "Hello?"

"This is Detective Wolfe. Who's this? Where's Cherry?"

"This is Ms. Compton. I'm the administrative assistant on the ground floor of the Valley National Bank building at Stone and

Congress. When I didn't let that woman use my phone she started to make a fuss and since I didn't want to upset my other customers I let her call you. You should know I've also called the police."

"I am the police. I'm a detective."

"I mean the real police. In the uniforms?"

There wasn't any time to argue the point so I got her back on track. "Ms. Compton, where did Cherry go?"

"She threw the phone at me and ran towards the back of the building. I assume she used the doors on that side of the building, although I can't see around the corner. I think she was on drugs because of the way she acted. I'm sure she's a meth user because of her teeth being all black and—"

"Was anyone chasing her?"

"No one but the boogie man in her drug addled imagination. I tell you—"

I ended the call and turned to Casey. "Cherry called from the Valley National Bank building, Stone and Congress. She ran away though before she could tell me anything. She said, 'he's chasing me' when I first answered the phone."

"Who's chasing her?"

"Hell if I know." I slammed the gearshift into drive and Casey followed me as I flew out of the parking lot. I grabbed the mic but had to jam on the brakes when some moron cut me off in traffic. I pulled next to him and badged him when he started speeding to keep me from going around.

The driver, a twenty-something moron, immediately slowed down when he saw the badge. I retrieved the mic from the seat where I'd thrown it when I'd grabbed my badge. I keyed it and gave my designator. "9David72."

The dispatcher answered. "9David72."

Do you have a call at the Valley National Bank building?"

"10-4 with no units 10-8." That meant all the patrol units were busy. An unwanted subject would be pretty low on the priority list anyway and probably wouldn't get dispatched for a few hours, if at all.

"Show 9David72 and 73 en route."

The dispatcher gave us the call info, "Call number 463, unwanted female at the Valley National Bank building, Stone and Congress. Showing 9David72 and 9David73 en route."

As we approached the building, I radioed Casey. "9David72 to 73. I'll go in the front, you check around back." Parking is notoriously bad downtown and when I couldn't find a parking space I parked illegally in a tow away zone. I threw a business card on the dashboard and ran into the building.

I'd clipped my badge to the outside of my coat and a woman hurried over to me. She wore the 1950's style cat-eye glasses that had recently come back into vogue. Above them, she'd penciled in half-moon eyebrows that gave her a permanently surprised lift to her forehead. Her overly full lips were painted an odd pepperoni red and I found myself staring at them as she spoke. "Was I just speaking with you? I'm sorry we were cut off somehow but—"

I didn't want to give her time to ramp up into her non-stop monologue so I held my hand in front of her face, which surprisingly had the intended result. Her painted eyebrows rose even higher and she stopped speaking. "Ms. Compton? I'm Detective Wolfe. Has the woman who used your phone returned?"

"No." She turned and pointed to a door in the back. "The doors around that corner aren't to be used. We keep them locked at all times but that woman ran out of them without a by your leave."

"Thank you." I ran to the back of the lobby, skirted the corner and pushed the door open, eliciting a "You can't—" before the door swung closed behind me. The emergency exit opened onto a parking lot and I saw Casey's sedan stopped in the middle of the lot with the door open.

I ran to the car to check inside, but then heard Casey calling to me from off to my right. "Alex, over here." I jogged to where she was standing over a pool of bright red blood.

She was a little out of breath as she pointed south. "I saw some guy running this way so I chased him. He got into a brown pickup." Unclipping her radio from the back of her belt, she called in the make of the truck and a partial plate.

While she was doing that, I walked a wide circle around the perimeter of the lot looking for a body or more blood. When I saw more drops, I let Casey know. "More blood over here. I'm gonna follow to see what I find."

She had moved her vehicle closer to the blood and waved to let me know she'd heard. I came to a blue dumpster and mentally girded myself to find Cherry's body tossed inside. I peered over the edge and was relieved to see the normal detritus you'd expect to find in a business dumpster. I moved past it and luckily registered movement out of the corner of my eye.

Reacting instinctively, I twisted to my right and barely missed getting skewered by a wild-eyed Cherry, who let out a feral scream as she lunged at me with a pair of kitchen shears. I knocked her arm aside and then grabbed her by the wrist and twisted it behind her back.

She continued to scream and buck and I had to take her to the ground to control her manic gyrations. I managed to get both hands behind her back but she continued to grip the scissors with a death grip and I couldn't let go of either hand to get my cuffs.

Casey came running around the corner, but instead of being able to cuff her, she had to pry both of Cherry's ankles off my leg where she'd wound them around so tightly I couldn't get my leg beneath me to gain any purchase.

Once Casey freed my leg, I put one knee in the small of Cherry's back and knelt on the other. I still had the problem of trying to get to my cuffs and as I was trying to figure out how to release a hand while still maintaining control, I heard the distinctive sound of a zip tie behind me. Glancing back, I saw that Casey had secured Cherry's ankles and was reaching behind her back to pull out her cuffs.

She ratcheted them onto Cherry's wrists and I could finally pry the scissors out of her rigidly spasmed fingers. They were clamped so tightly around the rings of the shank that I thought I might have to break them to get her to release. In the end, I had to pry off one finger at a time and when I released each one, they curled inward so forcefully I worried her fingernails were carving gashes in her palms.

When I rolled her over, Cherry's face morphed through a series of twitches and tics that confirmed Ms. Compton's initial assessment. Cherry was torqued on Meth.

"C'mon. Sit up." I helped her up and saw exactly what I'd expected to see, a round, dilated pupil, black with a tiny sliver of green circling the circumference. "Cherry, you said somebody was following you. What happened?"

The involuntary twitching around her lips intensified as she opened her mouth to speak. "I got 'im. I got 'im. Did ya see 'im? I got 'im. I got 'im." Her rapid speech came out both clipped and slurred at the same time. Meth tends to rev a person up, and it's really hard to keep up with what they're trying to tell you.

"Who'd you get, Cherry? Who was following you?"

"Don't matter. I got 'im an' he's gonna die." Her eyes opened wide and she began laughing a choppy, insane kind of laughter.

I took her by the shoulders and lightly shook her. "Who did you get, Cherry?"

"That man. That man. That man that got Tom. Tom's dead. That man got 'im and I got that man!" The triumphant glaze that popped her eyes wider than should have been possible sent shivers down my spine. We couldn't take anything she said at face value because she was having a difficult time separating fantasy from reality.

I took out my phone and called dispatch. My friend, Sheralyn Davies, one of the communications supervisors answered the phone. I liked Sheralyn but had only recently gotten to know her better when we'd both attended a retirement party for our mutual friend, Pedro Martinez. "Hey, Sheralyn. How's it goin' today?"

"Nothing new under the sun, Alex. How about you?"

"Not much. Do you think you could you do me a couple favors?"

"Depends. Can I get demoted, fired or jailed for them?"

I laughed. "You've been listening to the rumors. This is perfectly legitimate and case related. Could you check the records and see whether there have been any bodies show up recently, like the last twenty-four hours, either in the city limits or in the county?"

"I assume you mean besides the one you're working from Saturday night, right? Hold on, let me look."

While I waited, Casey called the paramedics for Cherry, who hadn't stopped babbling about the man she'd "gotten." We both walked her to Casey's car, which reminded me that my car was double parked in a loading zone. "Shit." As I headed around to the front of the building, I called over my shoulder. "Gotta get my car."

I rounded the corner in time to see a tow truck backing up to the hood of my sedan. "Hey! Don't even think about it!" I ran up to the driver's side window and badged the guy. The door opened and two huge, telephone pole legs swung down out of the seat. I looked up into an untrimmed beard that hung down over a massive chest and immediately recognized the driver who'd pulled Kate's car away from a caved-in basement a while back.

The last time I'd seen him, he'd worn a t-shirt sporting a squirrel with boxing gloves. The words, 'protect your nuts' had been prominently displayed across the top. Today, he wore one that read 'English is important, but math is importanter.'

I pointed to it and asked, "Your granddaughter again?" She'd been the one who'd given him the squirrel t-shirt.

Slightly yellowed teeth peeked out from beneath the shaggy beard as he grinned at me. "Yeah. She's a math whiz. Me? Not so much." He pointed to my car. "You call about this?"

I shook my head. "No, that's my car. I had an emergency inside."

We both looked to the double doors of the bank as Ms. Compton came scurrying out. "I called about that car. This is a loading zone and we can't have people blocking this space."

"I parked here when I was rushing to help you. Remember me? The one who came to help out with that crazy woman?"

"Of course, I remember you. You're just lucky I don't call the police and have them give you a ticket."

"I am the police."

"I mean the real police."

It was at that point that I remembered I had Sheralyn on the phone. "Sheralyn? You still there?"

She chuckled and said, "I can only give this information to a real policeman. Would you put one on the line please."

I grinned into the phone. "Bite me."

The tow driver smiled and climbed back into his truck.

I on the other hand waved to Ms. Compton before climbing into my car and following a paramedic truck around to the back parking lot. On the way, I chatted with Sheralyn, "So, any new bodies?"

"Other than a couple suicides, two drug overdoses on the east side, and three old people who died in their sleep, no."

"Okay, second question. Is there any chance you could call around to the hospitals to see whether any new stabbing victims have been brought in? And if not, can you ask them to let us know if one does come in?"

"Sure, I'll have someone call around, and if we come up with anything I'll let you know."

"Thanks." I hung up and got out of the car just as one of the paramedics poured disinfectant over Casey's hands.

They both looked at me and the medic held up the bottle and recited a litany of questions I was sure he must ask people several times per day. "Did you get any blood on you? Do you have any open cuts on your hands or did you get any blood on your face or in your eyes?"

When I checked my hands and coat, I was surprised to see there was no blood...anywhere. I walked over and held my chin up. "Do you see any blood on my face? How do I not have any blood on me?"

The medic, a tall, thin man who kind of folded over in the middle to pick up a wipe he'd dropped, straightened and peered into my face. He might have been good looking if he actually had any muscle on his bones. As it was, his arms barely had any definition and he looked like he had, maybe, one or two percent body fat. I briefly wondered how many anorexic men there were in the world before he said, "I don't see anything. You're lucky. The arrestee didn't get cut herself, a good thing since she's a meth addict and probably has hep C. And, she actually got very little of her victim's blood on her."

He motioned to the spot where a small pool of red had begun to coagulate. "The victim, on the other hand, may not have long to live, judging by the amount and color of that blood there. Hold out your hands." He poured disinfectant on my hands and pushed up my coat sleeves so he could use a wipe to spread it on my wrists and forearms.

When he'd finished, he pointed at Cherry. "She's coming off her high now. We don't have any reason to take her to the hospital, so if you want her, she's all yours."

"Thanks." As he and his partner packed up, I dried my hands on a paper towel and pulled out my phone to call Kate.

Casey finished drying her hands and when she saw me she motioned for me to stop. "I already called Kate if that's what you were gonna do. She wants us to bring Cherry to the station. I guess she has some questions she wants to ask." She glanced sideways at the listing hooker. "Good luck with that..."

Casey helped Cherry up from the back step of the medic truck and walked her over to her car. She had to help her into the backseat because the woman was coming down hard and could barely walk.

I doubted Kate would have any luck talking to her. I still had some questions so I thought it wouldn't hurt to give it a try before we sent her off to the station. I leaned in before Casey shut the door. "Hey, Cherry. Do you know who was following you? Do you know his name?"

Her head was resting on the back of the seat and she rolled it to the side so she was facing me. "Who was following me?" She squinted while trying to focus.

"Do you remember stabbing somebody?"

Her words were beginning to slur. Badly. "I stabbed somebody? Shit."

"Okay then." I shut the door and leaned my elbow on Casey's open doorframe while she sat in the front seat writing in her notebook. "Do you need me to go with you? If not, I want to go check out that desert area where I think Tom might be staying."

"I called for a patrol unit to come transport her to the main station and take her up to the third floor. If you wait a few I can go with you."

"If it weren't for the blood, I'd think she made the whole thing up, but..."

"I know. The man I saw jump into the truck was moving pretty fast. I don't think he was the one she stabbed."

"So, there were two of them?"

She shook her head. "Three I think. The guy jumped into the passenger seat and someone else drove off. Those two plus whoever was stabbed makes three. The man I saw could have been going back to kill Cherry when he saw me and changed his mind." She shrugged. "Either way, we know that more than one person is worried about something Cherry might have seen."

When the patrol car pulled up, we both smiled to see that Terri had come to pick up our second suspect of the day. She got out shaking her head. "Don't tell me, this lady was somehow having sex with a dead man. How'd she manage that?"

Cherry overheard and was momentarily pulled out of her stupor. "What? No way." Her eyebrows came together in serious contemplation. "You sure he was dead?"

I rolled my eyes and waited while Casey got her out of the car and exchanged handcuffs with Terri. With that done and Cherry safely on her way to chat with Kate, I checked the time and realized we'd gone past quitting time. "How about we find Tom in the morning? It's late."

Casey checked the time on her phone. "Sure. Are you going back to the office first?"

"Nope. I don't want to be stuck babysitting Cherry."

"Yeah, I need to get home to feed my critters. I'll see you in the morning, Alex."

I took one last look around and then called it a day.

CHAPTER 3

Megan's car was parked outside my house, which definitely surprised me since it was Thursday and I happened to know Megan had a beginner's dog obedience class at her business, The K9 Academy Thursday afternoon. What puzzled me even more were the 9 or 10 other cars parked in my driveway and up and down my street.

I knew the people weren't visiting my agoraphobic neighbor, Newton Goren. In fact, my guess was Newton had retired to his bed when he saw this many cars pulling up—that would be under his bed, not on top.

I approached my door with trepidation, knowing that whatever Megan was up to, I wasn't going to like it. The cement walkway went straight to my stoop, and the closer I got, the louder Creedence Clearwater Revival became.

Megan's mom had been a groupie for the band in the 70's and had obviously listened to too much of it while Megan was still in the womb. My best friend had followed in her mother's footsteps and had developed an obsession with the band. She'd driven to five Creedence Clearwater Revisited tours, had the originals of all seven of their albums and had cried for days after Tom Fogerty's death.

I put my ear to the door to see if I could get some kind of hint about what was happening inside. I heard laughter and some glasses clinking and decided there was nothing for it but for me to pull up my big girl panties and go inside.

I slowly opened the door and was immediately greeted by five doggy noses stair-stepped one on top of the other in the opening between door and jam. None of them belonged to either one of my two dogs, and I didn't see Megan's dog Sugar's nostrils sniffing at me through the crack either. I didn't recognize a bark from inside the room, the one that set the rest of the pack howling and carrying on over the presence of an intruder breaking into the house.

I heard Megan shout, "Hold it, Alex." Right before the door slammed in my face. The barking gradually subsided and after a few minutes, Megan came to the door holding out a margarita and a huge slice of pepperoni pizza. "Namaste!"

"What?"

"Namaste. It's an Indian greeting."

"I thought 'how' was the way Indians greeted each other. But you're trying to distract me from...that." I pointed to the loud party going on in my living room. "It's not going to work. What the hell are you doing in my house?"

"Here." She handed me the margarita and held out the pizza. When I didn't take it, she stuffed the tip in my mouth and smiled her huge, innocent, playful smile, which I never have been able to resist. When I rolled my eyes and grinned back, she lifted my hand holding the margarita to my lips and I washed down the pizza with a drink. "Better. C'mon in."

"You're inviting me into my own house, Numbnuts. Who *are* these people?"

"My Thursday beginner's class. I'm repainting the walls of the Academy and the place smells like paint. I couldn't have the graduating party there for Pete's sake and you know my apartment's too small."

"So, you bring fifty people and their dogs to my house, without asking, I might add, and serve them pizza and alcohol—" Suddenly suspicious, I looked over at my liquor cabinet where the doors were standing open and the shelves empty. "Megan!"

She pulled me inside and straight though the kitchen to the backyard. "Not fifty, Alex. Only twenty-two. Besides, look at how much fun Tessa and Jynx are having playing with the other dogs! You couldn't ask for better socialization than this! And I promise, we're picking up the poop as it happens. This is a responsible party, Alex, relax!"

"Relax! Get these people and their dogs out of my house! Now!"

"Geez. You used to be fun."

I glared at her. "I am fun."

Her face transformed into a ball of sunshine again. "That's the spirit!" Disappearing into the kitchen and leaving me standing in my backyard watching my two dogs romp with their new friends was Megan's way of escaping from doing the adult thing and getting these people out of my house. Looking around, at least half were too drunk to drive and I knew I was going to have to play door guard and make sure those guests and their dogs took an Uber or Lyft.

Rubbing my eyes, I walked back into the living room and saw Megan had joined a drunken game of coed strip poker. The doorbell rang and thinking it was another of the K9 academy students, I walked over and pulled it open.

There stood Kate with a perplexed look on her face. Just as she glanced down at the margarita in my hand, two cocker spaniels raced outside with their topless owner running after them in her blue sequined bra. The woman was easily a triple D and she shouted at me over her shoulder as she bounced past. "Shut the door for God's sake or they'll all get out!"

Megan, pant less now—she never did have any kind of a poker face —pushed me out onto the stoop into Kate. Just before she slammed the door, she yelled, "Sorry. Gotta keep the dogs in!"

I looked at Kate who now, unintentionally, stood shoulder to shoulder with me. "Hi Boss."

"Megan?"

I pursed my lips and nodded sadly. "Yup." I raised my glass to take a drink, but Kate pushed my arm down.

"How much have you had?"

"Just one sip. I haven't had time for more than that."

"Good. Commo called and said a man with a stab wound in his belly went to a vet's office and made the woman," she pulled out her notebook and opened it, "a Dr. Connie Slythen, stitch him up. We need to go interview her."

I looked back at my closed front door and scratched my head. "Would you mind helping me clear the place out? Some of these people need an Uber or Lyft because I'm not letting them leave my house as drunk as they are."

Kate used two hands to rub her tired eyes, took a deep breath and walked into the living room. "Listen up!"

As is usual when Kate uses her authoritarian tone of voice, everyone quieted and turned their attention on her. I've never known anyone who has more of a commanding presence than my sergeant. She held up her badge. "I'm a police officer. Now, I'm going to stand at this door until this house is empty. Those of you who need to call a ride, do so now. If anyone crosses this threshold intending to drive but too drunk to drive, I will have a DUI unit standing by to make sure that doesn't happen. Any questions?"

A chorus of 'No, Ma'ams and Yes, ma'ams sounded before everyone began pulling out cell phones and arranging for rides. Megan and her poker buddies got dressed and over the course of the next half hour, people left in groups of two or three, some of them sharing a rideshare between them.

Megan was the last to approach the door.

I know for a fact Kate scares her shitless, and when she tried to walk past, Kate stopped her with a hand to her chest. "Not you."

"But—"

"No buts. You're going to stay here and clean every dish, every glass, every bottle and every crumb from the tiniest bite of pizza crust. I'll be back with Alex in about an hour. You *will* be here. Understood?"

Megan blinked a few times before finally nodding. "Understood. I didn't mean for the party to get so out of hand." She turned a cheeky grin on me, "But it was fun while it lasted."

"You owe me a ton of booze. And they better not have drunk any of that special bottle of Glenlivet we're saving for Casey's birthday."

She looked slightly panicked at that and I thought I'd leave her with that parting jab. I doubted she could afford to replace the bottle but I wanted her to know I wasn't a happy camper. I pushed past her, grabbed two pieces of pizza, belatedly said hi to Sugar, Tessa and Jynx with an elbow pat, and walked out the door. Handing a piece to Kate, I turned and pulled my door closed behind us.

Kate drove us to the twenty-four-hour pet clinic on the corner of Oracle and Calle Concordia. The parking lot was empty except for three cars I guessed belonged to the night employees of the clinic and a Pima County Sherriff's patrol car.

A skittish receptionist jumped when we walked in and Kate immediately put her at ease. She pulled out her badge case and held out her identification for the woman to read. "I'm Detective Sergeant Brannigan and this is Detective Wolfe. I assume Deputy Harris is in the back with Dr. Slythen?"

The tiny woman, who honestly reminded me of one of the mice in the movie Cinderella, nodded. She pointed down a hallway to our left.

Kate and I sidestepped a droopy basset hound, probably the clinic's mascot, and continued past two closed doors on the left until we came to an office where Deputy Harris stood towering over Dr. Slythen.

The doctor, an aristocratic looking woman, was sitting behind a desk, a cup of hot tea cradled between two hands. She glared at us with a haughty superiority that immediately put me on edge. Some plastic surgeon had obviously gotten several large paydays from this woman and I couldn't help staring at her almond shaped eyes that I could swear hadn't started out in that particular configuration.

Deputy Harris held his hand out to Kate. "Sgt. Brannigan?"

Kate shook hands and nodded. "Yes, and this is Detective Wolfe. And you're Deputy Harris, correct?"

"Yes Ma'am." The deputy, who appeared to be in his late twenties, easily stood six-three and filled out his uniform with a broad chest and muscular arms that did him proud. He held up a sealed evidence bag. "The suspect knew what he was doing. He collected all of the bloody rags, gloves and even the needle she used to sew him up and took them with him."

He flashed a set of perfectly white teeth over his shoulder at the doctor. "Almost all of them. The doc here set a small swab with his blood on it on the desk over there before throwing it in his bag."

The doctor's nostrils flared angrily when he referred to her as "the doc."

Oblivious to her ire, Deputy Harris continued his report. "Neither of them noticed the small streak it left behind, mainly because she'd accidentally covered most of it with her prescription pad. Not all of it though, because I saw it after she moved the pad into her briefcase. I bagged the pad and took swabs off the desk. Those are in here." He lifted the small bag again. "It's marked with our case number, but I'm sure you'll be able to get it out of our evidence section tomorrow once you've cleared it with our Aggravated Assault sergeant."

He took out his notebook and wrote their case number on it. "We received the 911 at 1830 and I arrived at 1840. If it's okay with you, we're slammed tonight. My sergeant said to turn the interviews over to you and we can coordinate the whole thing as a joint investigation."

Kate took the piece of paper and nodded. "Thank you, Deputy. We'll take it from here. Are your detectives coming out on this?"

"No Ma'am. Like I said, we're slammed and we have detectives working several different scenes already. The Agg Assault team is actually working a case out in Ajo, so they won't be back anytime soon." He dipped his chin respectfully to her and left the room.

Kate pulled up a chair and motioned for me to do the same. She didn't sit, however, so I remained standing as well. "Dr. Slythen, we're with the Tucson Police Department Special Crimes Unit. I'm—"

"Sgt. Brannigan and Detective Wolfe. Yes, I heard." She reached down and pulled her briefcase into her lap as though ready to put an end to our interview before it ever got started. "It took you long enough to get here. I've been waiting almost an hour."

Her stylish, reddish-brown hair didn't have a strand out of place, which I though was unusual given that she'd just been forced to sew up a dirtbag at knifepoint. She wore it short and swept to one side where it hung down to just past her ears. The front part of the sweep had been died a blondish red, done by someone who probably charged a ton of money to get every strand just so.

Kate nodded. "That's right." She pulled a recorder out of her bag and set it on the desk. When she'd gotten the preliminaries out of the way, she started with the actual meat of the interview. "Now, I know you probably told your story to Deputy Harris, but we're going to need to go through it again. Could you please start at the beginning, from a few minutes before the suspect walked in and move forward from there?"

"Honestly, can't you get it from that deputy? I told him everything and I don't really have time to go through it all again." She fidgeted with the handle of the briefcase to emphasize her point and moved to stand.

Kate beat her to the punch. To emphasize exactly who was in charge, she stepped to the side of the desk, placed a hand on it and leaned in toward the woman, who was obviously trying to wrest control of the interview. Kate was having none of it. "The sooner you fill us in, Dr. Slythen, the sooner we can all leave. Deputy Harris did the preliminary investigation and we're here to get more details if we can. Now, please begin with the few minutes before the suspect entered the clinic."

With a huff and a muttered, "Fine." Dr. Slythen lowered her briefcase to the ground and sat back in her chair. "Emily, my receptionist and I were here late. She was finishing some filing and I was working on notes from the last surgery of the day. Oh, do sit down. I don't like people hovering over me."

Now that the woman was talking, Kate sat down to give her some space and I followed suit. "Just the two of you were here?"

"Emily and I were here."

The way she repeated her statement rather than answer the question made me curious. "Do you always prepare your notes immediately after surgery?"

Her steely, blue-eyed glare went from the top of my head and moved down to my feet, as though I was a distasteful child speaking out of turn. "Yes."

"What animal and what type of surgery?"

Even Kate tilted her head slightly, wondering where I was going with this.

The Doctor's nostrils flared as she pointedly looked at Kate. "Who is conducting this interview, Sergeant? Are you in charge or is she?"

Kate gave the woman a deceptively cordial smile. "We're both conducting the interview, Doctor, and I would appreciate it if you would answer the questions without asking ones of your own. As I said before, the sooner we get the answers we need, the sooner we will all be free to go home."

The doctor's lips thinned as she angrily consulted her notes. "Honestly, you'd think I was a suspect here instead of a victim. It was a two-year-old beagle. He'd fractured his leg and we had to reposition the bone and apply a cast."

I knew exactly when the penny dropped for her because she froze for a fraction of a second before raising her gaze to meet mine. I didn't want to seem confrontational so I gave her an out. "Emily doubles as your assistant? Does she administer the anesthetic?"

Her eyes narrowed. "Of course not. With all that happened I forgot about my tech."

"So, it wasn't just you and Emily. Your tech's name?"

"Veronica Ahern."

I smiled my best 'you're doing great' smile and with a look, turned the interview back over to Kate. I was used to tag teaming interviews with Casey but hadn't done too many with the sarge.

She picked up my intent though and asked, "What happened then?"

"As I said, I was back here at my desk and Emily was up front. I think Veronica, my tech, had left by then but I'm not sure. The bell above the door jangled, which surprised me because we had already closed. Or we should have been closed if Emily had done her job correctly." An irritated glare in Emily's direction told me the receptionist would be out looking for a new job sooner than later.

I piped in, "I thought you were a twenty-four-hour emergency vet?"

I guess people didn't deign to question the doctor because she lifted one side of her lip when she looked down her nose at me. "We have limited hours two days of the week, Detective. We closed at five and I was surprised by the jangling of the bell we keep on the door. I stepped out to ask Emily why she hadn't locked it, and she was standing at the end of the hall with—" Her voice wobbled. "That man had her in front of him and he was holding a knife to her throat. He asked if I was the doctor and I nodded. He used Emily like a...a..." She groped for the right words, "like a ram to push me back into my office. He shoved her to the side. She fell and then he..."

I held up my hand to stop her. "Where exactly did she fall?"

Dr. Slythen seemed to resent any type of questions from the hired help, a category she'd obviously shoved me into. She gave Kate a look that we both translated to mean she really should control her underlings. When she turned back to me, irritated condescension flew my way as she pointed to a corner off to the right.

I stood and positioned myself at the door. I mimed throwing something to my right with my right hand. "Like this?" When she nodded, I asked, "Where was the knife?"

"In his hand."

"Which hand?"

Her brows came together and she once more glared at Kate. "I don't remember. I can't say for sure. Are all these questions really necessary?"

Kate didn't answer, subliminally sending the message that I was just as much a part of the interview as she was. Even though the woman had pointedly asked Kate the question, I just as pointedly answered. "Yes, they're necessary if we want to catch your assailant. I know that's our intent. I assume that's your goal as well?"

She slowly turned her gaze toward me and spoke with a frosty bite to her words. "Of course, it is."

"Good. So, back to my question. When he threw her, did he throw her with the hand holding the knife?"

Her eyes tracked back and forth as she tried to remember. "No, the other hand. He pulled the knife away from her throat and then just threw her into the corner with the other hand."

"Thanks. Go on." At least we had a reasonable suspicion that the man was left-handed. Not a lot to go on, but more than we had before.

"When he threw her away from himself, I saw his shirt was covered in blood. He lifted it to show me he'd been stabbed and told me to sew him up." She scoffed at that. "I told him that I wouldn't. That I'm a veterinarian and it would be illegal for me to work on him."

"How did he respond to that?"

"He said if I didn't want to be a dead veterinarian, I'd sew him up. Otherwise he'd slit both our throats and be done with us."

"So, you treated him?"

"What do you think...Alex, is it?" She said my name with clear, pointed derision.

Ooh, this lady was treading on dangerous ground. The hackles on the back of my neck were spiking, and I was proud of how calm my next question sounded. "You may call me either detective, or Detective Wolfe." I put the same amount of derision in my voice when I said her name, "*Doctor* Slythen." I paused to let that sink in and then asked, "Can you describe him to me?"

She waved the question away as though it was completely nonessential. "He was tall."

"How tall?"

"Tallish. You know."

I raised my eyebrows and waited for a more detailed description.

"Oh, for heaven's sake. When he was holding Emily, her head came to about here." She held her hand up to her chest. "He had black hair, dark brown eyes..." She looked up at me. "Dead eyes. It didn't look like there was anything human in there."

"Yeah, I've met people like that." I held her gaze a moment to make my point and then continued, "Can you describe his hair?"

She glared at me, irritated that I wasn't impressed with the guy's dead eyes and apparently oblivious to my unspoken implication. This time when she answered, the edge to her voice ratcheted up a few notches. "What do you mean, can I describe his hair? I already told you. It was black."

I sat forward and spoke quietly to keep myself from blurting out 'What do you mean what do I mean, you Moron?' Instead I said, "Straight, long, short? How was he wearing his hair?"

"Oh. Well, curly and short, kind of."

"Kind of." I pursed my lips and thankfully, Kate dove in.

"Did he have any tattoos?"

"I only saw one. Across his chest." She ran her hand across the top of her breasts.

We both waited for her to elaborate. She didn't and instead dabbed her eyes with the tissue.

I didn't see any sign of tears from this cold-hearted harridan, so I sighed and prompted her for a more detailed answer. Honestly, I couldn't figure out why she was being so uncooperative. It's usual for domestic violence victims not to want to talk to us, but a woman who was kidnapped and threatened with death? It just didn't compute. "Can you describe it to us?" Dipwad.

She sighed dramatically, wanting us to know our time and her patience were both growing short. "It was very ornate. Probably paid a lot of money for it. It said, 'quae familia est,' which means 'family is everything' in Latin."

The condescending tone she used when she translated set my teeth on edge.

Kate leaned forward before I could say anything. "Any others?"

"Not that I saw."

"Was he thin? Muscular? What kind of body type did he have?"

"Muscular but... not like a body builder. Just normal."

"Did he speak with any type of an accent?" I was impressed with how patient Kate sounded when I just wanted to throttle the woman.

"Not really."

Not really? I was ready to have words with the lady, but once again Kate took her abbreviated answers in stride.

She prompted her again, "What does that mean? Either he had an accent or he didn't." She said it so nicely the woman didn't blink.

If I had said it, I would have had a complaint coming down the pike.

"Well. Really, there wasn't much, but if I had to put a name to it, I guess I'd say midwestern with a little bit of a Texas accent thrown in." She dabbed at her dry eyes with the tissue again.

Without looking up from her notes, Kate asked, "Could you tell what type of weapon made the wound?"

"No. I do know it wasn't completely smooth, like the kind of incision you'd make with a scalpel or medical instrument. Maybe a knife of some kind? But I'm only guessing on that."

"How long was the gash?"

"Well, I put in ten stitches, so I'd say around two inches. But that's just a rough estimate. I kept telling him he really needed to go to the hospital, and the last time I mentioned it, he put the knife to my throat and told me to shut up." She reflexively put her hand to her neck.

Seeing the movement made me wonder whether she'd gotten a good look at the knife. "What kind of knife was he holding?"

"Just a knife."

"A folding knife? A hunting knife? A steak knife?"

"I don't know. Something sharp, okay?"

I must have looked ready to throttle her because Kate said, "Why don't you go interview Emily, Alex? I'll finish up in here."

"Fine." I glared at the doctor as I walked out and found Emily sitting in the same spot as when we'd come in. My interview with her didn't take long. Her story matched the doctor's, except she'd definitely focused on the knife.

"What do you remember about it?"

Her arms and legs were crossed, giving the impression she wanted to curl up into a little ball and hide. As I mentioned before, her features were mouse-like, with a little pointy nose, a small mouth and close-set brown eyes. "He didn't have it in his hand when he came in, and then all of a sudden it was there."

"You mean he reached somewhere and got it?"

She shook her head.

"Where did it come from then?"

"I don't know."

"Did you hear anything when it appeared?"

She squinted and processed that a moment. "Kind of a snap, or a shick sound."

Probably a switchblade, then. "How long was the blade? What color was it? And finally, was there anything distinctive about it that you can remember?"

She began to unwind a little. I guess she realized the questions weren't going to be as scary as she thought they'd be. "About this long."

"So, eight- or nine-inches maybe?"

"And the blade was black. But I didn't see anything else."

"One more question. How wide was the blade?"

"It wasn't. It was really thin and...sharp looking."

"Okay, that's about it...oh...if the clinic was closed, why didn't you lock the door?"

"I thought I did. I always lock it."

"Were you out here the entire time from when you locked the door until the man came in?"

"Yes. Wait, no. I went in to use the restroom, but that was all. I'm sure I locked it, Detective Wolfe. I wanted to finish everything so I could get home to let my dogs out and I wanted to make sure no clients walked in on us at the last minute. But when I came out of the bathroom, he grabbed me"

She shook her head trying to forget. Like so many victims, she tried to move the interview away from the most painful part of their experience with the suspect. "I just now called my friend to go feed my animals and everything because of, you know...this and I really need to get home. Are we almost done here?"

"Almost, for the recording, could you give me your full name, please?"

"Emily Bohdana Goldstein."

I made her spell her middle name and then asked, "That's pretty. What does it mean?

She blushed slightly. "It means 'God's gift' in Czech."

I smiled to put her more at ease. "Your family is Czech?"

"My great-grandparents were. My great-grandfather was a chazzan, a cantor, in the Czech Republic." A bright smile lit her face. "I'm studying to be a cantor in our synagogue. I love chanting the prayers. My mother and I flew to Prague a few years ago and visited the Maisel Synagogue where my great-grandfather sang before the war. It's a museum now, but they allowed my mother, who is also a chazzan, to stand where he might have stood and lift her voice in prayer." She closed her eyes and lifted her chin, probably hearing her mother's voice again.

When she opened her eyes, her obvious delight at the memory had transformed her terror from the assault to a peaceful feeling of contentment.

Once again, I couldn't help but smile back at her. I wished I didn't have to ask any more questions, but I didn't have a choice. "I'm really sorry to bring you back to what happened this evening, Emily, but I do have one more question I need to ask. What time did the vet tech leave?"

"Veronica? I'd say, maybe four-forty?"

"So, a half hour before closing. Is that normal?"

"Yes. If they finish the last surgery early, she'll go home."

"And you locked the front door a half-hour after that?"

She blushed and lowered her voice, probably so Doctor Personality wouldn't hear. "No, sometimes, if I need to get home, I'll lock it a little early. Tonight, I think it was around four-forty-five."

"What time do you think the man came in, then?"

She lifted one shoulder, "Maybe...five?"

I gave her a warm half-smile. "Are you asking me or telling me?"

Her head bent toward her raised shoulder as she answered. "It was five."

"And how soon after the man left did you call 911?"

She shot an angry glare down the hallway. "Dr. Slythen pushed me out the door almost immediately and told me to call the police." There were obviously no warm feelings towards the harridan, that was for sure.

As if on cue, Kate and Dr. Slythen exited the examination room and came walking down the hall. I barely had time to give the date and time before Slythen snarled at Emily, "Make sure you lock up properly this time, Emily." Her tone indicated the entire incident was the receptionist's fault.

Pointedly ignoring me, the doctor stalked out to her $70,000 sportscar and drove away.

Both Kate and I could tell Emily was rattled and we waited for her to turn out all the lights and lock up. I assumed she'd jump in her car and head home, but instead, she walked to the bus stop on Oracle and sat waiting for the bus.

Kate and I watched her a minute, hesitating to leave until she was definitely on her way. As luck would have it, a blue and grey Suntran bus pulled up and Emily got on.

Kate pulled out onto Orange Grove. "That's that, then."

"Okay, I'm dying to know why you came on the interview instead of sending Casey."

"Are you making the work assignments now?" She smiled at me to soften her words, but I got the message. She would do what needed to be done and didn't need me questioning her methods.

"No. You've just never done that before. Not a big deal."

"I should hope not. So, does the description of the man match any of Gia's bodyguards that I might not know about."

I tried to keep from looking at her as though that wasn't the stupidest question she'd ever asked, but apparently I didn't succeed.

"Just answer the question, Alex."

I was a bit touchy about the Gia connection and my answer came out sharper than I actually meant. "Well, yeah Kate. About three-quarters of Gia's people match that description. So do most Mexican men in Pima County. A guy with curly black hair, muscled, but not really, stands anywhere between five-seven and six-three depending on where Emily's head really came to on the guy, who talks with some kind of accent, maybe midwestern, maybe some Texas thrown in? Hell, for all the bitchy Dr. Slythen knew he could have been an itinerant farm worker who's picked up various accents from the different farms where he's worked. And what kind of name is Slythen anyway? Sounds like she should be married to Draco Malfoy or something."

That got a smile out of her. "She really got to you, didn't she?"

"I hate hoity-toity people who look down on us peons from on high."

"You're better than that, Alex. I've seen you do interviews where the person calls you things that make most people blush, insult your family and threaten to do all kinds of nasty things to your dogs, and you keep your cool and ask all the right questions. You let her get to you, and that's not something a seasoned detective should do."

"I know, but we were there, on overtime, I might add, investigating her aggravated assault and kidnapping and she acted like we were keeping her from a very important bridge game."

"She was more shaken than she let on. Some victims feel like they've lost so much control during the assault that they need to put us in our place to regain that control." She turned to look at me before returning her attention to the road. "I know you know that, but you're tired and need to go home and get some sleep. If Megan hasn't cleaned up the place, leave it until tomorrow and I'll personally get her ass back to your house to finish what I told her to do."

I grinned over at her. "I guarantee you I'm gonna need to shove her and Sugar and Tessa off my side of the bed and I'll have to reclaim my pillow from Jynx." Jynx was my five-pound papiwawa, a scrappy little Chihuahua Papillon mix who could easily hold his own with my white, long-haired hunting dog, Tessa, and Megan's chocolate lab, Sugar.

"As long as you get some sleep. You haven't been on your best game recently and I need you in top form for this investigation. I know you don't think Gia is responsible for Pito's execution, but..."

"But you think she is."

"I didn't say that. I don't convict anybody without proof and I always keep an open mind until I know the facts. What I am saying though, is I want you to get back in the game. If you don't think you'll sleep well with a bed full of Megan and the dogs, then send them home. I expect you to be completely rested when you show up at work tomorrow."

We pulled into my driveway and Kate chuckled at Megan's car still parked in front of the house. "You two know each other way too well. You might as well be married."

I smiled back. "What can I say? I've known her since our days in the cradle. Most days I want to strangle her, but I'm not sure what I'd do without her. Goodnight, Boss."

I shut the door and walked toward the house. Megan had left the porch light on and it didn't take me long to unlock the door, shove everyone to the side of the bed and fall into a deep, much needed sleep.

CHAPTER 4

The next morning, I awoke to the wonderful sound and smell of bacon sizzling on the stove. The only problem was, I knew I didn't have any bacon in the fridge. I stumbled into the kitchen in my underwear and t-shirt, only to find Casey sitting at the table and Terri, in full dark blue TPD uniform, standing at my stove turning pieces of bacon in the frying pan.

Casey looked at me and took a bite of toast. "Nice uniform. You gonna come to work dressed like that or what?"

I still felt groggy and I sleepily raked my hand through my hair. My mother used to tell me I always woke up looking like Phyllis Diller and after I finally googled the woman's name, I had to admit she was right.

Terri threw an oven mitt at me and pointed to the oven. "Get the cinnamon rolls out, will you, Alex? I don't want 'em to burn."

I stumbled to the oven and obediently pulled the door open. "Where's Megan?"

"Right here." Megan walked in totally naked toweling her hair dry. I'd recently knocked down the half wall separating the kitchen from my living room and she stood there dripping on my faux oriental carpet.

"Sorry I asked. Would you please go get some clothes on? And stop dripping all over everything."

She looked me up and down. "As if you're outfit is any better than mine. At least I'm clean."

Casey shook her head. "How about both of you go get dressed and by that time Terri will have a gourmet breakfast waiting for you."

Terri was without a doubt one of the best cooks I've ever met. Her lemon scones were to die for and her vegetarian lasagna, which, when made by anyone else makes me gag, had me asking her to marry me.

Kate chose that moment to walk through the front door and Megan and I both stood there staring at her with a deer in the headlights kind of look. Kate blinked several times before turning and pushing Nate and Allen Brody, who'd followed her in, back out the door.

Megan waved cheerfully, "Hi Nate."

He twisted his head around while Kate was giving him a final shove, "Hi Megan."

I looked over my shoulder at Casey, pointed at Kate's retreating back and mouthed, "What the hell?"

Casey took another bite of her toast. "Kate called this morning and said she wanted us all to meet early this morning and Terri said if we met up here she'd cook us all a good breakfast before her shift started."

I shoved Megan down the hall to my bedroom and yelled back to Casey, "A little head's up would have been nice." Didn't anybody realize a woman's home is her castle? I grabbed a pair of khaki's off the floor, pulled a clean shirt from my closet and clean underwear from my dresser drawer and grumbled my way to the shower.

By the time I emerged, Tony Rico had joined the group and all seven of them were sitting around my kitchen table eating scrambled eggs with melted cheese, bacon bits and what looked like chopped up chunks of green chilies in the middle, toast, cinnamon rolls and coffee. I grabbed my Eeyore coffee cup, which everyone was smart enough to know I'd hit the roof if they'd taken it for themselves, poured my coffee and added creamer and six green packets of sweetener.

About a month earlier, Megan had been on a health kick for about five minutes and had invaded my kitchen and thrown out all my blue packets of sweetener. She'd replaced them with these green ones, and I had to admit, I actually liked them better. I'd never tell her that though. I didn't want to encourage her eccentricities when it came to running my life.

Kate set down the roll she'd been enjoying and wiped her hands over her plate. "Good. We can start."

I shook my head. "Uh, no we can't."

Everyone turned to look at me and I pointed at Megan. "Unless you want everyone who takes dog training lessons from Miss Mouth over here to know every detail of our investigation—"

Megan piped up, "You mean the one where Gia's bodyguard had his head blown off his shoulders?"

Kate lowered her forehead onto her fingers and sighed. "Good point, Alex." She raised her head and looked pointedly at Megan. "What makes you think he was Gia's bodyguard?"

Megan cheerfully spoke around the bite of toast she'd just put in her mouth. She at least had the good manners to cover it with her hand. "It was in the papers this morning."

I shook my head. "What papers? I don't get the paper delivered to my house."

"No, but your weird neighbor, Fig Newton does. When I took the dogs out to pee, I saw it on his front porch and looked through it while I was waiting for them to finish." She popped up and started for the door. "I'll go get it."

I stepped in front of her. "Oh no you don't. I'm sure you've already traumatized Newton enough this morning."

"Naw, we're friends now ever since I yelled in his window and told him that since I call him Fig Newton he can call me Meg-the-Peg-Leg." She straightened one of her legs and walked around in a circle. "I wave at his window and he usually wiggles his fingers out from behind the curtain to say hello."

Casey glanced up from her smartphone. "Never mind. I found the article." She adjusted her glasses and peered down at her screen. "Let's see, blah, blah, blah... oh, here it is. '...Agapito Mancini, the bodyguard for Ms. Gianina Angelino, the matriarch of the Angelino family...'" She glanced up and smiled. "Matriarch. I bet Gia appreciated that.... 'was murdered sometime Sunday night and left in a dumpster behind a local restaurant. As of the time of this edition, Ms. Angelino was unavailable for comment."

I sat back in my chair. "Whose byline is it?"

Casey scrolled back to the top. "Conner Smith."

I turned to Kate. "Dempsey's nephew."

She pursed her lips but didn't say anything.

Megan did, though. "Who's Dempsey?"

I shrugged, hoping she'd take the hint. "Nobody important."

"Is he a cop? I thought cops weren't supposed to talk to the press." Okay, so, Megan never has been very good at taking hints.

Kate pointed at her with the piece of cinnamon roll she'd just picked up. "Drop it, Megan. Nothing you've heard goes beyond this table. Understood?"

Shrugging, Megan popped her last forkful of scrambled eggs into her mouth. "Sure. I need to go, anyway. I have an appointment with a neurotic Doberman coming in this morning and I don't want to be late. See ya, Alex." She shot a "come hither" grin at Nate. "Byyeee, Nate."

Nate grinned back and waved his fingers. "Byyeee."

He jumped when Kate cow-kicked him under the table. He lowered his head, but not before I saw a playful smile tugging the side of his lips. "Sorry, Boss."

I rubbed my cheeks with my thumb and fingers trying to hide my amusement, but when I looked up Kate was staring at me with the squint I'd learned to steer clear of.

We all watched as the front door closed behind her and Sugar, and then Kate got down to business. "Casey, give everyone a recap of what you and Alex found yesterday."

I ate while everyone went around the table and briefed us on what they'd found so far. I didn't learn anything in the way of new information.

That is until Tony Rico had his turn. "I talked to all of Pito's neighbors. Most of them knew nothing about him, but one old lady who sits next to her window all day knitting for her thirteen great grandchildren..." He paused while we all took that in. "...said that up until a few days ago some guy lived there with him. Her eyesight's shot-that's why she has to sit at the window to knit to get the better light-so she didn't have a good description other than 'big.'"

I looked up, triumphant. "Ha!"

Kate tilted her head my way. "Care to share, Alex?"

"Remember that big jock strap I collected? I knew there was no way Pito's Lilliputian balls would fill it up." I raised my fist in the air. "Yes! Who's good? That would be me."

Most everybody in the room had no idea what I was talking about, but Kate grinned and nodded her acquiescence. "Okay then, it's up to you to figure out which Jolly Green Giant's peas fit into that jockstrap."

Did Kate actually just make a joke? About a jockstrap? Just knowing I might be influencing her toward the dark side made my whole day.

She pushed back from the table and folded her napkin across her plate. "Terri, thanks for the best breakfast I've had in a long time."

"Anytime."

"Okay, everybody. Let's get to work. Let me know what you find today because I want to wrap this up sooner than later."

Terri placed one of the leftover cinnamon rolls into a plastic container, and I quickly grabbed a plate and pointed to the biggest one. "Can I have that one for Newton? I always try to give him little things to thank him for letting the dogs out while I'm at work and putting up with Megan."

"I can do you better than that." She took the plate from me and piled it high with eggs, toast and two cinnamon rolls. "Anybody who has to put up with Megan deserves all the extras we can give him."

I took the heaping plate from her. "Thanks."

After everybody had filed out, I gave the dogs their daily chew toys, locked the door and carried the plate to Newton's living room window. I couldn't see him hiding behind the curtains, but after living next to the guy for a while now, I knew he was there watching everyone leave my house. "Hi, Newton. I brought you some breakfast. Don't worry, I didn't cook it. Terri did. I'll just leave it on your front stoop, okay? But you need to get it right away before any neighborhood cats or dogs get to it." I left the plate and headed to my car.

Casey was already waiting in hers and she once again followed me on our way to check out the desert area where I hoped to find Tom. As I pulled past Newton's house, his door opened just enough for his hand to slide out and take the plate inside.

The desert area I was looking for sat on the edge of the city limits, away from most of the hustle and bustle of the city. With the absence of homes and businesses, the remoteness drew the homeless to its forests of creosote bushes, overgrown patches of desert grasses and shoots of barbed yellow foxtails blowing gently in the cool desert breeze.

With the help of shears, a good knife or a pair of scissors, a homeless person could cut out a nice warren surrounded by sticks and stalks. They often covered the low-lying mesquite trees or creosote bushes with whatever spare material they had to hand. As we bumped down the dirt road, we passed several dens, some covered with old blankets and sleeping bags and others piled high with discarded clothing.

At one encampment, two women sat in low-to-the-ground folding chairs watching us with the suspicion of anything new and different ingrained in them from years of living in the open. Without a doubt, they knew we were cops, and I could tell by the way one of them lifted her chin that she recognized me at the same time I did her.

She'd probably been a pretty woman at one point, but years of hard living had taken its toll. Her brown hair hung limply across her shoulders and she had a permanent squint because some teenagers out on a lark had broken her glasses a year or so earlier.

I slowed as I drove by, and since we hadn't spotted any other vehicles whatsoever, I decided to stop and see what these two women had to say.

Casey pulled to a stop behind me and together we approached the camp.

As we walked up, the woman whom I'd had dealings with before pulled her heavy sweater close around her ample chest and watched my approach with more than a little apprehension.

I knew, and she knew, that if I ran her name through the system, she'd have a warrant for either shoplifting or burglary. Her specialty was property crime, and whenever I needed to know who was working a particular neighborhood, I'd track her down and ask.

"Brigid Duffy. Fancy finding you out here."

Brigid gave me a rueful smile. "I was about to say the same about you, Detective Wolfe." She nodded at Casey. "And you, Detective Bowman."

I looked at the younger, dark-skinned woman seated to her left. "Are you going to introduce us to your friend?" The dirty brown blanket they had stretched between two creosote bushes flapped up and down in the breeze. Without thinking, the other woman reached out and steadied it, holding it taut until the breeze let up.

Looking at the other woman out of the corner of her eye, Brigid lifted one shoulder. "She's nowt t' worry 'bout, Detective. How can we help you?" Was that a touch of unease I detected in her normally friendly banter?

Possibly having heard the same hint of disquiet in Brigid's reply, Casey stepped forward and motioned to the other woman with a flick of her fingers, a move universally understood by the homeless and disenfranchised to mean they needed to produce some identification, pronto.

The woman reached into her inner jacket pocket and Casey and I both rested our hands on the butts of our Glocks. She wore large, gaudy rings on three of her fingers, one of them a match to the blue stone earring piercing her left nostril.

I stared at her hand. "Easy."

"I'm jus' gettin' m' I.D. ain't I? Fuckin' cops think you're gods or sumpin'." The massive wad of gum in her mouth made it difficult to understand her words and from the looks of it, even more difficult to chew. With mocking and exaggerated care, she slowly brought her hand from beneath her coat and handed the I.D. card to Casey, who took it and walked a distance away, pulled her radio off her belt and ran a records check on the woman.

She held a paperback in her lap with her finger holding the page where she'd been reading. I read the title upside down. "Snake Eyes. Is it any good?"

Sneering at me, she shut the book with a snap and shoved it into her coat pocket.

So much for the friendly approach. I decided to get down to the reason we were here. "Have either of you seen Tom Handy around lately?"

Brigid, a round, plump lady with tired, hazel eyes, an aquiline nose and white, almost translucent skin pursed her lips. "No, can't say we have. Last I saw him he was beggin' at the light at..." She scratched behind one ear to help her remember.

One trait I appreciated about Brigid was she always told the truth. She had no qualms about breaking into somebody's home and stealing their possessions, but it was a point of honor for her to tell the truth, no matter what.

She'd told me once that she'd lost her husband and daughter in a car accident and after their funerals she'd walked away from normal society and had never looked back. In all the time I'd had dealings with her, which added up to several years now, I'd never known her to use drugs. Alcohol was another thing altogether. Brigid liked her amber nectar and drank it with the best of them.

"...it was Ruthrauff and that light just the other side of the freeway."

"When was that?"

"A few days ago."

I turned to the other woman, who couldn't have looked more different from Brigid if she tried. Her dark skin stretched tightly over high cheekbones and her jet-black dreadlocks hung down past her shoulders. I guessed she was in her late twenties or early thirties and healthy enough that I doubted she was an addict, although it could have been early days. "How about you?"

"Don't know no Tom Handy." She squinted up at me. "What you lookin' at me like that for?"

I'd subconsciously tilted my head to the side while I studied her face. She looked familiar somehow but I just wasn't placing her. "How do I know you?"

Casey came back and handed the woman her I.D. "One arrest for a

Delores Mefisto for simple assault a few months ago. Is that your real name?"

"It is. Why you askin' me if that's my name? Jus' cuz I don't got no felonies and no warrants, you think I'm lyin' 'bout who I am?" Her fingers flew down the front of her coat, unbuttoning every button and pulling it wide open as if to get some air. She looked everywhere except directly at us. "Fuckin' cops."

My Spidey senses were going off, but I had no clue why. She wasn't acting any different than a lot of the homeless we dealt with and she hadn't done anything particularly suspicious. I knew it would be easier to momentarily change the subject than get into an argument, so I went with what we'd originally come for. "Tom Handy drives a motorhome. He's in his seventies, balding on top, kind of a pug nose, round face?"

Both women shook their head and Delores said, "Haven't seen him." She leaned forward, "Is it true what they sayin' 'bout Hermie?" She pulled the coat closed again and her fingers flew up the middle in reverse, buttoning each button they passed.

Casey and I glanced at each other before Casey answered, "What are they saying?"

A sneering glint sparkled in the woman's eyes. "You know. They said he was batter dipping the corndog with a dead lady."

I curled my lip in disgust. "Batter dipping the—that is disgusting."

Brigid poked her friend with her elbow and said in all seriousness, "Wouldn't be any batter if she was dead."

"Stop." I put my fingers in my ears while Casey rubbed her eyes. I lowered my hands. "Can you just answer my question? Have you seen a man looking like the one I just described? Or, have you seen an old motorhome parked anywhere around?"

Delores leaned forward and rested her forearms on her knees. "They was one in the desert over by 22nd and the freeway 'bout four days ago."

"No, he's already left there. How about in the last day or so?"

Both women shook their heads.

"Have either of you heard anything about a body being dumped in a dumpster Saturday night?"

Delores shook her head. Her fingers undid the top button but stopped without going any further and did it up again. It seemed to be an unconscious mannerism, one that I'd never seen before.

Brigid asked, "I did. Who was it? One of us?"

"Nobody you'd know."

Brigid, whose intelligence rivals that of a lot of cops I know, asked, "What's Tom have to do with the guy in the dumpster?"

"I didn't say he did."

She batted her eyes at me and grinned, "You didn't say he didn't." Her eyebrows drew together and she asked in a more serious tone, "And what about Cherry? I heard she was somehow involved."

"Where'd you hear that?"

She lifted a shoulder. "Around. Cherry and Tom don't run in the same circles. I can't see 'em both involved in a murder of somebody you say we wouldn't know." Unlike the other woman, Brigid could actually hold a friendly conversation with cops. She didn't resent us and there'd been several times I'd taken her to a drive through to get a good meal before dropping her off at jail.

Not that I took her to jail that often—mostly when the weather was miserable out and she hadn't had a decent meal or shower for a while. She was looking good now, though. Healthier than I'd seen in a while. If I had to put a word on it, she actually seemed happy and maybe even content.

Casey refocused the conversation, so we were the one asking the questions instead of the other way around. "Okay, listen up. I want to know three things." She held up a finger. "One, how did you hear about the body in the dumpster?" A second finger joined the first. "Two, who told you?" Another finger popped up, "And three, what made them think Cherry was involved?"

Brigid chuckled and held up her middle finger in a saucy bit of rebellion. "One, I heard it from the smoke around the campfire last night. Two," A second finger popped up next to the first. "Smoke. And three," a third finger joined the rest, "straight outta Cherry's mouth."

I'd always liked Brigid. She was cheeky and irreverent, but like I said before, honest and for the most part helpful. "I assume you're talking about Smokin'?"

She nodded. "Smokin' an' Puffin' both."

Smokin' was a low-level dealer the whores and hookers went to whenever they needed a quick score and Puffin' was his common-law wife. Word spreads among the homeless like an unbridled racehorse but it still surprised me that these two already had the details of the murder. "What did Cherry tell him?"

"Not much. That's why I asked you. He said she was jonesin' and didn't do much more than mutter about the body in the dumpster. Do you think she killed the sod?"

Casey cocked her head. "Do you?"

She shook a finger up at Casey, "The old 'answer a question with a question' routine, eh Detective Bowman?"

"You know I can't discuss an ongoing case with you, Brigid. You on the other hand, are required by law to tell me everything you know about said case." Not exactly true, but close enough.

"Do I think Cherry killed some guy in a dumpster?" She shrugged. "How was he killed? Shot? Then no. I've never seen Cherry anywhere near a gun. Stabbed? Then maybe. She can go cockeyed when she's burnin' and you need to steer clear cuz you never know when she'll go off. Everybody knows that. Choked to death? Beat to death? Not likely. Not strong enough." She thought about that. "On second thought, if she's flyin', she'd have 'nuff strength to bash somebody's head in with a baseball bat or somethin' like it."

Delores nodded and I thought back to when Cherry had fought with me behind the bank building. The meth had certainly made her strong enough to give me a run for my money. Up to this point, I hadn't really considered her as a suspect in Pito's murder, but now I realized that was a big mistake. Who's to say she couldn't have gotten her hands on a gun?

For that matter, she could have grabbed Pito's semi-auto and capped him, although I highly doubted it. His murder had all the hallmarks of an execution, and if she'd have grabbed his gun, it would have been an all-out battle as Pito fought to get it back. A gut shot would have been more likely than a blast to the back of his skull. But still, everyone associated with the case should have been a suspect in my book, and I began to broaden my thinking as far as who could have capped the little weasel.

Delores' long fingers unbuttoned the coat again but instead of pulling it open, they immediately reversed course and had the coat closed so fast I marveled at their efficiency. It was one of the more peculiar affectations I'd seen over the years, but certainly not the strangest.

Neither Casey nor I had any more questions, but before we left I pulled out my phone and snapped a quick picture. The two began arguing as we walked away and I glanced over my shoulder while they bickered about who was going to make a beer run.

We'd been partners for a long time, and Casey could read me better than most. "What's bothering you?"

"Delores mostly. Did she seem familiar to you at all?"

She considered my question and then stood outside my car while I unlocked the door. "I know I've never met her before, but I also don't think Delores Mefisto is her real name."

Still trying to get a handle on where I'd seen her before, I looked back at Delores. She'd apparently lost the argument because she'd gotten to her feet ready to a hike to the nearest store. I squinted at her, trying to get my mind to take her out of the present context and put her anywhere but here. Nothing clicked so I lowered myself behind the wheel. "It'll come to me. Probably at one-thirty in the morning, but it'll come."

Casey pulled out her notebook and flipped to the page where she'd written Delores' information. "I'll see if I can come up with anything when we get back to the office, but for now," The notebook went back into her pocket, "there are a lot of other campsites out here and we really need to find Tom. Let's keep driving. I'll follow you."

We meandered our way down rutted dirt paths barely wide enough for our cars to pass, let alone a small RV. The trails wound around the spindly creosote bushes that filled the landscape as far as the eye could see. Their tiny dark green leaves covered the stick-like branches shooting straight up from the plant's base. Not much else grew out here except the occasional towering saguaro, prickly pear cacti and the aforementioned stalks of desert grass.

At one point, the main dirt road intersected our path and on a whim I turned left and followed it for about a quarter mile. "Gotcha." As I approached yet another small path leading off to the right, I saw creosote bushes on either side with their branches broken, the ends pointing toward the ground instead of straight up. On others, tires had completely run over their branches, pushing the spindly stalks all the way into the dirt.

I turned and followed the path, and about a quarter mile in, I spotted some tracks leading off the top edge of an arroyo, a deep, wide, sheer sided gully carved into the desert by our yearly torrential monsoon rains.

As I drove closer, the undercarriage of a vehicle came into view and by the time I parked, I saw enough to know Tom's RV had somehow flipped over onto its roof with the bed compartment over the cab caved in. Judging from the tracks, someone had driven it over the edge fast enough for it to sail through the air and hit the ground at just the right angle to send the back up and over the front where it came to rest with all four tires pointing to the sky.

I parked and walked to the edge of the arroyo and waited for Casey, who whistled softly. "Wow. That doesn't look good."

I squatted and jumped down to the soft sand cushioning the overturned vehicle. Casey did the same and we walked around the RV trying to find a door that worked. It was one of those motorhomes that look like a truck in front with doors on either side. Neither of those would open and I put the side of my hand against the driver's window to check for Tom. I didn't see him anywhere so we went to the door on the side of the living area.

The door, upside down now, stood partially open.

When I took a step toward it, Casey put her arm out to stop me and pointed at the dirt below the opening. Two sets of footprints faced into the door and the same two prints came back out again. That didn't bode well for Tom Handy.

The one set of prints were from a man's boot, size ten or eleven. It had a lugged sole like one you'd find on a hiking or working boot.

The second set were from a much smaller person, probably a woman, but I suppose it could have just as easily belonged to a small man. In one of the smaller prints, a black bead shone up at me in the midday sun. I pulled out a small bag, scooped the bead into it, sealed it and shoved it into my coat pocket.

I moved to the open side of the door, careful not to step on any of the prints.

Casey slid in behind me and both of us unholstered our Glocks.

Shoving the door open, I waited a moment and then yelled, "Tucson Police. We're coming in." The only sound was a set of curtains billowing in the breeze wafting through the camper from one of the broken windows.

Inside, the place was a mess. Cabinet doors hung open, dishes and pans were scattered and the air conditioner that usually sits on top of the roof had pushed up through what had now become the floor. One long cabinet door near the front had a full-length mirror attached to the inside, and when I looked at it to try to see into the back, I became momentarily disoriented by what I saw.

Another closet door stood open at the other end of the camper, and it, too, had a full-length mirror attached to it. One mirror reflected the other, which reflected the first, which then reflected the other. The pattern continued far into the imaginary distance and I had to adjust my perception to take the infinite repetition of reflected mirrors into account.

When my brain waves adjusted, I saw the soles of two boots sticking out beneath the back-closet door. I turned my head so Casey could read my lips and whispered, "Body on the floor. There's a door obscuring it. I'm going in and moving left."

I had to step over the lip of the door since there is normally six to nine inches between the top of the door and the ceiling. I swung left, holding my Glock at the ready. I waited for Casey to enter.

She stepped over the lip and immediately swung right. I waited a moment for her to check the front to make sure no one was hiding behind the open cabinet door. When she was satisfied, she turned and since I had my back to her, she quietly said, "Clear."

I moved forward, ducking or closing cabinets as I passed. The refrigerator door was blocking the aisle and I pulled it toward me trying to shut it. It wouldn't stay closed and Casey moved around me slightly to put her foot in front to hold it.

I heard a thumping on the other side of the closet door. Thumping didn't fit into my mental equation of what was back there, and I gingerly pushed the door closed with one hand, while keeping the Glock ready in the other.

A worried and submissive Max lay on the other side of Tom's body, near his head. When the dog saw me, the thumping became louder and faster as he tried to tell me he wasn't a threat. Max has the body of a whippet and the coat of a grey wirehair terrier. He put his head down on his paws and continued his wagging.

"Hi Max, buddy. It's okay boy." I holstered my weapon and lowered myself to one knee so I could feel Tom's carotid artery. "Shit!" I looked up at Casey. "He's still alive."

While Casey stepped out to radio for meds, I quickly assessed Tom's injuries. He lay partially on his side and blood had pooled beneath his bald head. It had somewhat coagulated which meant the bleeding had stopped on its own. There was a gash in his ear where someone had yanked out an earring and a nasty bruise covering the left side of his forehead.

He still had on the navy blue peacoat and I unbuttoned it and his shirt to get a better look at his torso. Deep, dark bruises the shape of someone's fist covered his stomach, but other than that I didn't see any outward, obvious injuries. I visually checked his pants for holes indicating he'd either been shot or stabbed. Again, I didn't find anything.

When Casey returned, I asked, "Should we move him to check the other side for injuries?" Casey had been a medic prior to joining the police department and I always deferred to her when it came to medical emergencies.

"No. From the looks of that blood under his head, he's been here a while. I don't think there's any more injuries that would require immediate attention."

"How long do you think he's been here?"

She shrugged. "Hard to say. A while anyway. If I were to guess, I'd say this happened sometime during the night. When I went out to call for meds and call Kate, I looked more closely at the tire tracks. He never braked, which makes me wonder if he was running without lights trying to get away from someone chasing him and didn't see the arroyo."

"Could you see any other car tracks?"

Nodding, she reached over me to pet Max, who'd sat up when she'd walked up behind me. "More like truck tires to me. I guess it could have been the same one I saw when we found Cherry behind the bank building." She shrugged. "That's just a guess."

She stepped back and patted her thighs. "Come here, Max. Here boy."

The lurcher lay down and put his muzzle on Tom's chest.

Casey tried again without any better luck. "He's going to have to come out of there before the meds come in. Can you get him by the collar and bring him out?"

I squinted at her, thinking she was way more qualified for that job than me. Strange dogs made me nervous, no matter how friendly they seemed. Turning to Max, I cooed, "Easy boy. C'mon," while slowly reaching for his collar. A low growl came from deep in his chest and I immediately retrieved my hand.

Casey chuckled and pulled back on my shoulder. "Move. How many times has Megan told you it's your fear dogs react to?"

Thankful that she'd decided to take my place, I quickly stepped back to let her in. Somewhat chagrined at the way she easily grabbed Max's collar and half pulled, half cajoled him out the door, I spotted a leash in the closet and grabbed it. "Here, this might help."

Grinning at me—she knew and I knew that between us she'd always be the animal whisperer on our calls—she took the leash and clipped it on. "I'm gonna put him in my car. It's cold enough he'll be perfectly comfortable in there."

She managed to get him outside, but when she walked to the end of the leash hoping Max would follow, he had other plans. He had no intention of leaving Tom and he planted his butt in the sand and refused to move. She tugged a little harder but only succeeded in pulling him a few inches.

I pointed to the outdoor light, which, because of the inverted position of the camper, now hung about nine-inches from the ground.

"Why don't you just tie him to that for now and let him chill?" I left her to it and went back inside to wait beside Tom. His breathing was shallow but steady and every now and again he'd groan or mutter something I couldn't understand.

It took a while, but I eventually heard the wailing of the sirens in the distance. The sound gradually became louder as they neared until it abruptly cut off.

I heard Casey talking in the distance and figured she'd gone back to our cars to wave them in. She was a little too far away for me to hear exactly what she was saying, but as she moved closer her words became clearer. "Could you step off to the side of the door, over there on that side and try not to mess up those prints? I'm getting ready to photograph them. I'll be finished by the time you're carrying him out, but it would sure help if you missed them on your way in."

Casey came into the camper first carrying several small, numbered cones which she quickly set over spots of blood on the floor. Thankfully they were in close to one of the lower cabinets and we hadn't stepped on them when we'd first entered. Once the cones were placed, she jumped out to allow the medics to enter.

A few moments later, a heavy medic box was lowered with a clang over the lip of the door and a stout woman followed shortly after. Once inside, she picked up the box and headed my way, carefully avoiding the cones. I had to shuffle around to get out of her way and then backed up even further when her partner, a fortyish man who looked pretty good in his coveralls, came in behind her.

The woman set her box down and knelt next to Tom. She began checking him out, and I stood in the doorway until Casey finished photographing the prints. While I waited, I glanced over at Max to see how he was handling new people going in to check on his human. He sat straight and alert, his full attention riveted on me, or rather on the door I was standing in.

A tiny spot of red around the lower muzzle caught my eye and I swung to the side of the door and hopped down. "Hey buddy. C'mere." He wagged his tail and walked toward me until he reached the end of his leash, at which point he strained against the collar wanting to get closer to the door. I knelt and stroked his head, all the while trying to get a closer look at his face. "Hey Case. Come here."

She came and knelt beside me.

I put my finger beneath Max's jaw and pushed up.

"Holy crap. Is that what I think it is?"

"It sure looks like it to me."

She pulled out her Swiss Army Knife and pried out the scissors. Before she cut a sample of Max's hair, she grabbed a small paper bag from her coat pocket, opened it and set it on the ground. "Hold his head up a bit."

For the most part, Max had an easygoing personality and I wasn't too worried my poking and prodding would upset him. I lifted his chin, which he accepted with a resigned raising of his eyelids and a downward tilt to his eyes so he could keep an eye on what was happening at the door.

Casey held the bag below the bloody chin hairs and snipped off a sizeable chunk. She sealed the bag and labeled where the hair had come from, opened another bag and carefully snipped off more hairs along his upper lip. "The stuff beneath his chin could be from Tom's head wound, but I'm hoping this stuff around his mouth came from one of Tom's attackers."

"That's what I was thinking but Max seems too genial to actually bite someone."

"He growled at you just because he wasn't sure why you were afraid. If someone actually went after Tom and hurt him, I don't think anything would keep him from protecting his pack." She sealed the second bag and labeled it as well. "Lurchers were bred to bring down game. He has aggressive genes in him all right, they're just well hidden behind his wonderfully calm personality. Aren't they, you handsome devil?" Her baby talk seemed to ease the worried look in his eyes as he continued to fixate on the camper door.

I didn't need to wonder what we'd do with him. Casey had registered her property as a licensed foster home for just these types of situations. She couldn't stand having an animal that belonged to a sick or injured homeless person go to Animal Control and possibly get adopted out because the person couldn't afford to claim him.

The female medic stuck her head around the corner. "We've got him stabilized. Are you finished with the footprints?"

Casey nodded, "Yup. Thanks."

The lady disappeared, then after a few moments, carefully stepped backward out of the door and down onto the ground. She'd set the stretcher down just inside the door and she reached back in, picked it up and backed up until her partner was at the door.

I grabbed his end and moved to the side to give him room to jump down. "Where are you taking him?"

"Over to Kino." Kino hospital was located on the southside of Tucson and it was where most of the homeless were taken when they needed emergency medical care.

We followed them to the edge of the arroyo and helped them lift the stretcher up and over the side.

Kate pulled up just as their back-up beeper sounded. They maneuvered around until they had a straight shot down the dirt path that led out to the wider one and finally out to the main road.

I returned to the camper and climbed inside. If it weren't for those two sets of footprints going into and coming out of the door, I could have believed that Tom had gone flying during the crash and had come to rest where we'd found him.

Except the footprints, and the blood spatter fanning out on the inside of one of the open cupboards on the passenger side of the camper. Kate stepped in behind me and quickly assessed the situation. She saw me studying the blood, and since she's an expert in blood pattern analysis, I stepped aside to give her a better look.

Kate always took advantage of a teaching moment and I never passed up an opportunity to learn. "You know what type of spatter this is, right?"

I wasn't exactly sure but I took a guess. "Cast off?"

She smiled, "Good guess, but it was a trick question. If you look closely, you can see both cast off and blood spatter. Why?"

"Well, cast off blood usually happens when an already bloody object is raised a second time to hit the victim again. The blood is cast off the object onto something else. I guess the blood spatter came off his head the first time he was hit, and then the cast off came when the attacker raised the weapon a second time to hit him again."

"So, the doctors should see at least two impact wounds on his head. Since Casey said there was blood beneath his head I'm making an educated guess as to where he was injured. Where was he standing and where was the suspect?"

"I'd say Tom stood here," I stepped between her and the back of the camper, "and the suspect was standing where you are."

"So, the suspect hit him like this?" She held up her right hand and swung at me twice.

I looked at the cast off and then shook my head. "No, because then the cast off would be over there." I pointed to the cabinets on the driver's side. The only blood on that side of the camper was a different shaped spatter down low.

"How do you know?"

"Because that's the way you'd pull your arm back to swing again if you were right-handed, and the blood would go flying that way."

"Okay, both the cast off and the blood spatter are on the passenger side of the camper. What does that tell you?"

I thought a moment. "He back-handed him with the weapon in his left-hand, causing the spatter to go to the passenger side, then raised the weapon quickly to his left side, casting off blood from the first hit, and hit him again."

Her smile of approval made my day and when she clapped me on the back and said, "Excellent," I thought I'd died and gone to heaven. Kate believes detectives should know their job and do it competently. As a result, she doesn't generally compliment her people on doing or knowing things they should have already done or known. Her compliments were few and far between and I'd just gotten one.

I looked over at Casey who'd been watching from the doorway. Her grin told me she knew exactly what I was thinking and the slight raising of her eyebrows said, "Good job." She pointed to the cones she'd placed over the spots of blood. "So Sarge, at first, I assumed that blood on the floor was from Tom, but Alex found blood around Max's muzzle. I'm wondering now whether the drops might be from the suspect instead."

Kate picked up all the cones and set them to the side. After a moment's consideration, she said, "You're probably right. Look at this one. It looks like something, possibly a paw, was dragged through it, and you can see what might be marks from his pad here, and here."

She pointed to some striations in the blood. "To me, that could mean Max was holding onto the suspect's arm with his teeth and the suspect dragged him towards the door as he tried to get away." She moved to another set of drops. "But these drops are round, meaning they dropped almost straight down, which would happen if blood was dripping from the suspect's bite wound. Let's get them photographed and take samples from these and from these." She indicated the floor, the spatter inside the cupboard, the blood on the cupboard door.

"Alex, I want you to look around for whatever they used as a weapon, and when Casey is done, I want you to remove the bloody cupboard door, and this one as well." She pointed to one close to where we'd come in.

I stared at the second one, wondering why she wanted me to take that one too. And then I saw it. A couple strands of hair had gotten caught on the cabinet catch. How Kate had managed to see that in the few minutes she'd been in the camper was beyond me. I nodded. "Tom's bald."

She pointed her finger at me. "Exactly." Moving to the doorway, she held her hands out as if going for someone. "Let's try this on for size. The suspect comes in. Tom shoves him aside," She mimes falling to the side and hitting her head on the latch. "That puts the suspect in this position." She faced the front. "Now, we've already decided the weapon is in his left hand, making his first swing at Tom, who is headed for the back of the camper, a backhanded one as he shoves his way past the attacker. After the first hit, the attacker turns and quickly raises the weapon, casting off the blood into the cabinet and onto the cabinet door and brings the weapon back down onto Tom's head, sending blood flying down onto the kitchen counter. Max attacks and bites the attacker's arm. The suspect backs toward the door pulling one of Max's hind legs through the blood, manages to get free and takes off without finishing off Tom."

Casey, who was still listening from just outside the doorway, nodded. "So, Max probably saved Tom's life."

"Probably. Where is he, anyway?" Kate stuck her head around the door to where we'd tied the dog.

"I was finally able to get him to my car when they took Tom up to the ambulance. He's waiting for me in the back seat like a perfect gentleman." She shook her head. "Tom is that dog's life. I sure hope he pulls through, both for his sake and for Max's."

It took Casey and I a couple hours to process the scene. Kate left shortly after we started, taking Max with her to the station. She was a dog lover too and didn't want the poor thing waiting in Casey's car until we finished with the camper.

We were finishing up the details when the tow truck arrived. Lo and behold, my furry giant friend climbed out of the cab. He stood at the top of the arroyo instead of climbing down the bank, and when he smiled down at me, his teeth fairly sparkled. The whiteness shone out from between his mustache and beard like freshly fallen snow wedged between two patches of dried grass.

He must have seen me staring because his smile widened. "You're wonderin' 'bout the teeth. Everybody's ribbin' me 'bout it. My granddaughter thought I needed whiter teeth, so she gave me these plastic tray-like things, you know, that are shaped like your teeth? Anyway, she told me to put 'em in my mouth until she tells me to take 'em out. Well, she forgot an' I thought the time was normal so I left 'em in for about an hour and a half." He pulled back his lips and pointed. "Whaddya think?"

"I think if you're out at night you won't need a flashlight."

The guffaw he let out brought Casey out of the camper to see what was up. When she saw his teeth, she shaded her eyes with her hand and chuckled. "Kept the bleach in too long, I guess?"

"Yup." He turned serious as he studied the motorhome. "Looks like I'm gonna need help with this one. Give me a second and I'll order up our other big rig." He disappeared back into the cab and it wasn't long before he reemerged with the good news. "My buddy just dropped a load an' he's on his way here now. Shouldn't take him long to get here, but we'll be a while pullin' this puppy outta here."

Casey and I did rock, paper scissors to see who had to wait with the tow trucks and who got to take the evidence back to the nice, comfy, warm office. My rock smashed her scissors and she helped me load the paper bags into my trunk. I waited around long enough for her to make a coffee and burger run—to somewhere other than the Sling 'em—and when she got back, I headed into the office.

Kate was waiting for the elevator when I stepped out with my arms piled high with paper bags full of evidence. She grabbed the two on top and followed me into the auxiliary evidence room to the right of the elevators.

This wasn't the main evidence section. The department used this room primarily to store new evidence until the techs could make time to process it into the master storage facility. The room was pretty much empty except for a small seating area the detectives used as a quiet break room consisting of a low, uncomfortable sofa, two chairs and a wooden coffee table.

A shelf about four feet high ran along the left side wall and cops used it to fill out unfinished paperwork. The acrid scent of bleach hit me as I walked through the door and I nodded to the cleaning lady who was busy wiping down the long, narrow shelf. She acknowledged my greeting with a smile and continued her work.

Off to the right, two rows of refrigerated cabinets were stacked one on top of the other. There were ten in total, and we filled four of them.

Kate closed and locked her cabinet and then turned to me, "Did you find the weapon?"

"No. I looked everywhere; in the desert, all around the camper, up and down the wash. If it's there, I didn't see it."

The cleaning woman dropped her rag in the bucket with a plop, causing the water to splash up to the edge and almost, but not quite, spill out onto the floor.

"Where's Casey?"

"She's waiting for the tow trucks to haul the motorhome out of the arroyo."

We absently watched the woman ring the excess water from the rag. The twisting motion released more fumes and I wondered how she could work with that chemical smell all day long.

Kate's puckered nose meant she'd noticed it too and she quickly checked her watch before shooing me toward the door. "It's quitting time. Stay close to your phone. If Tom regains consciousness I want you to go talk to him. Same for the man from Pito's apartment. By the way, did you get his I.D?"

The fresh air hit me when we left the room and I pulled in a big breath, savoring the distinct lack any type of odor whatsoever. I'd forgotten about the guy's driver's license and I pulled it out of my pocket and held it up. "I did. You want me to run it before I head home?"

She pushed the down button for the elevator. "Yes. And remember, no Glenlivet with Gia or hard lemonade with Megan. I want you standing by and ready if I call. Got it?"

I gave her a mock salute. "Got it." I headed into our office and was glad to see only a few detectives left at their desks. It had been a long day and I didn't feel like chatting to anyone.

I set the driver's license on my desk, pulled off my coat and hung it over the back of my chair. I heard a child's voice, followed by the deeper voice of a detective, and looked across the room to where Burney Macon, one of the child abuse detectives sat hunched over his tape recorder.

Burney was nearing retirement age and he looked it. He was a short, African American, maybe five foot four inches and weighed in at around two hundred and fifty pounds, most of it hanging down over his belt. As I said, he was hunched over his desk, giving me a perfect view of the half circle of grey hair that stretched from ear-to-ear beneath an otherwise bald head. He glanced up, saw me looking at him and motioned me over. "Listen to this for me, will ya? Anderson thinks the kid's sayin' 'Daddy did it,' but I'm not sure." He rewound the tape a little way and then hit play.

Closing my eyes when I listen to a tape is a habit I've picked up over the last couple of years. Usually the office is too busy and too loud for me to concentrate on what I'm hearing. When a child's voice began speaking, I close them and leaned in close to get the best sound possible.

I couldn't be sure what the girl was saying either and I asked him to rewind it several more times before finally giving him my opinion. "I think she's saying the doggie did it, not the daddy."

His hand slammed down on the desk so fast and so hard I jumped. "Yes!" He hit the desk several more times, each time punctuating his pounding with a "Yes. Yes. Yes!"

I grinned at him. "If you knew that's what she said, why ask me?"

"Because Anderson was convinced the dad did it, and I said he didn't. She was dropped off at daycare this morning with a black eye so they called us. I talked to the parents who seemed like good people." He shrugged and I thought what a loss to the department when he retired. He'd been a child abuse detective for seventeen years and had a sixth sense when deciding how a child had gotten injured and who had done it. And in this case, who hadn't.

I headed back to my desk. "You're welcome." Suddenly, that little itch that had started at the back of my mind when I'd met Delores Mefisto came to the fore. I blinked several times, but still couldn't place her.

Since I'd just listened to a child speaking and that had triggered thoughts of Delores, I decided to go with whatever it was my subconscious was trying to tell me. I pulled out my phone, scrolled back to the picture I'd taken at the camp and returned to Burney's desk. "Hey Burney."

The clasps on his briefcase clicked as he snapped them shut. "Yeah?"

"There was this homeless lady Casey and I saw today. She gave us a name, but neither Casey nor I thought it was her real one. I thought maybe I recognized her, but I can't place from where. I know it's a long shot but do you by any chance recognize her?" I turned the phone around so he could see the picture.

He gave it a cursory look as he grabbed the handle of his briefcase and then did a melodramatic doubletake. Setting the case back onto the desk, he clicked the clasps open again, rummaged around inside and finally pulled out a pair of drug store reading glasses. He settled them onto his nose before taking the phone from my hands.

After staring at the photo for at least thirty seconds, he picked up the receiver on his desk phone and dialed. After a moment, he said,

"Ginny? Burney. Could you do me a favor and check your records for a Sandy Hoffelder?" He listened a moment and then nodded. "So, she's still there, right?" He brought my phone up again and studied the picture. "In Tucson? Okay, thanks."

He hung up and handed it back to me. The troubled look on his face fueled my already burning curiosity. I took my phone from him and he shrugged. "Whoever that is, she's a dead ringer for Sandy Hoffelder." He looked at me as though I should know who that was and then guessed from my blank expression I didn't have a clue. "You know, Hoffelder. The one the media dubbed 'The Baby Burner.'"

My mouth dropped open as my mind suddenly kick into gear. That's where I'd seen Delores, or at least someone who looked exactly like her. Several years back, the child abuse unit had convicted Sandy Hoffelder of lowering her toddler into a pan of boiling water up to his knees to punish him for running around their apartment. Her picture had been all over the news. "That was your case? I knew I'd seen her before. But the jail says she's still there?"

He motioned to my phone with a flick of his stubby fingers. "That lady could be her identical twin"

"How many years did she get?"

"The baby died in the burn unit. Got an infection. Hoffelder was found guilty but mentally ill and sentenced to life, which is too short as far as I'm concerned. I'd've gladly stuck the needle in her arm myself but the judge thought she should be a drain on the tax paying public for the rest of her life." He angrily threw his glasses into his briefcase and snapped it shut again.

"So, she's in prison?"

"No, she's at the state hospital in Phoenix. Well, usually she is. They transferred her down here for some kind of tests. If and when they decide she's suddenly sane again she'll be transferred to the Arizona State Prison system. Anyway, thanks for the help with the recording. I gotta run. Danny's playing middle linebacker for the U of A tonight and I'm gonna have front row seats."

"Wish him luck for me." Burney had four children and Danny was the youngest of the bunch. I'd met him a couple of times at office parties and always enjoyed his easygoing but driven personality. He was going far and there wasn't much that would ever stand in his way.

I sat down at my desk. The driver's license I'd taken off the intruder sat on top of a stack of reports next to my computer. I turned it to face me, placed my fingers on the keyboard and typed in his last name. Unfortunately, the little gnome who sits on my shoulder and gently warns me when I might be missing something hauled off and punched me on the side of the head.

I paused, hit backspace and erased what I'd just typed in. Instead, I entered "Delores Mefisto" and pulled up her records. Her mug shot from the assault was a bit grainy and when I held the phone up next to the computer screen I couldn't really compare the two pictures.

I cleared the screen again and typed in Hoffelder, Sandy. Her mugshot wasn't much better so I grabbed my phone and called my friend Kelly at the library.

I had to wait a bit for them to find her, and when she finally answered she sounded frazzled. "This is Ms. Bruster. How may I help you?"

"Kelly, it's Alex Wolfe."

"Alex! I haven't heard from you in a while. Are you still working Special Investigations?"

"I am. In fact, that's what I called you about if you have a few minutes?"

"I do now. I was just having an issue with a homeless man who decided to bathe himself in the third-floor bathroom." When she paused, I pictured the way she habitually adjusted her white and pink striped cat eyeglasses whenever she stopped to think. I heard a smile in her voice when she said, "You would have been proud of me Alex. I walked in, threw his shirt and coat at him and marched him out the front door."

I scratched the side of my head while I thought how to chastise her without curbing her enthusiasm. "Kelly, cops have training when it comes to dealing with the mentally ill. Some of the homeless can be violent when given even the slightest provocation."

"Oh, I know that." I could just see her lopsided grin. "I had Charlie come with me for back-up. You remember Charlie don't you?"

"You mean the guy who used to play professional football?"

"That's him. He finally finished his degree in library sciences and we were lucky enough to snag him right here as a fulltime employee."

"Well, next time send him in instead of going yourself. Anyway, could you pull up some old newspaper articles for me?"

"Of course. Let me grab a pencil. Do you have the dates?"

"I don't think you'll need them. If you could find any pictures of Sandy Hoffelder—"

"The Baby Burner? Why in all that's holy would you want to dredge up that monster again?"

"I just need to see some good pictures of her. One straight on and one in profile. It would—" I'd forgotten how Kelly's mind worked ten times faster than my own and had to get used to her interrupting me all over again.

"Here we go. There's a lot of them."

My computer dinged and I looked down to see an email from her in my inbox. "How do you do that so fast?"

"Do you need more?"

I opened the email and clicked on the first attachment. The photo had been taken as Hoffelder was coming out of the courthouse. It was a full-frontal photo of her face and I could have sworn that was the lady I'd seen earlier in the day. I opened the second one, which was a profile shot of her being put into a patrol car. "No, those are perfect. Is there any history on her or her family? I mean specifically her parents and any siblings?"

"Hmmm. That might take a little longer. Can I call you back with the information?"

"Sure. I won't be near my computer, but I'll have my phone with me. I have to do something and then I'm headed home, but feel free to call me as soon as you have anything."

"Will do. I just love doing police research with you. It makes me feel so grown up."

I smiled at that since Kelly was somewhere in her late forties and had a very high-end job at the main library. "Thanks. I'll wait to hear from you then." I hung up and swiveled my chair around so I could stare out the window and think.

There were too many unanswered questions floating around Delores and they just weren't sitting well with me. How could someone who looked so much like Hoffelder be staying in a homeless camp with Brigid? If she was a family member, like maybe a twin sister or something, could she be just as insane as Hoffelder and if so, was Brigid in danger? She may be a thief, but she wasn't evil and I still worried about her well-being.

I grabbed my coat and briefcase and headed for the door. I needed to go back out to talk to Delores, and I needed to do it now.

When I stepped out of the elevator into the parking garage, I was momentarily taken aback to see my Jeep parked right in front of the elevator doors. When I saw Megan sitting behind the wheel, I strode over to the driver's door and pulled it open. "What the hell are you doing here in *my* Jeep?"

No matter how angry I got, it never phased her. She reached over the passenger seat and pushed open the door. "You promised to take me to get my car after work and I knew you'd forget so I broke into your house, stole your keys and then stole your car." She batted her eyes at me and grinned. "Get in."

"You have a key to my house. I know you didn't have to break in and besides, I can't go right now, I need to go do something."

"Fine. I'll follow you and then we can go get my car."

"You're not following me."

Her eyes narrowed and I recognized her "I'll do whatever I want to" look. "Try to stop me."

I growled under my breath and went through a dozen possibilities in my mind trying to figure out my best plan B. I couldn't drive Megan around in a police car, even if it was an unmarked detective one. Nothing brilliant occurred to me and I couldn't have her following me out to a homeless camp by herself in my Jeep. "Fine. But I'm driving." I grabbed her arm and pulled her out. "Get in the other side."

When she hopped out, I was suddenly ambushed by three dogs who were overly excited to see me. Sugar, Megan's chocolate lab, of course stayed in the back seat where she'd been told to go. Tessa put both paws on my shoulders and began slathering me with kisses while Jynx jumped out and ran in circles barking at me.

"Megan! What the heck? They can't come with us..."

"Then take me to get my car and I'll take them with me."

I didn't exactly know why, but my gut was telling me I needed to get back out to talk to Delores sooner rather than later. I grabbed Jynx and pushed her and Tessa into the back seat next to Sugar.

Angry with myself for giving in and angry at Megan for putting me in this position, yet again, I climbed behind the wheel and sped out of the garage. Megan scrambled to get her seatbelt on and she yelled at me over the sound of the revving engine. "Slow down, Alex! Are you trying to kill us?"

I turned and glared at her. "The dogs? No. You on the other hand..." I realized that in my anger I had passed sixty miles-per-hour in a thirty-five mile-per-hour zone. I forced myself to let up on the gas and slow down.

Megan finally clicked the seatbelt into the receiver and sat back in her seat. "Jeez, Alex. What the hell? You said you'd take me to get my truck. I don't know what the big deal is. Slow down."

I didn't even dignify her comment with an answer. I headed west into the desert where Casey and I had found Delores and Brigid. There were no lights in the area and the sun had set early because it was the dead of winter.

"Hey, where are we going? It's dark out here. You know I hate the dark. Turn around and I'll wait back at the station."

"I need to talk to some people who live out here."

"What? Out here? Oh hell no. Turn around, Alex. I mean it. Turn around." When I didn't immediately stop the Jeep, she grabbed the wheel, jerked it toward her and grunted through gritted teeth, "Now!"

The Jeep spun in a full circle before I was able to wrestle her hand off the wheel. "Megan. Let go, you Moron!" I jammed on the brakes and the poor dogs ended up bracing against the back of our seats to keep from flying forward. All except little Jynx who'd already scurried beneath the back seat to wait it out.

I faced Megan and was startled to see her face covered in the soft glow of an eerie orange light. I spun around and saw the glow of a fire out where Brigid had erected her makeshift tent. "Shit."

I gunned the engine again and raced across the desert hoping

Brigid had gotten out from under the blankets in time. Strangely enough, I wasn't worried about Delores because something told me she hadn't needed to get out in the first place. I skidded to a stop and leapt out of the car. I ran toward the campsite until I heard Megan's footsteps behind me. I turned and shoved her backward toward the Jeep. "Get back inside and stay there!"

She must have seen something in my eyes because instead of arguing like she usually does, as soon as she caught her balance—with my adrenaline spiking I'd shoved her backwards pretty hard—she raced back to the Jeep and jumped inside.

I circled the inferno, darting in as close as I dared hoping to get a glimpse of what was inside. "Brigid! Brigid!" I ran a full circle around it, knowing if she was in there she was long since dead.

I jerked around when I heard a woman screaming in the distance. "Brigid?" I took off running toward a second, terrified, high-pitched screech and that was the first time I saw small spots of fire dotted throughout the desert.

The screaming continued and I kept calling Brigid's name hoping she'd hear me and run toward my voice. There was no moon out and since the fire had destroyed any night vision I had I was basically running flat out through the desert like a blind woman. I fell over more than one creosote bush and counted myself lucky they hadn't been prickly pear cacti.

After my last faceplant in the dirt I heard what sounded like a human growl. I stilled to try to zero in on exactly where the noise was coming from.

Off to my right, Brigid, out of breath and crying, yelled, "Get off of me! Get off of—" There was a grunt and a thud accompanied by another thud.

I pushed to my feet and ran toward her voice. Another large bush loomed before me, but this time I had enough warning to skirt around it. Just as I did, Brigid came tearing around from the other side. We collided and since she weighed at least a third more than I did, I went flying backward and landed with her sprawled on top of me.

In her panicked state, she didn't know who I was. Screaming directly into my ear, she kneed me in the groin before lumbering to her feet and taking off. I don't care what anybody says, that hurts on a woman too-maybe not as much as a man but still enough to force out a grunt of pain.

The pain lasted until I heard another woman cackling in the distance and the hair on the back of my neck stood straight on end. "Fuck." I jumped up and chased after Brigid—not too difficult since her extra weight gave me an advantage in the speed department—and managed to grab her by the arms and pull her around to face me. "Brigid. It's Alex! Detective Wolfe. Stop a minute." I needed to get her to stop panicking and focus.

Brigid's terrified eyes were looking everywhere but at me. I shook her hard enough to make her teeth rattle until her gaze finally riveted onto mine, at which point she began screaming at me. "She's crazy! She tried to burn me in my sleeping bag! She'll kill both of us!" She pulled out of my grasp and ran off into the dark.

The cackling sounded again, this time closer than before. I looked over my shoulder and saw Delores, illuminated by the lighter she held in her hand, bending down to light some dry branches on fire. I was tempted to pull my Glock to keep the crazy witch away, but I knew if I had to drag Brigid with me while running blindly through the desert there was more than a good chance I'd fall and accidentally fire off a round.

It had been a dry winter and the desert grasses had dried into dead yellow stalks. The entire desert floor was covered with it, along with tinder dry foxtails and desert shrubs. To my horror, the fire took hold and with a slight wind blowing into my face I knew it wouldn't be long before it overtook me.

I heard Brigid, whose breathing had become harsh and ragged, stumbling through bushes off to my left. After tripping over rocks and catching my shins on the spines of a prickly pear leaf, I finally found her bent over with her hands on her knees, gasping for breath between sobs.

I grabbed her hand and jerked her after me as I ran in the direction of what I hoped was the fire from the original camp. I hadn't paid much attention to where I was running when I was trying to find her and with all the small fires dotted around, I really couldn't be sure which direction we were running.

In the distance, too far for comfort since the fire was rapidly gaining on us, I heard the Jeep's horn sound several times. I pictured Megan, eyes the size of saucers, panicking at the fires springing up all over the landscape. Then, to my amazement, I heard the engine roar to life and saw the headlights come on. The Jeep sped in our direction and I was dumfounded how Megan knew which way to come.

My lungs burned from the smoke and Brigid, who was in worse shape than I, gasped for air between sobs. Normally when I smell creosote I think of rain, but what choked me now was an acrid, black scent that seemed to coat the inside of my throat making it nearly impossible to breathe.

I knew I couldn't go much further and also knew, without a doubt, I wouldn't be able to carry Brigid any distance to safety. I prayed Megan would find us in time.

As I followed her erratic driving as she missed the more obvious bushes and trees, I thought it uncanny the way she drove right for us, until I saw two dogs running full out ahead of the Jeep bathed in the light from the headlights.

Tessa and Sugar raced up to us seconds before Megan slid to a stop not ten feet in front of Brigid and me, adding billowing dust to our already compromised lungs. The fire had circled around now and I shoved Brigid toward the passenger side door. "Get in back!"

For a hefty woman, it was a miracle the way she was able to throw herself over the seat as quickly as she did. I ran to the driver's side and was relieved to see Megan had anticipated my move and was already climbing over the console into the passenger seat.

I scooped Tessa into my arms and followed Sugar as she leapt onto the driver's seat and then into Megan's lap. I jumped in after them and threw Tessa onto Brigid, who gathered her into her arms and held her tight. I shot a glance at Megan and yelled, "Jynx?"

"Under the seat! Get us the hell out of here!"

Not needing that last bit of instruction, I slammed the gearshift into drive and spun in a circle heading back the way Megan had come. A wall of flame had sprung up between us and our way out. Sending up a quick prayer, I gunned the engine and had to listen to Megan's shrill shriek reverberating in my ear as I drove directly into the flames.

We flew out the other side and I drove like a maniac, bouncing over plants and anything else that got in my way until we were well away from danger. I quickly opened the door and stood on the side rail, checking the canvas roof to make sure nothing had caught on fire. When I was satisfied all was well, I bounced back onto my seat and slammed my door before pointing to the radio that had fallen at Megan's feet. "Give it to me!"

When Megan didn't react, I looked over and realized she still had her eyes scrunched shut. I punched her in the arm and yelled loud enough to get her attention. "Megan! God damnit give me the fuckin' radio!"

Her eyes flew open and when she saw where I was pointing, she grabbed the radio and threw it at me. It was a good thing my window was closed, otherwise the radio would have gone flying out into the desert. Megan never has been very good in tense situations, but I had to give her credit, she'd saved our bacon this time.

"9David72. I'm in the desert area west of El Camino Del Cerro and I-10. There's a large 10-70 and I need you to send fire to this location."

"10-4 9David72. We've already had reports and fire is on the way. Are you Code 4?"

"Yes, we're fine. The person who set the fires is still in there. A number three female, five-foot-six, one hundred forty-five pounds, black hair, brown eyes. Goes by the name of Delores Mefisto." I looked back at Brigid and only then noticed her swollen eyes and cut lip. "On second thought, we're gonna need meds for an assault victim and smoke inhalation."

"Your 10-20?"

I'd forgotten she didn't have our exact location. "I'll drive out to the intersection and will be waiting on the southwest corner. I'm in a white Jeep Wrangler."

"10-4."

"2U6 I'll be en route. Let's get the helicopter up and see if we can find her."

2U6, AKA Jack Dougherty, was a sergeant in Team Two and luckily, also a good friend of mine. I sat and listened as he had officers set up quads around the area to try to catch her when the fire flushed her out. The way the fire had taken off, I wondered whether she'd be able to get out.

Megan told Sugar to hop into the backseat and then made rolling motions with her hand. "Let's go, Alex. I want to get out of here."

"We'll go as soon as the fire department arrives. I'm waiting to see if Delores comes this way. If she needs help, we're gonna have to go in after her."

"Go in after her? Are you crazy? I'm not goin' in after her."

"If I see her, you can get out and wait here, okay?"

"Why? She was stupid enough to start the fire, why should you risk your life to go save her?"

I just smiled at the windshield and let her rant. Megan and I had come from two very different molds and I think that's what had kept us friends for so long. While we waited, I swiveled around so I could talk to Brigid. "What happened?"

She pulled Tessa in close to her chest. "She tried to kill me, that's what."

I pulled up the console and grabbed a small notebook and pen. "How long have you known her?"

"Too long, that's how long. The bitch is insane."

"How long?"

"About a week."

"Was she staying with you in your camp?"

"Not 'till tonight. After you left, she lost the toss and ended up bein' the beer bitch. I thought she'd get something from Circle K, but she went down the road to the liquor place and bought some expensive ass tequila. Tequila? Who the fuck drinks straight tequila? Not me, that's who. She ended up drinkin' the whole fuckin' bottle and she got completely shit-faced. I mean bat-shit crazy! We got into a fight. Fuck her. I wanted beer and she brings that shit back and then drinks it all herself? Shit. I went to bed, and the next thing I know my feet are burnin'."

I hadn't noticed the smell of burned socks before but now that she'd stuck a foot in my face to show me I almost gagged. Her feet were dirty and bloody from running. "Get that away from me!" I pushed her leg down and when I did I noticed some blistering on the top of her foot. My windows zip open and both Megan and I quickly unzipped ours and pushed the flap out to let a cross breeze in.

Unfortunately, there was a spattering of smoke in the air and we all three ended up coughing and choking so much we had to put the windows up again. I sent up a prayer of thanks when I finally heard sirens heading our way and not long after that, the darkness lit up with red, blue and white strobe lights from several different kinds of fire apparatus that came barreling down the dirt road. As soon as they passed, I gunned the engine and drove out to the intersection where a medic unit was already waiting.

I jumped out and didn't waste any time pushing my seat forward and helping Brigid out of the backseat. The medics escorted her to their truck and I was just about ready to leave when something she'd said registered.

I walked over to the truck. "Hey, Brigid. When you say, 'expensive tequila' that can mean different things to different people."

She smirked at me. "You mean what's expensive to a bum like me might be normal for most..." she held her fingers up in quotation marks, "normal people?"

"Something like that, yeah. So, what do you call expensive?"

"Try a bottle of Don Julio 1942. That's what I call expensive."

I had no idea what a bottle of that would cost, but not wanting to seem a total rube I nodded sagely. "Oh yeah. That's expensive all right. Where'd she get the money for something like that?"

She shrugged. "Beats me. Ow!" She hit the paramedics hand away from her foot.

The woman gave her an apologetic nod and poured more distilled water onto her toes. "Sorry, I need to clean it out. It's going to hurt but I'll be done soon."

Jack Dougherty pulled up and rolled down his window. I walked over to say hi. "Hey, how've you been? Kids all good?"

"Kids are great, thanks for asking. I take it you're not on duty?" He indicated the desert area. "Heck of a place to hang out on your free time, but hey, each to their own."

"I kinda am and I'm kinda not."

He gave me a knowing look. "Ah."

"What does ah mean?"

"It means if anybody else gave me that kind of answer, I'd want specifics. When Alex Wolfe says it, I just shrug and say, ah, and think to myself 'I sure am glad she's Kate's and not mine.' Speaking of Kate, have you let her know about this yet?"

Before he'd finished the sentence, I watched Kate pull up across the street and park. He glanced over his shoulder and gave me his little boy smile. "See ya."

"Thanks a lot." As his car inched forward I called out to him, "If you find the lady who did this, I need to talk to her."

Kate came and stood next to me, "Who did this and what did you have to do with it?"

"I thought you went home."

"I stopped to get some groceries, and lo and behold, who do I hear out in the middle of the desert where we just happened to find a motorhome that may or may not be involved in a homicide we're working?" She turned and held my gaze. "Off duty I might add."

I was busy sending telepathic messages to Megan to stay in the Jeep and keep quiet and hadn't worked out exactly what I was going to say to Kate. "I hope you don't have any frozen stuff in your groceries." Okay, that was pretty inane, but what was I supposed to do? I had hoped Kate wouldn't find out about our little escapade and here she was standing beside me staring at Brigid.

"Who's she?"

"Well, that's the thing. She's nobody as far as the case is concerned, but the lady who was with her this morning when we were looking for Tom, well, probably isn't anybody either, but…"

"But?"

"But…do you have any idea how much a bottle of Don Julio 1942 tequila is?"

She squinted at me, then cocked her head to the side and shoved her jaw to the right, a sure sign she thought I'd lost my marbles. "No, Alex. How much does a bottle of Don Julio 1942 tequila cost?"

"No, that was a real question because I don't know. But it's curious that the other homeless lady bought a bottle. Where'd she get the money?"

"And we care because..?"

"Because I thought I recognized her, but I didn't because I couldn't have because Burney Macon says it wasn't her."

The jaw pivoted to the left, which meant she'd moved from irritated to slightly pissed off. "Alex, you're making even less sense than you usually do. And, you didn't answer my first question. Who is this lady getting treated by meds?"

"Brigid Duffy. She's a burglar, but an honest one. I like her. And I got worried about her when Burney looked at the other woman's picture and thought she was the baby burner, but he called the state hospital and she's still there. So, how did this other homeless lady look just like her? The baby burner was insane, and if this lady is related to her somehow—"

"She's related to Sandy Hoffelder?"

"No. I don't know. No. But if she was, I started to worry about Brigid because the little gnome started pulling my hair and—"

Kate sighed loudly and began massaging her temples.

"—and now that she's done this I'm wondering where she got the money for the tequila."

My shoulders went up to my ears when Megan yelled out her window, "Hey Alex! C'mon. I need to go get my car."

Kate and I stood in silence watching the medic wrapping Brigid's foot. My heartrate had jumped tenfold and I decided silence might work better than anymore babbling so I kept my mouth shut. When she finally looked at me, her jaw was clamped shut and the eyes, well, livid might be too mild a word.

"You're covered in dirt, you have soot on your face, and Megan is in your Jeep."

I wiped at my face with the cuff of my jacket. "I was trying to find Brigid because her blanket tent was on fire and I heard her screaming out in the desert. I was running in the dark and couldn't see anything and I fell over bushes and then Brigid ran into me and knocked me into the dirt and then the other lady kept lighting fires and we couldn't get out and Tessa and Sugar helped Megan find us and—"

Kate slowly spun on her heel to stare at the Jeep. "Tessa and..." I heard a soft growl, from her, not the dogs, and she lifted her hands in surrender. Without another word, she crossed the road to her car.

I watched her drive off and wished she'd have yelled or something. It's always so much worse when she has to go away to keep herself from throttling or firing me...or worse.

The medics strapped Brigid onto a stretcher and loaded her into the back of their medic truck.

I walked to the Jeep, got in, turned the key and sat with the motor idling. My phone rang and when I answered, Kelly chirped, "Hieee. It's me!"

I didn't say anything and she tried again. "Alex? You there? I have that information you asked for."

"Yeah, I'm here. Sorry, what did you find?"

"There's a ton of information on Sandy Hoffelder. As you can imagine, the reporters went crazy with digging up dirt on her background. Apparently she had a sister and brother. Both younger. The brother drowned in the bathtub when he was seven, but it was suspicious because he had bruises all over his body. Most of the bruises were old, though, so they couldn't prove one way or another if there was any foul play involved in his death."

When she stopped for breath I jumped in. "And the sister?"

"The sister disappeared when she was fifteen. Her name was Annie Lee Hoffelder. I tried to find her but there's no record of anyone with that name and date of birth showing up anywhere in the United States after the date she disappeared. She hasn't paid taxes or held a job or had a library card for that matter. I did find a picture of her though from her ninth-grade yearbook. Both she and Sandy went to Beaumont High in Evanston, Illinois."

"Could you email the picture to me, please? Do they look alike?"

"Oh heaven's no. Annie Lee is almost white. A mulatto."

"Were there any other sisters? I wonder if she had any female cousins who might have looked like her."

"I'll look in the yearbook. Maybe I can find something for you. I need to get home tonight, though. My husband has dinner almost ready and I hate to keep him waiting."

"Wait, what about the parents?"

"Oh, yes, I forgot to mention. They're both dead and the papers made a big deal over the fact a boiler exploded in their home, killing them both."

That got my interest. "What was the big deal? I mean, of course it was tragic, but you said they made a big deal about it. Why?"

"Well, it was about four months after Annie Lee disappeared without a trace. Their neighbors—from what I can gather it's a very rural community and the closest house was about one hundred and fifty yards away—thought they heard arguing. The neighbor's seven-year-old son came home and said Mrs. Hoffelder, the mother, was throwing all of Sandy's clothing out the upper story window and screaming at her to get out of their life while the father stood at the front door with a shotgun daring Sandy to try to get past him."

Megan saw the puzzled look on my face and began poking me in the arm and whispering, "What? What's she saying? Is it Kate?" She pulled my hand away from my ear to read the display and she whispered again, "Who's Kelly?"

I held the phone to my chest and said, "Megan. Stop it. You're like a little kid sometimes, you know that?"

"Put it on speaker, that way I don't have to ask."

I put the phone back to my ear in time to hear, "...so nothing came of it."

"Kelly, wait a second. I have a child in the car who won't leave me alone."

"A child? You have children?"

"Just one twenty-nine-year-old. I'm gonna put you on speaker, okay? And I didn't hear anything after the dad and the shotgun."

"Sure, sure. That's fine. I was saying, apparently the boy was known for his tall tales..."

Megan piped in, "He was a liar, you mean."

"Yes, exactly, so his story was so fantastical that no one believed him. The boiler exploded that night, and by then the neighbors didn't want to get involved so they kept quiet and it was put down as an accidental explosion."

Megan opened her mouth to say something but I clasped my hand over her mouth and asked, "So how did the reporters find out about it?"

"Because, the Burned Baby trial happened eight years later and by then, the boy was fifteen and when a reporter did his homework and talked to Sandy's neighbors, the boy told him what he'd seen."

"Hm." I let that sink in. I knew she needed to get home so I'd save any other questions I might have for later. "Thanks, Kelly. I'll call if I need anything else."

"You're most welcome. I really have to run now. Goodnight!"

When she disconnected, I pulled up the number for the evidence section and gave the night crew a call.

"Evidence. Andrews speaking."

"Hey Andy. This is Alex Wolfe. Would you mind pulling out the interview tapes Detective Macon did with Sandy Hoffelder? I'll stop by first thing in the morning to pick them up."

"Sure. I'll have them up front waiting for you."

"Thanks. Talk to you later." I hung up and turned to Megan "Okay. Where's your car?"

"It's too late. The garage closed ten minutes ago. But you look like you could use some Chinese takeout and a movie. My treat."

I looked at her and realized that's exactly what I needed. "That would be awesome and just might make up for Kate getting so pissed off. Of course, that's partly my fault, too, so how about I buy us some ice cream to eat on the way home?"

She pulled her seatbelt across her chest and buckled it. "Deal."

CHAPTER 5

The next morning, I showed up at the evidence section at six-thirty. I don't usually get in before eight, but I wanted to get a head start on watching Burney's interview. A counter separated the detective's area from the row upon row of shelving that stretched floor to ceiling and ran the entire length of the west end of the police station. Each shelf held bags and boxes of evidence, all catalogued and placed in precise locations.

During the busiest time of the day, an evidence tech manned the counter, but the morning crew had just come on duty and I knew they were having their usual morning briefing. I popped the dinger on the silver call bell and waited.

I've always thought the evidence section was a great place to study unusual weaponry. Scattered in among the bags and boxes are various items that, for whatever reason, hadn't been placed in sealed containers. From where I stood resting my forearms on the countertop, I could see several golf clubs tagged and laying on a bottom shelf. Pretty obvious how to use them.

Next to them stood a pressure washer and my mind took off with all the ways I could kill someone with it. I suppose spraying a person directly in the eye or ear could do it. Bashing someone with the wand would hurt, but I don't think it could kill unless you got lucky with your placement.

On a shelf directly across the aisle from the clubs was a dented x-box 360, which I happened to know had been used by a young man to bash in his mother's head after she'd pulled the plug on his game.

Above that sat a pair of dusty purple stiletto heels.

Speaking of stilettos, I heard the clip clop of high heels coming toward me and knew they could only belong to my friend, Marla Springer. No one got away with wearing six-inch heels in the police department except Marla, a beautiful oriental woman who wore her hair perfectly coiffed, her makeup expertly applied to the golden skin covering her heart-shaped face and manicured nails that could have been featured on the cover of Nails magazine.

Her face lit up when she saw me. "Alex. Andy said to expect you." She pulled a manila envelope out from beneath the counter and tore off the evidence sheet stapled to the top. She briefly read the description of the contents. "I remember this case." Her cheerful smile disappeared. "How anyone could do that to a baby." She sadly shook her head and then set the paper on the countertop. She turned it towards me and handed me a pen. "Why on earth would you want to listen to this monster's interview?"

"I don't know, exactly. I'm just following up on a gut feeling."

"Your little gnome jumping up and down again?"

Her smile had returned and I grinned back. My gnome had become famous among my friends and coworkers and they never missed a chance to tease me about it. "Yes, he is. Hey, I'm super curious. Did someone use that power washer behind you to kill?"

She looked over her shoulder at the device. "No, they used it to clean up a bloody garage after they disemboweled their ex-husband."

I scrunched up my nose. "Yuck."

She lifted her eyebrows in agreement. "Yeah. We never know what kind of bizarre evidence is going to show up. Last week Andy Montagne brought in a prosthetic leg. I guess the woman took it off and beat her husband's lover to death with it."

Before I signed the property sheet, I grabbed a pair of scissors out of the rack, cut open the envelope and checked to make sure that what I was signing for was actually in the bag. I signed the sheet, wished Marla a good day and took the tape down to our media unit, which is housed in the basement. They were the only ones who had the equipment to watch the old interviews done on a VCR tape.

As I sat down to watch, my cell phone rang with Casey's distinctive ring. "Hey Case. What's up?"

"Nothing, I saw your car in the garage but you're not at your desk. Where you at?"

"Down in the media department getting ready to watch Burney's interview with Sandy Hoffelder."

"Did you find anything interesting?"

I slipped the tape into the slot and watched the machine swallow it. "I haven't started yet. I'll let you know." I hit play and fast forwarded through the introductory parts.

Burney had been considerably younger then and his paunch didn't take up quite so much of the camera as it would today. Unfortunately, the quality wasn't great. I was getting tired of looking at subpar photos of Sandy Hoffelder. I watched and listened for a while just to get a feeling for the woman. Lines kept appearing horizontally through the picture and it flickered regularly enough that I swatted the side of the monitor several times in a futile effort to steady it.

Listening to her describe what she'd done to her son was disgusting enough, but to hear her justify burning the little boy turned my stomach. The interviews had taken place over a series of days since she'd originally tried to pin the blame on a non-existent babysitter. At least no one had been able to find the person she said she'd left the child with.

It was going to take more time than I had before work to listen to all the tapes, but I rewound the first to the beginning and began again. The problem was I didn't have the faintest idea what I was looking for. After five minutes, I rewound and started again. I did this several times, until I heard Casey open the door behind me.

"What? You couldn't live without seeing my face for half an hour?"

When she didn't answer, I turned to see Kate leaning up against the door with her arms crossed over her chest. I swiveled around to face her. "Oh, sorry. I thought you were Casey because she called a while ago."

Irritation shone in her eyes as she indicated the VCR with a lift of her chin. "What are you doing?"

Looking back at Sandy, whose smug eyes stared out from an unfocused, frozen screen, I shrugged. "I don't know."

Seemingly unable to hold in her ire, Kate launched into me without preamble, "What the hell were you thinking taking Megan to a transient camp? How many times have I told you not to bring her to any work-related situations?"

"I was off-duty in my own Jeep." Thank God.

"Off duty returning to the scene of an ongoing criminal investigation. And I want to know what you think those two women have to do with Pito's murder. You were making zero sense last night. Start from the beginning."

I always have difficulty explaining myself with her towering over me, but I didn't have much say in the matter. "Well, yesterday when Casey and I were looking for the RV, we saw Brigid sitting in her camp. I figured she might have seen Tom and I went over to talk to her."

Kate pulled out a chair and sat.

The room couldn't have been more than nine-by-nine and having her sit so close really crowded my personal space. I actually preferred having her towering over me.

She leaned back, crossed her legs and stared at me, waiting to hear the rest of my story.

"There was another homeless woman there. I thought I recognized her but didn't know where from. She was verbally aggressive and generally a bitch. When we left, I took a picture of her. Then, when I came here to do some paperwork, Burney asked me to listen to an interview with a little girl and for some reason that lady at the camp came to mind."

Here's where I wasn't going to be able to explain why I did what I did. But, Kate had always been pretty good about letting me run with my hunches as long as they didn't interfere with my current investigation.

"I pulled up the photo and showed it to Burney. He thought the lady looked a little like Sandy Hoffelder."

"The Baby Burner?"

I nodded. "Yeah. But he called the state hospital and she's still there."

"So why are you obsessing about her? The arson unit is taking over that investigation, so you need to drop it and get back on track. Got it?"

When I nodded, she pushed to her feet and pulled the door open. She glared down at me one more time before her gaze flicked to the screen again. She left shaking her head and mumbling something I didn't quite catch.

I stared into Sandy's eyes. There was humor behind those dark, deadly eyes and I pushed the play button in time to hear her say, "He wouldn't shut up."

I quickly hit end and ejected the tape. I knew these tapes weren't going to help me. I also knew I needed to go meet those crazy-ass eyes face-to-face.

CHAPTER 6

I called Burney to find out exactly where Sandy Hoffelder was being held.

He put me on hold while he called the hospital back to get the address. "Okay, you still there?"

"I'm here."

"She's at a private lockdown facility at 2202 S. Victoria Court. Some kind of medical tests they needed to do down here."

"Thanks, I owe you one." While I'd been waiting, I'd headed out to my car and as soon as I had the address, I headed that way. The building wasn't too far away, and before I knew it, I was sitting in a comfortable room staring at the baby burner.

Time, even the few numbers of years she'd been incarcerated, hadn't been kind to the woman. Even though she was relatively young —her file said thirty-two—her sallow skin and dark, half-circles beneath her eyes made her look much older. She'd yet to look me in the eyes and hadn't responded when I introduced myself.

I'd been right, though. Delores Mefisto bore a striking resemblance to this woman. Knowing that Kate would have a fit if she knew I was here, I wanted to get this meeting over as soon as possible. With that goal in mind, I cut right to the chase. "Sandy, are you related to anyone named Delores Mefisto?"

About all that got me were a pair of lowered eyebrows and a scowl.

"Do you have any cousins you haven't met?"

"Fuck no." Finally a response, albeit a surly one. But really, what did I expect?

"Were you adopted?"

Angry eyes turned my way. "What the fuck? No, I wasn't adopted." She stood. "Nurse!"

When a smiling woman appeared at the door, Sandy stalked up to her. "Do I gotta talk to this bitch?"

The nurse put her hand on Sandy's arm. "Of course not, honey. Let's go on back to your room." The woman mouthed the word, "Sorry," over her shoulder at me and that concluded my meeting with Sandy Hoffelder.

What a wasted trip. I'd learned exactly nothing except I'd confirmed what I already knew. Sandy and Delores looked almost enough alike to be one of those doppelgangers you always hear about.

On the way back to the station, I remembered I'd left the tape in the VCR. That could turn into a big problem if anyone found out I'd left evidence laying around, so before I went into our office, I made a quick side trip to the media room and retrieved the tape. Luckily no one else had needed the room and both the tape and evidence envelope were right where I'd left them.

The basement is a warren of small offices and storage units on the south side of the building with the SWAT bay on the north. As you exit the elevator that runs up and down through the middle of the police station, the offices are through a set of double doors on the right. If you turn left, there's a large bay that houses the SWAT unit. The cavernous bay not only accommodates their offices, but it also has room for a couple small tanks and armor-plated vehicles. The previous chief had the forethought to design the bay with large rollup doors that lead directly to the back parking lot, making it convenient to drive the tanks into the building.

The SWAT guys can be a boisterous bunch, so I wasn't surprised to hear someone pontificating behind me while I waited for the elevator.

CREDO'S HONOR

What did surprise me was hearing my name mentioned followed by a murmur of agreement from several rumbling male voices.

I glanced over my shoulder and saw the usually locked door wedged open with a forty-pound kettlebell. Stepping lightly so as to avoid being heard, I moved to the door to hear what was being said about me.

I recognized Dempsey's adenoidal tone immediately. "Can you believe they have her investigating a homicide? And don't you think it's a conflict of interest to have her investigating her best friend, who just happens to be the biggest criminal this side of New York *and*..." I could picture him holding up a finger to emphasize his point, "...the number one suspect in that homicide?"

Again, there was a round of indistinguishable murmurs. Sure, some of the SWAT guys were Neanderthals who considered women nothing more than an inconvenience on the department. But I always gave them the benefit of the doubt because I figured that when evolution happened, their ancestors had been placed into the control group. They basically couldn't help who they were and I never really paid them much mind.

But I also had friends in SWAT whose antennas at least picked up all the channels. As I stood listening to Dempsey, my blood began a slow simmer and I wondered where those friends were now.

Dempsey continued his diatribe, which I didn't particularly want to hear but I always followed the adage, 'keep your friends close and your enemies closer.' "Yeah, I know beyond a shadow of a doubt Angelino ordered the hit, but do you think either Wolfe or Brannigan will follow the facts to her doorstep? Wolfe's not smart enough and Brannigan knows which side the chief's bread is buttered on. Nobody wants to touch the mafia bitch." He snorted and I heard some shifting around before a second man spoke up.

"Didn't Alex solve a homicide last year that had you stumped? And before that, didn't she prove a man on death row was innocent after Fred Bulow botched the case? Can't be too stupid then." I smiled when I recognized Buck Paris' low, throaty baritone.

Buck had been in the SWAT unit for years and he and his German Shephard, Bear, were one of the most respected K9 teams on the department. And he was right, Dempsey had never forgiven me for solving his one and only high profile case last year. He'd been working double-time ever since to prove that it was a fluke that I had done something right for once.

A third voice piped up, "Yeah, and I've never known Sgt. Brannigan to nobble a case for political reasons. When she gets her teeth into a suspect, she hangs on like Lido when he's on a scent. She follows it until she either finds the perp or discovers she's on the wrong trail." That was another friend, Faraz Sexton, who worked in sex crimes. Lido was a bloodhound known throughout the country for his tracking abilities.

Dempsey grunted dismissively. "Eh, Kate used to be good, but ever since Wolfe got in her unit, things have changed. You'd think the two of them were havin' a ménage à trois with..." Here is voice took on a smarmy edge, "Gianina Angelino."

Buck Paris' voice came from farther away this time. He'd apparently wandered away from the group. "You're full of it, Dempsey."

Raising his voice, I suppose so Buck would be sure to hear him, Dempsey's next words sent me into overdrive. "Just watch. You think I was blowing smoke up your ass when I said I can prove she's guilty? It'll wipe that smile off your face when I bring her in wearing handcuffs."

Very slowly, so I didn't run in and throttle the idiot, I pulled open the heavy metal door and stepped through. I stopped about five-feet from the round briefing table they were all sitting around. Tubs of cream cheese and a flattened paper bag with bagels sitting on top littered the table.

One of the Neanderthals shoved an entire half-a-bagel in his mouth. His close-set eyes, which were too small for his block-shaped face, narrowed slightly. He not only chewed with his mouth open, but he apparently thought talking around his food made him look tough. "Look what the cat coughed up." Even from this distance, I could smell the garlic coming off the partially chewed bagel as he spoke.

A couple of the officers chuckled, but several grabbed their bagels and coffee and melted into the back part of the bay where Buck had apparently gone.

Dempsey, who stood six-one and was built like an inverted hourglass—thin top and bottom and round in the middle—smirked.

I was proud of the way I hadn't gone in sputtering and fuming at what an inane asshole Dempsey was. Instead, I turned my back and said over my shoulder, "Here ya go, Dempsey. Since you're not man enough to talk to my face, I'll help you out and turn my back. Go ahead and tell me all about what a topnotch detective you are. Oh wait, wasn't that guy who beat his wife to death released last week because the court decided your case was a piece of shit?"

Nobody laughed except Buck, who stuck his head around the corner of a door to one of the back offices. "It sure was. What a fuckup that was. I was in the middle of testifying, since Bear found the guy for him, and the defense attorney stopped me mid-sentence to say we didn't have probable cause to arrest the dirtbag at that point and we shouldn't have sent Bear after him until after the necessary legwork had been done. And the judge agreed. I'd only sent Bear after you assured me you had probable cause. Whooeee was that ever embarrassing, not to mention a paperwork nightmare." I guess Buck didn't care much for the asswipe either.

Red-faced, Dempsey stormed past me, but not before yelling over his shoulder, "Fuck you, Paris. And you, too Wolfe. You got a surprise coming your way and even Kate won't be able to protect you this time." The heavy door banged shut on the kettlebell.

The room was silent except for the jerk who had crammed another half-a-bagel into his mouth. He grinned as he chewed, opening his mouth wider than necessary and making loud, smacking noises just to irritate me.

I made sure to look each man in the eye and made a mental note of which ones hadn't had the balls to stand up for Kate. I never expected people to speak up for me, so the fact that Buck did meant a lot. But when they let the insults to Kate go unanswered, that told me plenty about the asswipes.

I waited long enough to hear the elevator ding and knew that Dempsey would be out of the hallway when I turned and left the bay. Too angry to chance getting stuck in an elevator with people who wanted to chat about the weather, I headed for the stairs behind the elevator shaft and took the treads two at a time.

By the time I stalked into our offices, I'd worked my way into quite a state.

Kate walked past our desks and motioned to Casey and me, "Alex—"

Without thinking, I blurted out an irritated "What?"

The normal buzz of a busy office went silent and Kate stopped dead in her tracks.

Still seething, I didn't notice anything until Kate walked to my desk and said in a quiet, dangerous monotone, "What I was saying before you interrupted me, was I need to see you and Casey in the lieutenant's office, now."

I really didn't feel like playing nice to the lieutenant right at that moment and I absently glared up at Kate who tilted her head sideways, bent forward slightly and asked, "Do you have a problem with that, Alex?"

I stood up and stepped close so that I could speak quietly enough that only she could hear. "Fucking Dempsey says he's heading out to arrest Gia because I'm incompetent and I've somehow made you incompetent as well. Oh, and apparently you and I are having a ménage a trois with Gia. The fucking asshole was down in the SWAT bay pontificating about how we're ignoring the facts and letting Gia walk."

If I thought she was angry before, I'd sorely misjudged her. I could actually hear her teeth grinding as her jaw worked beneath ever-reddening cheeks. I could have sworn her hackles actually rose on the back of her neck and she shoved the legal pad she was holding into my chest so hard I had to actually take a step backwards.

Turning, she headed down the aisle toward the door leading into the hallway. I followed and she turned and pointed to me the way Megan pointed to one of her K9 students. "Stay."

I was smart enough to know when to obey, well, this time anyway, and without hesitating I pivoted on my heel and went and sat at my desk. When the door slammed shut behind her, I turned to Casey who was staring after Kate with a wide-eyed amazement.

"What did you say to her?"

Everyone remained perfectly still, staring at me and probably wondering the same thing.

We'd just gotten a new lieutenant, Albert Dunhome, about a month earlier. He stuck his bald head around the corner from his office and glared out at us. "Who just slammed that door?" When no one answered, he turned and stared directly at me.

"Wasn't me, Boss." I asked around the room, "Did anybody see who just left?"

After a lot of murmured "Not me," and "Had my back turned," and "Sorry L.T." from around the bullpen, I looked at the lieutenant and shrugged.

None of us had really worked around Dunhome. He was older than everyone in the unit and had worked for the department for over thirty years. He'd mostly worked administrative assignments and knew very little about actual police work.

We'd discovered he was somewhat of a curmudgeon who liked his division run with clockwork precision. In all his thirty years' experience, he'd never worked in a detective unit before and I think he was discovering things didn't always go according to plan. There was one thing in his favor, though. He knew what he didn't know, and therefore allowed his sergeants the necessary leeway to run their cases the way they should be run.

We were fortunate in our division to have four excellent sergeants—one for child abuse, one for child sex crimes, one for domestic violence and us, the special crimes unit—who knew how to juggle the forty or fifty cases their unit might have open at a time.

The lieutenant retreated back into his lair, and after staring at Casey for a moment, I picked up my phone and called Ruthanne's cell. She answered on the first ring and whispered, "Whoa."

I didn't need to whisper, but I did anyway. "What's she doing?"

"Looking for Dempsey."

"He's not there?" That definitely worried me. If he was on his way to Gia's, I needed to warn her.

"No, but she went into Logan's office and slammed the door."

"Okay. Do you know where Dempsey went?"

"I have no idea. He barged in about ten minutes ago with his face redder than a baboon's ass, grabbed his stuff and stormed out again."

"Okay, thanks."

Casey raised her eyebrows, silently asking what I'd found out. I leaned in to answer but realized no one had gone back to work. We had all worked together for a couple years now, and I knew none of the detectives present would go running off to Dempsey. They were all staring at me, so after glancing at the lieutenant's door to make sure it was shut, I swiveled around in my chair and rolled it to the center of the room. Everyone else did likewise and I whispered, "She went to talk to Logan. Dempsey's gone somewhere. He said Kate—"

We all looked up when our office door re-opened, and luckily no one panicked when Kate came striding back in. She walked over to our impromptu group and, with hands on hips, sent a very pointed message without having to utter a word.

Everyone, including me, rolled our chairs back to our desks and pretended to get back to work. When Kate motioned for Casey and me to follow her to the lieutenant's office, Casey whispered, "The Lt's in there."

Kate pursed her lips. "We'll use the interview room then."

I knew the fact that this lieutenant stayed in his office a lot more than our previous one really irritated her. With her "office" being a glassed-in cubicle at the front of the open bullpen, it was difficult to have private conversations. Lt. Lake, our previous boss, had been out more than he'd been in, so it had been convenient for the sergeants to use his office whenever the need arose.

Before I followed them into the interview room, I held up a finger. "I need to use the little girl's room, Boss. I'll be right back." What I really needed was to call Gia and warn her about Dempsey.

"Get in here, Alex." I hesitated, and she tilted her head to the side and stabbed me with a heated look I assumed was residual, angry energy.

Sighing, I went in and sat on the robin's egg blue Bridgewater sofa the child abuse unit had appropriated from somewhere to make the room more comfortable for the kids they had to interview.

Kate shut the door and pulled her cellphone out of her pocket. She punched in a number, and I was shocked to hear, "Gabe? Sgt. Brannigan. I need to speak to Ms. Angelino."

Casey and I exchanged glances but very carefully kept our expressions neutral.

"Ms. Angelino? Kate Brannigan. How are you?" She listened to Gia's reply and then said, "The reason I'm calling is I never got the chance to thank you for offering your hospitality to Alex and me when we stopped by so unexpectedly."

Gia is smart, and I knew, and I'm sure Kate knew, she was trying to work out why Kate would be calling to chat. After a short pause to listen to something Gia said, Kate continued, "You've certainly turned Alex into a whiskey connoisseur. She said you took her down to your other home and showed her a special bottle you have there." Pause. "Yes, that's the one. She also said you were planning to take a trip down there today and I wanted to catch you before you left. I know you're *leaving*," She put a slight emphasis on the word, "in just a few minutes, so I won't keep you. Alex couldn't remember the name of the whiskey and we were both curious." Pause. "Yes, of course. Anyway, thank you for the information and have a great trip."

After a short pause, she disconnected and very pointedly held both my gaze and Casey's. Then she sat back, crossed one leg over the other and said, "So tell me what we have."

Since I couldn't say anything with my jaw resting on the floor, Casey started in. "Um…" Apparently the phone call had rendered her speechless as well, but she recovered quickly. "I found Cherry out walking Miracle Mile. I tried to get some more information from her about the man she stabbed. She didn't even remember stabbing someone. The meth definitely makes her swing between two different personalities. The sober one is almost childlike and when she's high, she's violent and paranoid."

Kate tapped her pen on her thigh while she gathered her thoughts. "I stopped by the hospital before coming into work this morning. The man who broke into Pito's house walked out of the hospital early this morning."

That shoved the whole conversation with Gia right out of my mind. "What? I thought he was under guard."

"He was. The officer left his post for a few minutes to use the john, and when he came back, the man had taken off."

"What, in his hospital gown?" I couldn't picture the hospital staff allowing a patient to walk out without questioning him.

"No, they kept his clothes in a closet by his bed. He must have quickly thrown them on and then walked out. The nurses were all busy and didn't notice him leave."

Casey brought up another good point. "The last time I checked in to see if he'd answer some questions, they had him handcuffed to the bed."

Kate nodded. "He picked the lock on Pito's door in next to no time at all. Opening a pair of cuffs was probably laughably easy for him. Anyway, the point is, we've lost him."

I slouched down in my chair, "Great." Not that it mattered very much since I'd also stopped in a couple times trying to get him to talk. The guy hadn't uttered so much as a hiccup both times. Then I remembered something. "Dempsey said he had proof Gia had ordered the hit on Pito. What did he know that we don't?"

"You keep away from him, Alex. Jon and I will handle him and you concentrate on what we know instead."

"That's not a hell of a lot."

"Then get out there and make it a hell of a lot. Where are you heading this morning?"

"I'm going to stop in that veterinarian's office and talk to the vet tech. I want to know whether she saw anyone hanging around outside when she left the office that evening."

Casey rose when Kate and I stood up. "I'm going to try and hunt down Grant Booth. I took a picture of him the last time I visited him in the hospital."

There were too many names floating around inside my head. "Grant Booth?"

"The guy you arrested at Pito's apartment."

Kate started for the door but I stopped her with a light hand on her arm. "Hey, do you think Gia got your message?"

Turning to face me, Kate cocked her head to the side and raised her eyebrows. "What message was that, Alex?"

I stared at her a moment, and then shrugged. "No message."

She turned to Casey who also shrugged. "I have no clue what she's talking about."

Nodding, Kate pulled open the door and as she headed out into the bullpen, I heard her say, "Me either."

CHAPTER 7

I pulled into the parking lot that fronted the vet's office and didn't see Dr. Slythen's midnight blue sportscar anywhere in the lot. "Thank God for small favors."

The receptionist, Emily was one of three now seated behind the counter and without looking up she pointed to the rest of the waiting room. "Take a seat please."

The open waiting room had benches pushed up against two walls that were covered with watercolors of various breeds of dogs. I hadn't noticed them the first time through, probably because I'd allowed Slythen to get under my skin.

Beneath each picture were smaller plaques with dog related sayings. One, by Marilyn Monroe, read, "Dog's never bite me, just humans." Big black letters on a red background had been placed beneath a photo of a cairn terrier and was attributed to Franklin P. Jones. It read, "Anybody who doesn't know what soap tasted like never washed a dog."

Having had firsthand experience with that brought a smile to my face. Beneath the watercolors and sayings, people sat with their cats and dogs waiting to be granted access to the inner sanctum.

"Can I help you?" A tall, friendly looking woman in yellow scrubs stepped out from behind the receptionist's area. In her mid-to-late forties, she had the professional air of someone who knows the inner workings of an office. Her gaze flicked down to the badge and gun affixed to my belt but didn't linger. I guessed she was hoping their clientele wouldn't notice my occupation.

Emily's head shot up and she put paid to that notion. "Oh! Sorry, Detective Wolfe. I didn't realize who had come in. This is Margaret Rutherford, our office manager."

I briefly wondered if Ms. Rutherford had been named for the famous actress, but due to the woman coloring slightly at Emily's rather loud pronouncement, I didn't take the time to ask. "Don't apologize, Emily. I can see you're super busy. And I asked you to call me Alex, remember?"

She nodded and Ms. Rutherford nervously glanced around the room. "Would you care to come back to the offices, Detective?"

Understanding her reluctance to air the clinic's dirty laundry, I followed her down the hall into the back room.

Turning, she indicated a plastic chair next to the wall. "Please, have a seat. How can I help you?"

I didn't sit since I wanted to be standing in case the vet tech was a mini Slythen. Subliminal messages were important in my line of work and I always used them the fullest advantage. "I was hoping to speak to Ms. Ahern. Is she working today?"

"Yes, she is, but as you can see we're terribly busy today. Dr. Slythen hasn't arrived yet so we're running somewhat behind."

That got my attention. "What time was she due in?"

"She's always very punctual. I can set my watch to her coming through the door at exactly nine a.m."

"And she didn't call in?" I glanced at my phone. It was coming up on ten o'clock.

"No. I've tried calling her cell and home phones and the answering service picked up on both occasions."

"Answering service?"

"Yes, all the doctors and techs receive their messages through a service."

"Is there any way to call her directly?"

The evident concern in her voice when she answered made me wonder if Slythen might actually treat her office manager with a modicum of respect. I highly doubted Emily would care one way or the other if Slythen never crossed the threshold again. "I've tried. Her cell phone has two numbers, one which receives calls from the answering service and a second private line that only a few people are allowed access to. When I tried her private line, it rang seven or eight times before I received a recording saying she wasn't available."

I pulled out my notepad. "I'm going to need that private number."

She hesitated before reciting the number. "I know Dr. Slythen will be angry that you have it, but this is unusual enough behavior that I feel justified in giving it to you."

"Thank you. How many veterinarians does your practice have?"

"We have five. Only three come in on any given day."

"And today is Dr. Slythen's day?" Nothing like asking the obvious, but if I didn't, I knew Kate would ask me the same question. She always admonished us to dot our i's and cross our t's.

As I figured she might, she gave me an exasperated look. "Yes, Detective Wolfe, otherwise I wouldn't be trying to find her."

"Sorry, but you'd be amazed at how many questions with obvious answers we ask that turn out with completely surprising answers."

She relaxed at that. "I understand. Just this morning I asked one of our clients how her dog was injured. She said, 'a car,' to which I clarified, 'a car hit him?' It turned out she had set the little guy on the roof of her car and he jumped down and broke both his radius and ulna. A very important distinction as far as the provenance of the injury."

"Yeah, I can see that. So, I only have a few questions for Ms. Ahern. Do you think she could break away from her duties to talk to me?" I knew I needed to let Kate know about Slythen, but I figured that could wait until after the interview.

"I'll go check, if you'd wait here please?"

I nodded that I would and after five minutes, Rutherford returned to say Ms. Ahern was just finishing up with a patient and would be in when she could. Since I had a few minutes, I decided it wouldn't hurt to let Kate know what I had. I pulled out my cell and called her.

"Hey Alex, I'm in a meeting. Can it wait?"

The fact that Slythen hadn't come in was curious, but I wasn't sure it merited pulling Kate out of a meeting. I must have hesitated a little longer than she was comfortable with because I heard her say, "Could you excuse me for a minute, Chief?" When she came back on the line I heard a door clicking shut in the background. "Ok, what is it?"

"Dr. Slythen, who is apparently always punctual, didn't come in to work today. Her office manager says she can set her clocks by her."

"What time does she come in?"

"Nine."

"And she definitely was supposed to come to the clinic today?"

I had to smile at that. "Yes."

"You asked?"

"Yes."

"Good. Okay. Get her address and have Casey meet you there. Do a welfare check and let me know what you find."

"Okay. I need to quickly interview the vet tech and then I'll get right on it."

"I'll be waiting for your call."

Translated, that meant hurry up with the interview and do the welfare check as soon as possible. I checked my phone and wasn't surprised to see she'd already disconnected.

It took another ten minutes before a woman wearing yellow scrubs identical to Margaret Rutherford stepped into the room. The color of her eyes struck me immediately. They were a deep, dark brown bordering on black. Her short, wavy hair was as dark as boot polish and when she saw me leaning against the desk waiting for her, she pushed a loose strand behind her ear. It wasn't a nervous gesture. More belligerent, if I had to put a name to it.

She couldn't have been more than five-two and I towered over her when I pushed off the desk to greet her. "I'm Detective Wolfe. Since I didn't get a chance to speak with you yesterday I thought I'd stop by and talk to you this morning."

I detected a definite chip on her shoulder when she crossed her arms and glared up at me. "I'm right in the middle of something. I didn't see anything when I left."

Okay then, she wanted to dive right in so I did the same. "What time did you leave yesterday?"

"Four-thirty." Her legs were spread shoulder width apart as though she expected to have to defend herself against me. Definitely odd. Judging from her fireplug figure and bulldog face, I guessed I'd have a pretty hard time arresting her without having to do some major damage first.

"Was the door locked when you left?"

She spoke slowly, as though explaining a concept to a dim-witted child. "It was four-thirty."

For whatever reason, her aggressiveness didn't bother me in the same way Slythen's had. Slythen's was a condescending, holier than thou attitude. Veronica's amused me more than anything because I'd dealt with this type of hostility my entire career. "Are you from Tucson?"

That took her off guard and she answered without thinking. "I'm from the upper Midwest."

"What part?"

She'd regained her equilibrium and shot back with a question of her own. "What difference does that make?"

I shrugged. "Just curious. So, you left at four-thirty and Emily hadn't locked the door yet. What did you see when you left?"

Her eyes narrowed, "I nearly stepped in a pile of dog crap one of our 'guests' left in front of our door. Would you like me to describe it to you?"

I had to smile at that. Aggression poured off this woman and I thought she'd be the perfect assistant for the bitchy Dr. Slythen. "What else?"

My lack of an angry retort irritated her and she dropped her hands down to her hips. "Look. I don't have time for this. I didn't see anything or anybody. I walked out to my car and drove home. End of story."

When I nodded and said, "Okay," she turned and stalked from the room. I certainly hadn't expected her combativeness, and when I walked past Emily at the reception desk I leaned down and whispered in her ear, "Can I talk to you outside a minute? I have another question for you."

Ms. Rutherford must have spoken to her about blurting out who I was, because Emily swiveled her chair so she faced her and whispered, "Can I go out for a minute? Detective Wolfe has another question she wants to ask me."

When Rutherford nodded, Emily and I stepped outside and moved away from the plate glass window and the curious looks from the awaiting clients. I leaned in and barely spoke above a whisper, "This is completely off the record, but is Veronica always so..." I paused to find the right word to describe her personality.

"Bitchy?" One side of her lip pulled up into a conspiratorial grin. "Yeah, most of the time. The only ones she doesn't act that way around are the doctors. She's as sweet as honey to them, but to everyone else, including some of the clients, she can be pretty nasty. I don't know why they put up with her. She's not even that great a tech."

"Well, I won't take it personally then. That's really all I wanted to ask. Thanks for all your help."

Apparently she hadn't finished because her brows came together and she shivered, not necessarily from the cold, which I'd forgotten about when I'd asked her to come outside. "Sometimes..." She caught and held my gaze. "...I can't prove it, but sometimes I think she hurts the animals. I've mentioned it to Ms. Rutherford, but she just tells me I'm being ridiculous."

"What makes you think she hurts them?"

"I hear animals cry out in pain when I know they're just in their kennels and should be resting. I'm not the only one who hears it, but I don't think the others suspect anything."

"Have you gone back to check on what's happening?"

Her face colored slightly, "I'm afraid of her, Detective Wolfe. God forgive me, I haven't. But I have been in the kennels when she goes in to get one of the animals for surgery or treatment or whatever. Animals that I know were friendly when they came in cower away from her. The cat's hiss and the dogs either snarl or whimper." Tears came to her eyes. "I'm not a brave person, but I don't know how to help them. Even though she's mean, no one wants to believe what I do."

Looking at her small figure, I understood her fear. "I can understand that. Just the way she's built could be intimidating. Look, give me a little while. I have a couple friends in the Animal Abuse Task Force who might have some ideas about how to handle your concerns."

Covering her mouth, she kind of shrank in on herself. "You can't let anyone know I told you. I need this job, badly. Please."

"Nobody will know you were the one who told me unless you give me permission to give your name."

"Like a confidential informant?"

I smiled. "Kind of."

"Okay, thanks."

"Welcome." I watched her walk back toward the door and then remembered I needed Slythen's address. "Oh, Emily!" I trotted over to her. "Could you give me Dr. Slythen's address?" When she hesitated, I pulled open the door and motioned for her to precede me. "That's okay. I can ask Ms. Rutherford. By the way, does she have a husband or children?"

"Ms. Rutherford?"

"No, Dr. Slythen."

"Oh, no, she lives alone." No surprise there.

We walked to the reception area where Ms. Rutherford sat in front of a computer screen typing as fast as our unit secretary, Sharon typed; and that's fast. She didn't question why I needed to know where Slythen lived. In fact, if I was reading her correctly, she seemed relieved someone was going to check on her boss without her having to actually call the police and report her missing. I'm sure she realized the department wouldn't do anything simply because the woman always came in at the same time 'like clockwork,' and was now over an hour late.

When I got in my car, I pulled out my cellphone and called Casey. I gave her the address out on the northeast side of town and headed that way myself. We parked a distance away from Slythen's Santa Fe style home and walked the rest of the way to her property line. Her home backed up to the Saguaro National Park to the East and there were no homes between her and about sixty thousand acres of undisturbed desert landscape. I got on the radio, gave the address and let dispatch know we were doing a welfare check.

This wasn't the normal, cookie-cutter type neighborhood. If I had to guess, I'd say every home had at least an acre if not two acres separating each lot. I hate to say it, because I dislike her so much, but her home was stunning. The burnt umber stucco made her robin's egg blue doors and window sashes come to life. Nothing looked out of place. In fact, the front yard was meticulously landscaped with desert cacti and pea gravel that exactly matched the color of the home covering the ground between plants.

Water bubbled pleasantly down a trendy waterfall fountain set off to the side beneath a canopy of a very large Chilean mesquite tree. We followed the winding, bluestone pathway up to a front porch that had nicer furniture than I had in my living room. I pushed the doorbell and heard a loud series of chimes. When no one came to the door, I put my hand to the brass door knocker and hesitated.

It was a beautiful piece, and I ran my finger down one side of the knocker, one of two arms that formed a circle. At the end of each arm was a hand, and the hands each held one side of a crowned heart. It felt cool to the touch, cold really, and I ran my finger over the heart.

Casey moved in to take a closer look. "A Claddagh ring. My grandmother used to wear one as a pendant. It passed to my sister, but she doesn't understand the significance of it. I always wanted it, but..." She shrugged, apparently accepting something she had no control over.

"What's the significance?"

"It an Irish symbol. My grandmother said the arms represent friendship, the heart is for love, and the crown represents loyalty." She hid her emotions well, but I could see the telltale signs of irritation—a twitch of her jaw muscles, pursed lips and lowered brows. "Things my sister will never understand. She's probably lost it by now in one of her drunken stupors. Or pawned it."

She grabbed the ring and rapped it angrily against the door. So much for accepting what she had no control over.

"I doubt Dr. Slythen ever understood any of them either. You should have met her. What a witch." I walked to the side of the house and saw a three-car garage. What would a woman like Slythen need a garage that size? Three rows of windows fronted each of the roll-up doors, and I put my hand against the smoky glass and looked inside. "Whoa. Would you look at that? I'll bet there's a quarter million in cars sitting in there."

Casey whistled when she looked in. "I wonder where she gets this kind of money. Veterinarians make good money, but not this good. Maybe she married into it."

"She's not married. I mean, she could have been at some point, but she's not now. It looks like she's probably home. She drove away from the clinic in that gold sportscar on the end." We walked around to the back of the home where the landscaping was just as manicured as in the front. A long lap pool took up much of the right side of the yard while a ceramic tile topped table with a single chair was placed beneath an extended overhang off the back part of the house.

There was nothing that suggested fun. Everything screamed single person lives here and likes it that way. Even the pool was utilitarian and I doubt anyone other than Slythen had ever swum in it. I could picture her going back and forth, from one end to the other, day in, day out, strictly to keep her body in shape. Heaven forbid she should ever enjoy herself.

I walked up to the french doors that opened onto the back patio. "Most vets I know have pets. A dog or two, maybe some cats. I didn't hear any dogs barking when we rang and knocked. I wonder if she has any cats. Or even a gerbil or something."

"Hey!"

When I heard Casey shout, my head shot up in time to see her racing around the corner. She shouted, "I've got this one! You check inside!"

I slid to a stop at the corner and watched her run to her car just as I heard a loud engine start up down the road. Someone must have hidden their car around the corner the same way we had parked ours down the street. I watched as a dark grey pickup sped past, already going at a high rate of speed.

Casey jumped in her car and fishtailed after them.

I pulled my radio off the back of my belt to call in the pursuit when

Casey's voice came over the speaker. "9David73 I'm in pursuit of a dark grey Ford F250." She went on to give her location and direction of travel. I was torn between following as her backup and doing as she'd told me to do. When I heard a patrol officer radio that he was in the area heading in her direction, that decided me.

Since she'd seen someone inside and had run toward the front of the house to intercept them, I assumed that's where the person had exited the residence. I ran to the front and saw the door standing wide open. I drew my Glock and holding it at the ready stepped about five feet away and slowly moved from the left to the right, "cutting the pie" by gradually exposing more and more of the interior as I moved.

"9David70 to 9David72, are you with 9David73?" Kate wanted to know if I was with Casey.

I stepped into the foyer and since I was clearing the home by myself, I didn't have time to answer.

Casey answered for me. "She's back at the residence doing a welfare check. We had to split up."

"9David70, I'll be responding to the home. Give me the address and get a patrol unit there as well."

"10-4 9David70." The dispatcher gave her my location and then dispatched a unit to come back me up. If Kate was coming from the main station, it would take her a minimum of thirty minutes to get to me, and that was dependent upon the traffic being light.

I shouted into the home. "Dr. Slythen. This is Detective Wolfe." I waited for her to acknowledge me and when I didn't hear anything, I yelled, "Tucson Police."

The home remained bathed in complete silence. I circled to my left, which brought me to a sunken living room that felt about as emotionally cold as its owner.

Everything was grey, black or white with small accents of gold. A low to the ground, grey L-shaped sofa sat off to the left with a square, off-white coffee table in front of it. A matching pair of modern, black accent chairs faced the sofa and behind them, there was what looked like at least an eighty-inch television screen hung on a black marble wall.

I moved past the furniture into what I thought was a bar area. The closer I got, I realized it was actually a kitchen with all black countertops and appliances. Even the sink and faucets were jet black. A dining island stood between the living room and the kitchen and I quickly moved around it to make sure the entire room was empty.

I retraced my steps to the front entry and moved down an equally stark hallway. The wall panels were textured and lit by floor level lighting that had been incorporated into the lower part of the wall. At the end of the hall stood an empty pedestal, and I wondered what should have been displayed on its marble surface.

As I moved forward, the hall veered to the left into another shorter corridor. On the floor, a bronze bust lay in the middle of the floor where it had fallen. I stopped when I saw a scuff of red on the grey marble next to the bust. My focus had been on people, and as I moved forward, I realized I'd missed a series of red scuffmarks moving from the door I was approaching, past me and out the front door. "Shit."

I didn't particularly care for the woman, but I didn't want to see her dead or injured in any way. I "cut the pie" around this door as well, and nearly gagged at what I saw.

A body, I assumed it was Slythen, lay on a rug that at one time had been completely white. The only reason I knew that particular fact was because one corner was still immaculately clean and white, while the entire rest of the rug was now soaked in blood.

The woman's intestines had been removed from her body and wrapped around her mouth and eyes. Her heart had been cut from her body and lay on her chest. I had to step closer to confirm what I thought I was seeing. It looked like a chunk of meat had been ripped from the heart. Possibly with someone's teeth?

I tore my gaze away and quickly finished searching the room, closets and adjoining bathroom. When I was satisfied no one was in hiding, I checked the rest of the home and the garage and then had to step outside to get some air.

As I've said before, I hate dead bodies, and I knew I'd never get the sight of this one out of my mind. The memory of what I'd seen would show up in dreams and at inconvenient times. It will pop up and I'll inadvertently close my eyes and shake my head to clear it, and whoever I'm with at the time will say, "What's up with you anyway?" and I'll respond, "Nothing. I don't know, just thinking that's all." and we'd never talk about it again.

The patrol officer's siren became louder the closer he got. Seeing Slythen's body had shaken me more than I thought, because I belatedly pulled my radio from my belt. "9David72, Code 4. Shut down lights and sirens." The siren immediately stopped blaring through the neighborhood and the officer got on the radio to say he'd arrived.

"4A62, 10-23."

I immediately recognized Jimmy Weatherby's bright red buzz cut when he stepped out of his car. Jimmy had spent four years in the Marines, although he's not bulky muscular like a lot of them are. He's built more like a gymnast, lean and strong and ready to take on the world. His bright smile lit his face as he strode my way. "Nothing, huh? Casey must be chasing the only suspect. Burglary?"

I was still feeling a little light-headed and I leaned against one of the porch posts and shook my head. "No."

He cocked his head sideways and studied me a minute. "You okay?"

I blinked out of my reverie and returned his gaze. "Yeah. Uh, no. This is a crime scene. I want the whole yard, from the mailbox here in front, around the sides and then all the way around the end of the pool." Having something familiar to do helped to clear my head and I pulled out my cellphone.

Jimmy nodded. "You got it. Do we need more units here?"

"One more to secure the back. When you're done with the tape, guard the front of the house. Don't go inside."

Curiosity shone from his eyes, but he was professional enough to just nod and begin doing what I'd told him to do. I hit autodial for Kate, who answered on the second ring.

"What do you have?"

Now that I had to verbalize what I'd seen, my voice wobbled a little when I began to speak. "Um, it's..." I cleared my throat and tried again. "It's bad..." I faltered again, swallowed and then gave myself a good kick in the pants. I was a professional who'd seen plenty of grizzly scenes before and I needed to buck up.

"What's bad?"

I realized I hadn't heard Casey on the radio and asked, "Did Casey get the suspect?"

Kate was quiet a moment, and then I heard her disembodied voice come over the radio I had hooked on my belt behind my back. "9David70 to 9David73." When there was no response, she repeated herself. My heartbeat inched up a bit when the radio remained still silent.

The dispatcher called Casey several times, and then hit the "tone," a high-pitched sound designed to get everyone's attention in case an officer had become distracted and hadn't heard their designator being called.

Still nothing. I grabbed my radio and asked if any patrol officers had caught up to the pursuit and when I was told "Negative," I began running for my car. "What was her last known location?"

I heard Kate yelling to get my attention through the phone and I put it to my ear. "Kate, we have to find her. These people are monsters. Slythen's dead. Butchered. I should have gone with Casey."

Kate got back on the radio. "9David70, go 10-39." A steady, repetitive emergency tone started up, telling anyone who didn't have a need to get on the radio to keep the airwaves open. Kate continued, "I need every available unit to converge on 9David72's last known location. Keep a lookout for a blue Ford Taurus, front end damage, Arizona license 592-GMW. Notify air we're going to need them up."

She'd apparently picked up on my panic because she was calling up every available resource, including the helicopter, to find Casey.

Just as I reached my car, she called me on the radio. "9David70 to 9David72. Stay there and maintain the integrity of the scene." I stopped in my tracks and stared at the radio. What? I spun around and saw Jimmy watching me as he reeled out the police tape. Then I listened while Kate coordinated the search with several patrol sergeants who would take over from her and direct their resources as they saw best.

The dispatcher gave the description of the truck Casey had been following, but Casey had apparently never gotten close enough to get a plate number because none was given in the details.

I wanted to jump in my car and join the search, but knew I'd just be driving in circles trying to find her. Kate was pulling out all the stops and I reluctantly stayed where I was. She didn't need me disobeying a direct order and distracting her from the search.

Weatherby looked relieved when I hooked my radio onto my pants and started toward him. Marine's follow orders no matter what, and that had never, and would never, leave him.

Me on the other hand, not so much. But I knew this time Kate was right. I got on the cell and when Sgt. Logan answered, I explained what I had. When I'd finished, I added, "I know this is part of our case, or at least part of the follow-up, but I wasn't sure if we should handle this or give it to you guys. If Kate hasn't called you yet it's because she's too busy right now."

Jon responded immediately. "We'll work it together. I'll send Ruthanne, Steve McShane and Andy Montagne out to you."

"Any chance you could keep Dempsey away?" I knew it was none of my business whom he sent my way, but I needed to ask. The last thing I needed right now was to get into a pissing match with the asshole.

"I sent him to do some follow-up interviews on the reservation for a different case. He won't be coming."

I breathed a sigh of relief and thanked him.

"Oh, and Alex, are you still with the body?"

"No, I'm outside."

"Go back inside and make sure she didn't have any cats or dogs in the house."

"I didn't see any, but I'll go check again." I didn't need it spelled out for me why we needed to keep animals away from the body and I fervently hoped my first impression had been right. Slythen was too self-absorbed to care for anything or anyone other than herself.

On a whim, as I walked into the house I tried calling Casey's cell. After several rings, the call went to her messages. Just as I pushed end, I got a call from Terri Gentry.

"Alex, what the hell's going on? Where's Casey and why aren't you with her?"

"Are you on duty today?"

"No, but I monitor the radio from home. What's going on?"

I wasn't sure how much to tell her and I stopped a second to think.

"Alex?"

I gave her the quick version of the story. "Casey and I came to do a welfare check on one of our victims. No one answered so we went around to the back of the house. Casey saw someone inside and took off running around to the front. She yelled at me to check inside the residence. She said she had the one who was running. They took off in a truck and she jumped in her car and followed." Guilt at not going with her twisted my stomach into knots and I grabbed a good hunk of hair in my fist and jerked on it, growling quietly enough that she wouldn't hear.

"And?"

"And we can't raise her on the radio."

"That's not enough to start the kind of search Kate's got going. What aren't you telling me?"

I sidestepped the question as best I could. "Kate'll find her, Terri. Look, I need to run and do something for sergeant...uh, for a sergeant. I'll get back to you, okay?" I didn't want to mention Logan, since she'd know Casey had been chasing a homicide suspect and now we couldn't raise her.

I heard her shout, "Okay? No, it's—" just as I ended the call. I realize that was pretty cowardly, but I knew Kate wouldn't want this case spread around and she definitely wouldn't want Terri running out to the field in a panic.

I turned and kicked one of the floorboards in the hallway, and immediately realized my mistake when I heard the tinkling of breaking glass. I'd forgotten about the lighting in the wall and I'd just compromised the crime scene. "Damn it." I decided to leave it and walked into the bedroom. Luckily, I didn't see any pets near, around, or on top of the body.

My phone rang. I pulled it out of my pocket again and saw Terri calling me back. "Shit." I knew it was unfair and cowardly not to tell her the truth, so I answered it by saying, "Look, I'm sure Casey is fine. You know she can take care of herself."

"What is it you're not telling me?"

Sighing, I decided I might as well go all in. "This turned out to be a homicide. We interrupted the killing and the perp took off in a truck.

I didn't know what we had and when Casey told me to do a welfare check inside, I figured she'd seen something...which...she had."

Terri was quiet for so long I checked to make sure we were still connected.

"So, now they're looking for her because she's not answering her radio. Okay, I supposed she could have jumped out of her car in pursuit and accidentally left her radio on the seat."

I tried not to look too closely at the body as I checked under the bed for any cats. "Yeah, I've known her to do that before." Not. I knew Casey was obsessive when it came to officer safety and she'd never accidentally forget anything.

"No, you haven't. And neither have I. I'm heading into town now to join the search. Let me know if you hear something before I do."

"Okay." I knew I would have done exactly the same thing, so I didn't try talking her out of helping to find Casey. We disconnected, and I pulled on a pair of gloves. I methodically searched for pets in cabinets and closets, in the bathroom and in the shower. When I was absolutely certain there weren't any animals anywhere near the body, I stepped out into the hall and waited.

I trusted the three homicide detectives who were coming and thought it would make everything cleaner if I waited to begin any type of investigation until they arrived and we could all get on the same page. After what seemed like hours—in reality it was about thirty minutes, as I very well knew from obsessively looking at the time on my phone—I heard the detectives radio in that they were on-scene.

Pretty soon Ruthanne called out, "Alex?"

"Down the hall." She poked her head around the corner, silently asking if there was any evidence she should watch out for.

"There are some red smudges, I'm assuming blood, at various intervals from the front door to the bedroom."

She knelt to get a better visual on the tiles. "Oh yeah." She glanced over her shoulder. "Hand me the tents." Someone handed her a stack of folded, v-shaped cards with numbers on them. They were handy indicators we placed next to or over evidence we didn't want to inadvertently step on as we walked around the scene.

Once she'd methodically made her way down the hall to my location, she glanced into the room. "Jesus, Mary and Joseph. Now there's something you don't see every day." Dead bodies didn't rattle her, so the fact that she at least displayed a little shock and awe made me feel slightly better about my still-queasy stomach.

Steve and Andy moved around Ruthanne and stepped into the room. Neither man said anything as they stared at the bloody mess that used to be Dr. Slythen's body.

Setting his case on the floor, Steve pulled a pair of gloves out of the bag's outer pocket. He straightened and gestured to the body with his elbow, since his hands were occupied with the gloves. "Well that's a new one. I've never seen intestines used as a gag and blindfold before."

Andy also pulled on some gloves. "No question we're dealing with a nutcase. You have any idea who did this?"

I shook my head.

Ruthanne brought her oversized case into the room and set it on the floor next to Steve's. She walked as close to the body as she dared without stepping into the blood pooled on the carpet. "Look at that. Is that a bite someone took out of her heart?" She studied the floor. "Were there any dogs or cats around when you got here?"

"I haven't found any pets. No food or water bowls, and I checked in this area really well."

"So, if there aren't any animals around, whoever did this probably ate some of the heart." She wrinkled her nose and looked over at Steve. "Remember that case..?"

Steve nodded. "Yup, but I know for a fact that guy's still in federal prison. His parole hearing is coming up again and I had to go sit in on a pre-hearing interview." He glanced up at me. "Casey was chasing the murderer?"

Guilt once again reared its ugly head and I felt I needed to explain why I hadn't gone with her. "I didn't know what we had and when I went to follow her, she told me to do a welfare check inside instead. She'd seen something through the window and saw the guy running. I hadn't. I heard a nearby patrol unit say they were on the way to back her up, so I did what she said."

He sighed, "Tough choice, but I understand why she wanted you to stay. Having a scene like this unsecured could have been a disaster if some nosy neighbor had come along and fucked up the scene. And you're right, patrol should have been plenty of back-up for her. Don't beat yourself up, Alex. Second guessing yourself will drive you insane."

Second guessing was exactly what I'd been doing for the last hour or so and without responding to the bone he'd just thrown me, I stepped into the hallway and called Kate.

"What's up, Alex?"

"Jon sent three of his people here. I want to come search instead of just—"

Kate interrupted and started in without preamble. "I want you to follow up on any lead you have as far as Pito's murder is concerned. Any lead, no matter how small or farfetched. This is all connected somehow, and the sooner we solve that case, the better chance we'll have of knowing who murdered Slythen. When we know that, we'll find Casey."

I swallowed the argument sitting on the tip of my tongue. I needed to be out there looking for my partner, but Kate's logic made sense. "Okay. Have you found anything?" The silence on the line really unnerved me. "Kate?"

I heard her sigh. "The helicopter just located her car. Looks like somebody rammed it. Still no Casey though."

I pictured the body lying in the next room and almost gagged. The people who did that to Slythen probably had Casey, and if—I stopped myself from going any further with that train of thought.

Kate's tone softened. "We'll find her, Alex. Just do your magic, okay?"

"As long as you do yours." There was no one I trusted more to organize a search for Casey than Kate, and I felt like I was putting Casey's life in her hands.

"Get going, Alex."

I stuck my head around the bedroom door. "Hey, Kate wants me working on our first case. She thinks they might be connected and if they are, that case might help with this one, which might help us find Casey."

Steve nodded. "Makes sense. If we find anything that might help, we'll give you a call."

I backed into the hall and turned to leave.

"Hey, Alex?"

Two backward steps allowed me to see into the bedroom again. "Yeah?"

"Good luck." The three of them looked pretty grim and I knew their concern for Casey was just as deep as mine.

I nodded and then headed out to my car. I sat behind the wheel a moment gathering my thoughts. I tried to prioritize the investigative steps I needed to take, but there was so much to do in such a short time they became all jumbled up in my mind.

I pulled a notepad out of my green, canvas briefcase, rooted around until I found a pen and then began jotting down my thoughts. Nothing was solidly related to anything else and everything we knew was circumstantial. We assumed Tom's attack had something to do with finding Pito in the dumpster. We assumed Cherry had been followed and had subsequently stabbed someone because of seeing Pito's body. We assumed the guy who had Slythen sew up his wound was the man Cherry had stabbed, but there had been several other stabbings that day and I hadn't had time to follow up to make sure all those victims were accounted for.

As I stared at the list, I realized the first thing I needed to do was to go talk to Tom Handy and see whether he could remember anything from the attack inside his overturned camper. I drove to the hospital and instead of waiting for the elevator, I ran up two flights to the floor housing the intensive care unit. I found Handy's name on the white board and hurried into his room.

"Excuse me!" A curly haired, female nurse followed me into the room. "You're not allowed to be in here."

I pulled my badge off my belt and held it up for her to see. "I'm Detective Wolfe. I need to speak to Mr. Handy."

She pursed her lips and pointed to the empty bed. The sheets had been pulled tight with hospital corners. A thin blue hospital blanket lay folded across the foot of the bed.

I turned back to her. "I don't understand. Where's Mr. Handy?"

Her tone mellowed somewhat from her initial irritated stance when she'd followed me into the room. "I'm sorry to say. Mr. Handy expired earlier this morning."

"Expired? How?"

"I'm afraid you'll need to speak to the attending physician about that." She stared directly into my eyes, apparently still annoyed that I'd flaunt the hospital guidelines about getting permission to speak to one of the ICU patients.

I didn't have time to play games. "Who would that be?"

A man's heavily accented voice spoke up behind me. "That would be me, Detective. I'm happy to help any way I can."

A swarthy gentleman in his mid-sixties stood in the doorway. His manner of speech sounded lyrical, like a bubbling brook with lots of ups and downs. Combining that with his shoulder-length, black, wavy hair, I'd guess Italy as his country of origin. I held up my badge again and once more introduced myself. "I'm Detective Wolfe. I understand Mr. Handy died earlier today? How did he die?"

The doctor smiled and shrugged. "What, no foreplay? No, how are you? Nice to meet you doctor?"

"Sir, we have a detective who is missing, and Mr. Handy might have been able to help us find her. I'm sorry I don't have time for the pleasantries. Did he ever regain consciousness? If he did, did he say anything? Like who might have hurt him?" I knew I was grasping at straws, but Handy's death couldn't have come at a worse time.

His smile faded and he lifted his chin and nodded. "Ah, I understand. As far as I know, he never regained consciousness. Nurse?" He tilted his head in the nurse's direction.

She shook her head. "No, he didn't. I'm sorry Detective. I wish we could be more help." Her attitude had definitely softened now, and I appreciated that.

"So, he died from the head wounds, Doctor..." I realized I hadn't gotten his name.

"Sciacchitano." When I took out my notepad, he spelled out the name for me. When he'd finished, he continued, "And yes, he had a depressed skull fracture and a diffuse axonal injury. Both very serious. Even if he had regained consciousness, which was highly unlikely, he would have had severe brain damage."

"What type of weapon would cause that type of injury in an enclosed space?"

He pursed his lips. "That's a better question for your coroner, but, just as a guess, you understand, possibly a metal pipe, or a bat of some kind." He shrugged, "Maybe even…oh what do you call those things?" He closed his fist as though holding something. "You know. What police sometimes used in the old days?"

"A nightstick?"

His brows lifted. "Well certainly a nightstick could do it, but I'm thinking more of the heavy bag with a small handle? Oh, the other man gave me its name…" He tapped his forehead trying to remember.

"A sap. A lead filled leather bag?"

He pointed at me. "Just so. When I saw the injuries and the pattern of bruising, that is the first thing that came to mind. Was he perhaps the victim of a police beating?"

I shook my head. "No."

"Perhaps a mafioso, then? On the island where I was born, Sicilia, la Cosa Nostra quite often use that type of weapon."

That I didn't need to hear. Another link back to Gia. "Thank you. You've both been very helpful."

The doctor stepped away from the door to let me pass. "You're most welcome."

As I walked out, his words came back to me. I turned and asked, "The other man? What other man?"

"The other detective. The one who came for the body." He began patting various pockets in his long white coat. "Dove l'ho messo?" He reached into the back pocket of his green scrubs. "Ah. Here."

I took the business card he held out and read the name printed in gold colored, raised lettering, "Detective Sean Dempsey." I looked up at him. "Did you mention La Cosa Nostra to Detective Dempsey."

He nodded decisively. "I did."

"Can I keep this card?" I wanted to show it to Kate once this whole debacle was over and done with.

"Of course."

"Thank you." On the way back to the car, I stopped at a seating area near the elevator and pulled out my phone. I didn't want to make the call, but if I was jumping at shadows and being pulled in the wrong direction, I needed to know.

I called Gia, and when she answered, I said, "Gia. It's me. Look, Casey is missing, and I think it's all tied to Pito's murder. I'm following some leads, but I *need* to know…" I didn't want to say more because she was always very concerned her phones, or mine, were tapped.

For a long moment, silence was her only answer. I knew I'd insulted her, but that was too bad. "Alex, on my honor, and on the honor of my brother, Tancredo, the answer is no." Apparently she understood the gravity of the situation and my need to know the truth. "Is there any way we can help?"

"Absolutely not. You need to stay where you are. And…thank you."

"Of course. I know you'll find her safe, Alex. If anyone can, it's you."

I returned to my car and held my notepad in my lap. Going over my notes, I couldn't shake the feeling that Delores Mefisto and Sandy Hoffelder were at the center of all the death and drama we'd lived through the last few days. I knew they were whack jobs, but only Delores could have committed one or both of the murders. And how did the guy who Cherry stabbed fit into it all?

I tossed the notepad onto the passenger seat and drove back to the station. Kate always said if you're stuck, go back to the beginning. I ran to my desk and grabbed the VCR tape and then raced down the stairs to the media room. I shoved the tape into the player and hit the play button.

I'd already listened to about the first half hour so I fast forwarded to where I thought thirty minutes would be and hit play again. My impatience grew with each mundane topic Sandy and Burney discussed. I pulled out my phone to call Kelly to see if she'd found anything new and only half-listened to the interview drone on.

Kelly answered with her usual cheerful greeting. "Alex! I was going to call you when I went on my break. Did you get the picture I sent you? I sent it to your email address instead of your phone because I know how busy you always are."

"No, I haven't had a chance to look and I'm not near my computer. Hang on, let me pull it up on my phone. What picture are you talking about, anyway?" I put her on speaker and then pulled up her email. I opened it and scrolled down. "It's going to take a second to download."

"Oh, you asked me to look through the yearbook to see if there were any girls who looked like Sandy Hoffelder. There was one, a cousin, maybe, or even an illegitimate child, although I couldn't be one hundred percent certain. Sandy Hoffelder's father, Benjamin Hoffelder, was served with a paternity suit about the same year Sandy was born. I couldn't find who filed the suit, though. That's the picture in the email."

While I was waiting for the download—my phone was ancient and sucked when it came to doing anything fast—I happened to glance back at the VCR. I blinked several times and then hit rewind so fast I painfully jammed my finger backwards into its joint. I stood up and then immediately sat back down again. I hit play, stood up again, and then forced myself back into the seat so I could get a good look at the tape. "Shit."

"What?" Kelly's voice came faintly over the phone.

"Shit, shit, shit. That can't be. There's no fucking way." I hit rewind again and played what I'd just seen a second time. Burney had turned up the heat on Hoffelder, and she'd begun to fidget. Not just fidget. She methodically unbuttoned her jacket and then buttoned it up again.

I ran my hand through my hair, stood and began to pace within the confines of the tiny room. I had to think. What I was thinking just wasn't possible. I had spoken to Sandy Hoffelder in the locked facility here on Victoria Court just that morning. I hit rewind and watched the scene again.

I remembered the phone in my hand and put it to my ear. "Kelly? Are you still there?"

"I'm here. What's the matter, Alex? Was it something with the photo?"

"What?" I'd completely forgotten her email. "Oh. I forgot to look. Hang on."

I clicked back to my email. The picture had finished downloading and I moved my fingers across the screen to enlarge it. The photo looked like a younger version of both Delores Mefisto and Sandy

Hoffelder. When I scrolled down to get the girl's name, I had to sit down again. "No."

"No, what? Don't you think she looks like Sandy Hoffelder?"

"Yes, she does. It's her name that shocked me that's all. Delores Mefisto. And you say she might be related to Sandy somehow?"

"I think she might be a cousin or an illegitimate sibling. Could be either one, actually. Sandy's mother had a sister. I haven't found any marriage records for her yet, but if she married one of the four or five Mefisto men I've found living close to them at the time, then Delores and Sandy could be cousins. I'm still searching though."

With the scene paused, I stared at Hoffelder. Her expression held just the hint of fear at whatever Burney had just said. The intensity of her dark eyes had sharpened. I had paused it with her long, beringed fingers worrying one of the buttons. To the left of her hand, I spotted something black at the lip of her pocket. The whole jacket was a dingy, dark grey and I leaned in to try to get a better look. The image was still blurry, but if I used my imagination, I might say it looked like the tip of a black bead poking up between the pocket and the jacket itself.

I ejected the tape, stuck it in the envelope and ran out to my car. I wasn't sure how this new information could help us and my mind was racing between various scenarios. I got in the car and sat a minute, trying to make sense of everything. When the phone rang, I saw that Kelly was calling me back.

"Kelly?"

"You hung up on me. I wasn't quite done. You'd also asked me to send you a picture of Annie Lee Hoffelder. I'd forgotten until just now, so I just sent you another email."

"Annie Lee Hoffelder?" My mind was full of names and that one didn't ring any bells.

"You know. Sandy's little sister who disappeared just before the explosion? I found her picture in the yearbook and you asked me to send it to you."

I looked at my mail and saw that a new email had just come through. "Okay, thanks. I'll call if I need anything else." I needed to get out and drive, so I tossed the phone onto the seat and drove out into the bright midday sun.

I decided to go with what I knew even if it didn't make sense. If, somehow, Delores Mefisto and Sandy Hoffelder had changed places, that would explain why Delores, AKA Sandy, had completely gone insane when she'd gotten drunk and tried to burn Brigid. Alcohol can trigger psychotic episodes in people who are seriously deranged to begin with, and Brigid had said Delores had drunk the whole bottle of tequila that night. But why would anybody take the place of an insane murderess and allow her to go free? Especially knowing the woman was serving a life sentence for killing her own child?

I hit the steering wheel with my fist. All these little pieces weren't getting me any closer to helping Casey. I needed to go talk to Sandy again to see if there was any chance she wasn't really who she, and the Arizona Prison System, said she was.

Ten minutes later I was walking into the locked mental health facility for the second time that day. A nurse, or a guard, it was difficult to tell them apart in this place, ushered me into the same room I'd been in before.

When Hoffelder came through the door and saw me standing there, she lost it. "What the fuck? I told you I didn't have nothin' t' say to you! Get the fuck outta here! Nurse! Get this woman away from me!"

A different nurse than the one who'd showed me to the room came running over.

I stepped between Hoffelder and the doorway and blocked her from leaving. "Listen to me! A woman's life is at stake. I need to know whether you're Sandy Hoffelder or Delores Mefisto." The widening of the eyes told me everything I needed to know. "Do you know what you've done? Do you know how many people she's killed in the last few days? Do you care?"

I didn't think she'd break so easily, but tears flooded down her cheeks and she screamed back at me. "Of course, I care! You think I'm scary psycho like they are? Well I ain't! I had two baby girls back in Evanston. Two!" She held up two fingers. The tears were really flowing now and snot ran freely from her nose. She wiped it with the sleeve of her hospital gown. "An' now I got one. They took my Misty, and I don't know where they keepin' her. They come 'n got me an' said if I didn't change places with that monster, they was gonna kill my little girl." Her big eyes practically bugged out of her head. "And you know they would. She's only six, but they would!"

My money was on the fact that little Misty hadn't lived past the first night Sandra had gotten out. I decided I'd get more information out of her if the atmosphere wasn't quite so charged with emotion. I spoke slowly, as though calming a child. "When did you make the change?"

The nurse, who was looking totally confused, held out a box of tissues.

Delores grabbed one and wiped furiously at her face and nose. "A week ago Monday."

"You said, 'they,' who did you mean?"

"My other cousin an' her husband."

"Your other cousin?" Who the hell did she mean by that? "What are their names?"

"I don't know his, but hers was Annie. I thought she been dead since we was kids, but then she shows up at my apartment sayin' she got Misty an' if I ever wanted t' see her again, I had t' come take Sandy's place. We always looked alike as kids, and I guess they hatched this plan t' get her out." She sat in a chair, rested her elbow on the table and put her forehead on her hand. "I'm sorry for whoever's dead, Detective, but I got m' girl t' get home. I'd do anythin' t' bring my girl home safe."

"Where can I find them? Do you know where they live?"

Her face crumpled again and she shook her head. She began sobbing and I knew I wouldn't get any more useful information out of her. I'd accidentally left my phone on the passenger seat of my car, so I left Delores to the nurse and ran to my phone to call Kate.

When I grabbed the cellphone off the seat, it was still open to the mail app and I remembered Kelly had sent me the yearbook photo of Sandy's missing sister, Annie Lee Hoffelder. I raised my finger to switch to my contact list, but I thought of all the times Kate had drummed into my head to dot all the i's before I make my report. I quickly punched download, and then waited impatiently for the picture to appear.

Once it did, rage gripped my mind and squeezed the air from my chest. "That fucking bitch." I jammed the gear lever into drive so hard I passed the D and accidentally shoved it into manual. When I punched the gas, the engine revved up to turbo and I realized I'd shifted into permanent low gear. I shoved the car into drive and spun out of the lot.

While the car was still fishtailing, I punched auto dial for Kate with my thumb. She answered immediately and I blurted out, "Meet me at the vets!" I almost sideswiped a car as I got out onto the main street and realized driving the way I was and talking on the phone wasn't such a good idea. I disconnected and shoved the phone into my coat pocket.

After running two red lights—I at least slowed enough at the intersection to know I wouldn't ram into anyone—and weaving in and out of traffic like a madwoman, I skidded into the parking lot in front of Slythen's clinic.

My little gnome had found a sledgehammer somewhere and he was busy bashing in the side of my head with it. Time was running short for Casey, and I needed to figure things out fast.

I ran into the office yelling, "Ahern! Where the fuck are you?" I caught the startled faces of Margaret Rutherford and Emily as I sprinted past the front desk, opening the doors to each treatment room and checking inside as I sped past.

When I shoved the third door open, the exit on the opposite side of the room slammed shut. Since a vet was standing at one end of the metal treatment table and a woman holding a Pomeranian blocked the other way around, I jumped up and slid across the top, barely landing on my feet on the other side.

I pulled open the other door in time to see Victoria Ahern's ass careening around the corner at the end of the hall. I managed to tackle her just as she pulled the door to the waiting room open. Both of us went sliding through the room on her stomach accompanied by the shrieks of hysterical clients, both men and women, and the excited barking of every dog in the place.

When we came to a stop, I wrenched her arm behind her back.

"Where is she?" I pulled up on her arm to the point where I was millimeters away from dislocating her shoulder.

Someone grabbed me under my arms and jerked me backwards and I heard Kate shouting in my ear. "Alex! Let go. We've got her, let go!" She practically lifted me off the woman and I had to let go of Ahern's arm or risk wrenching it from the socket.

A patrol officer took my place. He cuffed Victoria Ahern and hauled her to her feet.

Kate yelled over the cacophony of hysterical dogs to an astonished group of women standing next to the front desk. She pointed with her head, apparently afraid of what I'd do if she let go of my arms. "Emily. Clear out two rooms, now!"

We didn't have time for this and I spat out my earlier question. "Where are they, Victoria?"

She turned a frightened look my way before the patrol officer, at Kate's direction, escorted her into one of the quickly emptied rooms.

Kate and I went into another. Furious at the wasted time, I turned a murderous glare on Kate when she let me go. "We don't have time!"

Kate grabbed my collar and pulled me forward. "We don't have time for *this,* Alex. Get a grip and tell me what you know."

I pulled in a deep breath and blew it out with a growl. When she released me, I gave her the abbreviated version of events. "I don't have time to explain everything. All you need to know is Sandy Hoffelder's cousin, Delores Mefisto, changed places with her at the medical facility here in Tucson. It's Sandy Hoffelder, the baby burner, who's holding Casey."

"And Ahern?"

"Remember I told you Hoffelder's sister disappeared just before her parent's house exploded?" I raised my eyebrows, knowing she'd make the connection.

She did. "Why do you think Ahern is Sandy's lost sister? I thought she'd been declared dead."

I blinked and had to think a minute. Too many facts were swirling around in my brain and I couldn't remember why I'd made that connection. Then it came to me. I pulled out my phone and opened the picture Kelly had sent to me. I held it up so Kate could see. "This is Sandy's sister, Annie. Kelly sent me her yearbook picture from High School."

"Kelly?" She took the phone from me, enlarged the picture and squinted down at it.

"My friend at the library."

"That's Ahern all right. Her facial features are really distinctive." She handed the phone back to me. "And you think Ahern knows where they are?"

"She has to."

"Why?"

I realized I'd left out one important detail. "Because her husband's involved. I'm not sure, but I think he's the one who Cherry stabbed. Also, remember there were two sets of prints coming out of Tom Handy's camper? A big set, and a smaller set? And Sandy would have needed help getting Pito's body into the dumpster. You said Pito had to have been killed somewhere else because of the lack of blood in the dumpster."

I felt like I was babbling, but I needed to communicate all my thoughts in a short amount of time. "And if he was with Sandy when she killed Slythen, then he was probably driving the truck Casey went after."

Kate nodded, thinking everything through—something I was having a hard time doing right then. Thank God I have a calm, cool, collected Sergeant because where my friend's lives are concerned, I tend to lose it a little bit. "So, the vet tech...what's her name again?"

"Veronica Ahern, AKA Annie Lynn Hoffelder."

"It was probably Veronica who unlocked the door and let her husband in when Emily went to the restroom." She'd been looking around the room as she thought out loud, but now she turned her gaze my way. "We need to get Ahern's address. Hoffelder wouldn't have a home or place to stay. You said you first came across her at a homeless camp using the name Delores Mefisto. But Veronica and her husband have to have a home or an apartment somewhere. That's where we start looking for Casey."

I pushed past her to get the information out of Veronica one way or another but Kate grabbed the back of my shirt and jerked me back.

She pulled me around and spoke very slowly to emphasize her words. "I'm in charge, Alex. If you want to find Casey—"

I'm sure my eyes took on the laser-like intensity of a bird of prey.

She held up her hand. "I know you want to find her, but Casey's best hope right now is for us to work together. You do what I say. Understand?"

Knowing my eyes didn't lose any of their intensity, I nodded.

When we left the room, Kate walked right past the door into where the officer was holding Ahern. I stopped and nearly barged in, but then remembered I was supposed to be following her lead.

She went straight up to Rutherford. The woman had an obvious air of authority, which I'm sure Kate recognized. Kate pulled her badge off her belt and held it up. "I'm Sgt. Brannigan. I need Veronica Ahern's home address, now."

Probably because she'd already had dealings with me, Rutherford looked to me for...what? Validation? Permission? I nodded at her. "Please. We don't have much time."

It was Emily who wrote something on a yellow sticky note, ripped it from the pad and held it out to Kate. "This is where she lives. It's not far from here." She glared up at Rutherford, daring her to call her on the carpet for supplying the address without her explicit permission.

Kate grabbed the paper and hurried out the door. "Alex, you're with me."

No shit. Where did she think I'd be? Waiting at the vets until I heard what they'd found. I ran for my car, but Kate yelled, "No. I mean you're with me in my car."

I sprinted back, pulled open her passenger door and jumped in seconds before Kate jammed the pedal to the floorboard. The wheels spun in place for just a second before catching and hurling us forward. I hadn't had time to put on a seatbelt and I quickly pulled mine around and clicked it into place.

Kate grabbed her mic from the clasp on the dashboard. "9David70. I need patrol units to respond to..." She held up the paper and read it while traveling at over seventy miles per hour.

So, she was just as rattled as I was, she just held herself together better than I did.

She gave Ahern's address and then said, "No lights and sirens. Stand off until I get there. I repeat, no sirens."

That was kind of a moot point because at the speed we were traveling, there was no way anyone would arrive before us. The address turned out to be in Slythen's neighborhood, only in the not so pricey section. The homes were much smaller, but still had a good bit of land between each one.

We stopped one house down from the address and both of us ran full out to the front door, which was standing wide open. We pulled out weapons but didn't enter the home nearly as fast as we'd approached.

I stepped into the foyer and felt my breathing slow, as it usually did in tactical situations. A curved step led into a sunken living room off to the right. I slid around the wall and faced directly into the room while Kate did the same to the room on the left.

The first thing I registered was the copious amounts of blood that had been flung all over the room. Red fanned out on the far wall starting at floor level, forming a wide arch halfway up and then spraying all the way across and onto the adjoining wall.

Another similar pattern covered a long sofa that lay knocked over onto its back. The sofa's four feet pointed at me like rifle barrels and I stepped into the room dreading what I'd find lying behind it.

Kate called out to me. "Alex, let me look first."

I shook my head and continued forward. The first things I saw were a pair of lugged soled work boots. I'd been holding my breath and I let it out in a rush. I turned to Kate who was hurrying toward me. "It's not her." I moved forward to see how badly the person had been injured. A gaping wound bisected his throat from one ear to the other.

Kate stopped in the middle of the room. She'd gone pale, and when she knew it wasn't Casey lying there, I saw a little color return to her cheeks. Turning, she headed back the way we'd come. We searched the rest of the house and didn't find anything alarming until we walked into the kitchen.

It, too, was a bloody mess. The kitchen table lay on its side and all four chairs lay scattered about the room. Two had broken legs while the seat on a third lay in pieces near the pantry. Smears of blood covered the floor and walls where a knockdown, drag out fight had obviously taken place.

I followed a pair of bloody footprints to an open door that lead into the back yard. We scanned the area, trying to get a feel for where the two combatants might have gone. About ten yards north, there was a scuffed indentation in the dirt where the fight must have continued.

I heard Kate get on the radio. "9David70 to 4U6. Coordinate units in a search of the neighborhood. 9David73's out here somewhere, we just need to find her."

"4U6, 10-4."

I wasn't sure which sergeant 4U6 was, but I had to trust they knew what they were doing. Footprints in the loose, desert sand led away from the scuffed area. Kate and I followed as best we could. Unfortunately, they petered out after about fifty yards.

Kate said, "You're her partner, Alex. You're the best one to know how she thinks tactically. Where would she run?"

Where would she run? After the suspect, of course. I processed Kate's words and then came to the obvious conclusion. "Wait, you think Sandy's chasing her instead of the other way around?" It was a testament to the level of adrenalin racing through me that it hadn't occurred to me that Casey might be the one injured and running away. I'd just assumed she was chasing the woman to take her into custody.

Kate turned a full one-eighty. "If she's badly injured, yes, I think she'd try to find someplace safe to shelter until help arrives."

Like Kate, I spun in a circle, seeing the area from a different point-of-view. Where would Casey go if she needed a safe place to hunker down and wait?

There was a neighboring house southwest of our location, but I knew beyond any shadow of a doubt Casey would never lead a homicidal maniac anywhere near a home full of innocent people. She'd rather die before putting anyone else in danger. Even though there was open desert straight ahead, I could see several homes in the distance, and the same reasoning applied.

When I looked to the north, the spire of a Catholic church rose in the distance. Instantly, I knew that was where she'd head. She'd grown up Catholic, had gone to Catholic school, and although she didn't practice the religion, she still had a very deep, devout belief in the Almighty and the sanctity of the church and the sanctuary it would provide.

I sprinted toward the spire knowing Kate would be right behind me. I began to see more blood as we ran, and I hoped to hell it was Hoffelder's and not Casey's.

Just as we'd found at the home, the door to the knave stood open. It was dark inside and my eyes hadn't had time to adjust before an inhuman growl rose on my right. I only had a moment to react before, out of the darkened nave, the end of a heavy marble pedestal rammed into my chest.

The blow knocked the Glock from my hands and sent me toppling over onto Kate. The two of us fell in a heap with the heavy baptismal font attached to the pedestal crashing down on top of us. Only a turbocharged, insane, manic rage could give the woman the superhuman strength necessary to lift something that heavy.

My gun had sailed off to the right, but I saw Kate's Glock spinning to the left on the slick, black marble tile floor. It slid beneath a low side table and came to rest against the wall. Hoffelder dove for it, and I pushed out from under the font and dove on top of her. We slid into the table knocking it, a stack of pamphlets and two heavy candlesticks to the floor.

As Hoffelder stretched her arm out to snag the gun, Kate grabbed our legs and pulled us back and away.

Hoffelder screamed and wrenched her body around so that she and I were face to face. Her teeth were bared, and I knew she intended to bite into some part of my flesh. My forehead was the only weapon I had and I rammed her nose so hard I heard bones crunch beneath the blow.

Even that didn't faze her. She lifted me off her chest and literally threw me far enough away to give her fist a clear path to Kate's face.

Kate hadn't straightened yet and I heard a snap when her head jerked backwards onto her shoulders and she fell into a frighteningly limp, unconscious heap. I hoped to God Hoffelder hadn't broken her neck.

The woman twisted onto her hands and knees and I tackled her again, pinning her arms to her body in a desperation move. As we fell, I smashed her forehead against the marble tile hoping to knock her unconscious or at the very least try to disorient her.

With the strength of a demon from Hell, she lifted the two of us into a push-up position, reached one hand up to grab my collar and then rolled me onto my back, slamming her knees into my solar plexus and robbing me of breath and the ability to pull in more life-giving air.

I punched her in the jaw, a stupid move since that's one of the hardest places on a person's face.

She let out a combination shriek and howl, opening her bloody mouth wide the way a wolf raises its muzzle to the moon. A heavy brass candleholder had fallen from the side table and she grabbed it and raised it above her head.

The blow to my stomach had paralyzed my diaphragm and I couldn't pull in a breath. I tried to react to her attack, but black dots danced across my vision making it difficult to see. The candlestick plunged toward my head, but before it made contact, I heard a solid, wet crack above my head.

Hoffelder lurched off to the side where she finally lay lifeless and still.

I managed to pull in enough air to at least get a good look at my surroundings.

Standing over us, a broad-shouldered, muscular priest, dressed in a black cassock and white collar, held a golden cross with a figure hanging from the crossbars. He held it like a homerun hitter on a baseball field, and judging from his stance, he'd swung it like one, too. A fierce determination shone from his eyes and when a bubbling sound came from Hoffelder's throat, he raised the cross, ready to strike again.

I rolled to my knees and crawled over to Kate. I felt for a pulse and almost broke into tears when I found one. I turned back to the priest. "My partner. She came here. Where is she?"

He pointed to a heavy, oak door standing slightly ajar. He spoke with a strong Irish accent, which struck me as somewhat of a cliché under the circumstances. "When your friend stumbled in with that demon close behind, I managed to throw the malignant skut far enough away to get us both inside the sacristy and lock us in. When I heard you fighting out here, I knew I had to come help." He looked back at the door. "I put a tourniquet on your friend's arm, but she'll need surgery to repair the damage."

I pushed to my feet and hurried in to where Casey lay unconscious on a pile of dark blue vestments. Sure enough, he'd expertly wrapped a tourniquet around the upper part of her arm and had used an ornate candlestick to wind it tight. He'd secured the stick with strips torn from an ornate, maroon and gold table runner that lay crumped on the floor next to Casey's head.

I heard voices in the vestibule and in moments a patrol sergeant, presumably 4U6, hurried into the room.

"Meds are moving in. They'll be here in just a second. Is she alive?"

I hadn't had a moment to check and I quickly put my fingers to the artery in her neck. "It's weak, but she's alive. She's lost a ton of blood, if even half of what's at the house is hers."

He nodded and hurried out, needing to coordinate the scene and the medical response.

I glanced up to the wall where a golden cross bearing the figure of Christ hung near the ceiling. Beneath that and to the right, a second figure hung on a much smaller cross. An empty nail stuck out from the wall on the left. I turned back to the priest who noticed me staring at the cross he held down by his thigh.

Giving me a wan smile, he held it up. "It's one of the thieves. You didn't think I'd use our Savior to bash in her skull, did you?"

I shook my head. "No, I'm actually surprised you used the thief."

He moved to the empty nail and hung the cross back where it belonged. "This is only a symbol, while you, on the other hand, are flesh and blood. I always weigh my actions against what I believe Christ would do. I think if necessary, our Lord would have even used his own crucifix to save your life." He smiled ruefully, "Although I highly doubt most of my brethren would agree."

At that moment, Kate came into the room holding her fingers to her cheek. "She's alive?"

"Yes, thanks to the padre." I looked up into his face. "Where did you learn to apply a tourniquet like this?"

He straightened and loosened his collar with a tug. "Leftenant Mark Riggers, formally of the Royal Regiment of Fusiliers. I had to tie too many of those during my ten years of service, mostly in Iraq and Afghanistan."

Two medics, both women, came in; one carried a heavy case while the other held a bag of fluids attached to several coils of long, plastic tubing. Unaware of Kate's injury, one of them brushed past a little too closely, causing her to stumble backwards.

Father Riggers put out an arm to steady her and I hurried to her side. I pulled a chair up behind her, hoping she'd sit, but knowing she probably wouldn't.

She didn't. "How badly is she hurt?"

I looked to the Father to supply the answer since he'd have a better idea than I would.

He shrugged, "I wish I could be completely optimistic, but she's lost a lot of blood. She passed out the minute she knew she was safe in here. Quite a warrior mentality; if at all possible, stay conscious as long as you have to, by any means possible, in order to survive." It sounded like he was quoting an army manual. "I managed to staunch the flow of blood, and with the fluids these two are pumping into her, I say she has a better than likely chance."

We all watched as the two medics worked on Casey. A third came in carrying a portable stretcher to move her from inside the sacristy and out into the nave where they'd parked the regular gurney.

Kate spoke quietly as an aside to me, although I halfway suspected she was only speaking her thoughts out loud. "Why would anyone unleash such a monster on innocent people?"

That reminded me of Delores' daughter, Misty. I realized her kidnapping was one of the, at the time, non-essential details I'd left out when I'd explained to Kate what I knew about Sandy, Veronica and her husband. "Well, because Annie, or rather, Veronica, and her husband kidnapped Delores' six-year-old daughter and threatened to kill her if Delores wouldn't take Sandy's place." I made my way to the door. "I know it's probably a lost cause, but I need to see if maybe..."

I didn't finish the sentence, but Kate finished the thought for me. "You think there's any chance she's still alive?"

"No, I don't. But until we know for sure I have to try."

"*We* have to try, Alex. Our unit is a team, remember?"

I shook my head, "You need to go to the hospital, Boss."

That got some raised eyebrows, "Oh really? Are you giving the orders around here, now?"

"No, but—"

She motioned to the door. "Let's go outside. I'm sure most of the officers are still hanging around. Might as well put them to work. Do you have a photo?"

I shook my head. "No, all I know is a six-year-old, number three female." The number three referred to anyone of African American descent. One for Hispanic, two for Native American, four is Oriental and five stands for white.

I followed her out and listened while she organized the officers into teams of two and gave them a grid pattern to search in the surrounding desert area. "Alex, you go with Buck and Bear. Start at the house. Do a thorough search inside first and then leave the rest up to them."

"Boss, since you've got all these other people looking, I'd really like to go with Casey to the hospital. This many officers can—"

"Once again, you've put on stripes and taken over my job. That's becoming a bad," she cocked her head, "and irritating habit, Alex."

I hadn't seen Buck and his K9 partner sitting on a brick planter next to the bay window, but when Kate motioned him over he immediately grabbed Bear's leash and started walking our way. He peered at her bruised, swollen eye and then asked, "Sarge? You okay?"

Her response came out harsh and clipped. "I'm fine." She seemed to realize it was maybe a little too harsh, because she said with a softer tone, "I'm fine, Buck. Thanks for asking. Right now, I need you to go with Alex back to the house. She'll explain why on the way." Her eye had swollen completely shut and she massaged her temple with stiff fingers.

I wanted to argue, but again, this wasn't the time. Casey was unconscious and wouldn't know whether I was with her or not, and if there was even the slightest chance that little girl was alive, we had to move fast to find her.

The distance to the house seemed further away than it had when we'd been following Casey's tracks. On the way, I filled Buck in on who we'd be looking for.

He listened intently, and then asked, "Do you have anything that might belong to the girl? Clothes, a hairbrush. Anything? There'll be too many odors there for him to know which specific one we're looking for. If you think she's still in the house, we can go in, but you'd probably have just as much luck finding her if she is. If she's not, then we need something..." He raised a shoulder.

"I don't know if there is or not, I wasn't looking for that kind of stuff the first time through. We can look around, although the living room and kitchen will probably be off limits. There's a dead guy in the living room and the kitchen's completely trashed. Casey must have put up one hell of a fight."

He glanced over at me. "Would you expect anything less?"

I shook my head as I followed him through the front door. 4U6—I finally had the time to read his nameplate, Gonzales—met us at the door. The man had a severely pockmarked face, thick lips, and a head full of straight, black hair typical of most Hispanics. "This is a crime scene, guys. Unless you have something specific you need..."

Buck cut him off. "There's a little girl missing, Sarge. We need to look around to see if we can find something of hers." He motioned to Bear with his elbow. "To help him track her scent."

Gonzales studied the dog a moment, probably thinking about the best way to allow the request and still maintain the least amount of contamination of the crime scene. "All right. Since Detective Wolfe has already been in here, she can look around. You wait outside, Buck. If she finds something, should she bring it out to you or would it be better for Bear to come in and smell it where it is?"

"Better for him to come in at that point. His nose can literally smell one to ten thousand times better than us. If Alex finds an object, he might pick up a residual odor we don't know about inside the house."

Gonzales conceded the point. "Makes sense. All right, we'll call you if she finds anything."

Buck took Bear outside to wait and I turned to the sergeant. "Do you have an identification on the dead guy in the living room?"

He pulled out his notebook. "I.D. says Glenn Ahern."

Veronica's husband. Like I said, Casey is one hell of a tough woman in a fight and I guess Mr. Glenn Ahern found that out the hard way. "What are my parameters, Sarge?"

"If possible, stay out of the living room and kitchen. Obviously watch where you step because we've found smears of blood in the hallway. You know enough about crime scenes, Detective. I trust your judgement. The homicide dicks and internal affairs should be here anytime now. Make it quick."

I thought about that a minute. "If IAD is coming, I'd rather have someone with me while I search." They'd be investigating Casey's involvement in the death of the stiff in the living room, and God forbid they blame me for altering the crime scene in her favor for some reason.

He gave me a not unfriendly smirk. "Don't trust 'em? Don't blame you." He yelled out the front door. "Collins."

A youngish, lanky woman with a cheerful smile came forward. "Boss?"

Gonzales flicked a thumb over his shoulder. "You're with Wolfe."

The woman grinned at me. "You got it." Her blue eyes sparkled with a kind of mischievous enthusiasm I usually appreciated.

Today, I could feel myself flagging and I wanted to get this day over and done with. I gave her a semblance of a smile just to be friendly and then made my way down the hall.

Collins followed fast on my heels. "You're Alex Wolfe, right?"

"Last time I checked." My tiredness made me less chatty than I might have otherwise been.

"I'm Melissa Collins. But call me Mali. Everybody does. Well, except the Sarge. He just calls me Collins. What are we looking for?"

I turned to her. "You keep your hands in your pockets. Don't touch anything, got it?"

She dipped her chin decisively. "Got it."

"You're my witness. You pay attention to what I do, so if IAD asks you to clarify my movements, you can tell them what you saw."

The sparkle that never seemed to leave her eyes intensified. "I heard you and them don't exactly drink at the same watering holes."

I pulled the sides of my mouth up in a token grin and shrugged. "Somethin' like that." I was worried about Casey and Kate and Gia and just didn't have any cheerful banter left in me.

"She'll be okay, Alex. She's gotta be." I nodded, but she reached out and stopped me with a hand on my arm. "The two of you are like…I don't know, peanut butter and jelly." Those eyes that always sparkled? They'd lost their shine and were staring at me now with a different kind of intensity. "We're all pulling for her. She's gotta be okay."

I don't know why, but I without thinking I put my hand on her shoulder. I felt the tears I'd been struggling to hold back start to form and I shoved them down. I worried that if I said anything, they'd let loose, so I ground my teeth to maintain control, nodded my thanks and turned to enter the first bedroom.

It didn't really look lived in. More like a sterile hotel room with cheap, imitation watercolors on the walls and department store lamps on the dresser. Before I began my search, I wanted to see the other bedroom to get a feeling for which room was more likely to be the master and which would be the second, or guest bedroom. Not that Misty would have been a guest, but I bet, no I hoped, they hadn't taken her into their room.

The second room turned out to be the master. Dirty clothes littered the floor, lipstick, mascara and perfume bottles were scattered on top of a dresser, and magazines sat on nightstands bracketing both sides of the bed. Apparently they were equal opportunity voyeurs because there were copies of Mossy Cleft, a porn mag for men, and Dipstick, which wasn't filled with pictures of automobile engines.

I looked around, trying to get a feel for where they'd stick a little girl if they needed to keep her close enough she couldn't run, but also completely out of their way. The master bathroom was on the other end of a very short hallway and I stepped inside the door.

It wasn't filthy, but no one had bothered to clean in quite a while. Off to the right, a jacuzzi tub been built into a bay window. A light dusting of spider webs ran up the sides of the windows and dead flies lay on the shelf next to the tub.

Someone had thrown a straight razor and a can of shaving cream onto the countertop so that the can had rolled down into the sink where it lay with the spray nozzle resting on the strainer basket. Two toothbrushes, one blue and one green, lay on the sink's rim with their brushes hanging over the bowl. Their nod to cleanliness I guess, letting the wet brush drip into the sink instead of drying and leaving old toothpaste residue on the countertop.

I appreciated the fact that Mali had decided to keep quiet while I worked. I glanced back and was gratified to see her intently watching me as I moved around the room. I hadn't meant for her to catalogue my every step, but better that than not paying attention at all.

I was about to leave when I noticed something odd on the floor in front of the cabinet. I knelt to get a better look, and Mali squatted beside me.

"What did you find?"

I pointed to some brown dust on the tile. "That looks like sawdust. Why would there be sawdust? And over there, too." I motioned to the side of the cabinet.

"Huh."

I pulled on a pair of gloves and then gingerly opened the cabinet door. Shoved in with no particular order were packets of soap taken from hotel bathrooms, various bottles of shampoos and conditioners, and lo and behold, cleaning supplies. I pulled out my phone and took several shots of both the contents and the sawdust before methodically pulling each item out one at a time.

Someone had drilled several small holes in the cabinet's side wall, possibly thinking a little girl might need air if she was stuck inside such a tiny little space.

I hit pay dirt at the very back. A used zip tie lay under a rubber wash pan that sat directly beneath the U-bend of the P-trap. The zip tie had been sliced open and forgotten, or simply cut and left where it had fallen, if the bedroom and bath were any indication of Veronica's cleaning skills.

I left everything as it was and stepped to the door. "Sarge?"

Gonzales leaned into the hallway from the living room. "I need Bear."

He turned and yelled outside. "Buck?"

Buck stepped up to the door and both he and Gonzales looked at me.

"I think I've got something."

Buck came into the house with Bear close on his heels. He made his way down the hall, careful to direct Bear around the little number tents set next to the blood smears on the floor. The homicide detectives must have arrived while we were in the bathroom.

I pointed to the cabinet. "Under there."

Buck took bear to the sink and pointed. The dog's head and shoulders disappeared into the cabinet where he sniffed and snuffled around. Buck knelt next to him. "There are probably way too many smells in there for him to know which one we want."

"There's a used zip tie in there. I thought maybe they used it to tie the girl. There are also fresh holes in the sides, you know, like air holes?" I hoped I wasn't making something out of nothing, but when Buck pulled on some gloves and retrieved the zip tie, Bear sniffed and immediately put his nose to the ground.

Mali jerked a fist close to her side and hissed, "Yes!"

I don't think she realized there was a ninety-nine-point nine percent chance we were looking for a corpse instead of a living, breathing little girl. We followed Bear down the hall, but Buck had to pull him up short when he turned to go through the kitchen.

Homicide Sgt. Logan walked out of the living room. "Is there any chance you can go out the front and pick up the track outside?"

Buck shrugged. "I guess. That's assuming they took her outside." Blood covered a lot of the kitchen floor and Buck studied the layout, wondering, as was I, whether they'd kept Misty in one of those cupboards too. After a minute he shrugged. "Well, I guess we'll start from the outside, and if he loses the scent we can always come back and begin again." He turned to Logan. "Could you can keep people out of the kitchen at least until we see if he picks up the scent?"

When Logan nodded, the three of us filed out through the front door. Well, four if you include Bear.

I almost told Mali her assignment was over, but she was good company, so I let her make that call. I knew what it was like to be the patrol officer on a case who never finds out how things turn out. The detectives come and you return to your car to answer two dozen more calls before your shift is over.

We didn't have to guess whether Bear would pick up the scent. As soon as he rounded the corner, he ran to the end of the leash and pulled Buck past the kitchen door and out into the desert. A shed stood off to the side, and I was surprised he hadn't made a beeline to it.

Bear pulled on a track that led us away from the other houses. His nose brought him about a hundred yards to the south of the church, and he was coming very close to crossing over into the Saguaro National Monument, which would put us on Federal land. I hoped that didn't happen because there was nothing worse than the Feds barging in and messing up an investigation.

Luckily, Bear stopped in a sandy area and began traversing a left-to-right grid pattern between bushes, cacti, and various species of desert trees. He moved back and forth, nose to the ground, definitely on the scent. Buck kept encouraging him with "find her" until Bear pulled him to the base of a giant sycamore tree.

When he began clawing at the ground and digging up huge plods of dirt, Buck pulled him away. "I'd say there's something here, but I'm not sure what."

Mali and I stepped forward and took over from the dog. Both of us went down on our knees and began moving sand away from the area where Bear had been digging. I didn't have to go very deep before my fingers scraped against a smooth wooden plank. I redoubled my efforts. "Over here. There's wood or—" Mali joined me and together we uncovered the edges of a wooden door.

We flipped the door over and my heart sank when I saw the little body lying with a chilling, deathly stillness in the bottom of a shallow grave. The three of us stood on the edge of the pit, silently staring down at the tiny body wearing what had once been a pretty blue jumper and tennis shoes.

Bear surprised all of us when he dropped down into the hole and began nudging the girl's shoulder.

Not wanting to wreck the crime scene, Buck called him off and ordered him out of the pit. "Sorry, he never does anything like that."

I looked down at Bear. "He doesn't?"

"Never."

I stared at the girl. She looked dead, but Bear's actions suddenly made me doubt my assumptions. Even though it was against all crime scene investigative rules, I carefully lowered myself into the pit and put my fingers to the small neck.

I jumped when I felt a weak, thready pulse. "She's alive. See if meds have left the church yet. Get 'em over here!"

Mali shouted and pumped her fist into the air. "Yes! Yes!"

I really liked this woman's enthusiasm. Anybody who didn't feel they had to act a certain way to be accepted by other cops was okay in my book. She keyed the mic clipped onto her shoulder lapel, requested meds and gave our location.

Smiling, Buck got down on his knees and pulled Bear into a big hug. Then he took a pull toy out of a bag strapped to his leg and rewarded the big boy with his favorite ball, throwing it as far as he could and watching as Bear streaked into the desert to retrieve it.

I wanted to pick Misty up and run with her to the church, but I forced myself to stay calm. I took hold of her hand, which felt deathly cold. Belatedly realizing the child must be half-frozen, I pulled off my coat and covered her with it. Who knew how long she'd been out here? The temperatures at night dropped close to freezing and Veronica and her husband hadn't given her any type of blanket or covering. They'd basically buried a six-year-old child alive.

Kate, Father Riggers and one of the paramedics came running from the church.

I climbed out of the pit so the medic would have room to work.

I glanced at Kate. "Casey?"

"She's on the way to the hospital." She indicated the paramedic in the pit and the one pulling the medic truck around to our location with a flick of her hand. "These two stayed behind to check me out." Her skin had a ghostly pallor that worried me and, although I knew she was trying not to be obvious about it, she was leaning against the trunk of the tree to steady herself. She'd run a hundred yards with a possible broken nose and concussion, and still stood at the edge of the pit anxiously waiting to hear the verdict on the little girl.

I wondered how badly she'd been hurt and moved to where I could put my hand on her elbow. "Let me take you home, Boss. You're not lookin' so good."

She chuckled, "Yeah, I don't bounce as well as I used to. But no, once the girl is stabilized and on the way, we need to get to the hospital to wait until Casey's out of the woods." She fished her keys out of her pocket. "But I'll at least let you drive. I have a splitting headache."

"And Hoffelder?"

The medic in the pit spoke while working on the child. "Severely depressed skull fracture. I doubt she'll regain consciousness."

"Good."

The woman looked up at me from the pit, hesitated a moment and then nodded.

I had no doubt any of us wished Sandy Hoffelder well.

While we waited, I knelt and pulled Bear into a big hug. "Thank you, you big, magnificent beast." His tail thumped against the hard-packed ground and he responded with a wet tongue across my cheek. I looked up at Buck. "And thank you, too."

He pointed down into the pit. "This makes all the training and extra work worth every second. I hope we got to her in time."

Kate looked at us out of her one good eye. "We never would have gotten to her at all if it weren't for you and Bear. Good work, Buck."

He and Kate had known and worked with each other for well over twenty years, but I still saw the flush of pride most people get at one of Kate's rare compliments. He nodded, gathered up his leash and took Bear back to his patrol car. Since the K9 unit normally works nights, he was either headed home and then back to bed or, more likely, to the hospital to await word on Casey.

The second medic maneuvered the van close enough for them to stabilize Misty, load her up and get her off to the hospital.

I pulled out my cellphone and called the clinic where the real Delores Mefisto was being held to let her know we'd found her little girl. She didn't say much, well, actually, she couldn't say much because she'd begun sobbing uncontrollably. I had her hand the phone to the charge nurse and I explained the whole situation to the woman and finished by asking her to arrange transportation to the hospital.

With that out of the way, I drove Kate to Banner hospital where Casey had been taken into surgery. I called Megan to let her know what was happening, and then sat with Kate and dozens of other cops waiting for her to get out of surgery.

CHAPTER 8

At about seven that evening, the chief, who'd spoken to the surgeon, came into the waiting room to let everyone know Casey had come through the surgery like a champ.

Shortly after that, our friend, Maddie, an E.R. nurse, had convinced Kate to keep an ice pack on her eye and to my surprise, had gotten her to take a pretty strong pain killer. Maddie had also scrounged up a bed for her, which we put in Casey's room, and now, at eleven P.M, Kate was sleeping as soundly as Casey.

Terri slept in her own armchair on the other side of the bed, and Megan and I dozed together in an oversized bed-chair waiting for Casey to wake up.

Well, Megan dozed. The problem of connecting Pito's death decisively to Sandy Hoffelder ate at me. If I couldn't make the connection, Dempsey would twist his "facts" to point directly to Gia, and I couldn't allow that to happen.

I elbowed Megan. "Hey."

She elbowed me back. "I'm sleeping."

"Well wake up. I want to run something past you."

She rolled to the side, squishing her butt up against my hip.

I elbowed her in the kidney this time. "Get your butt off my leg. This chair isn't big enough for you to fetal up on me."

"Ow. Stop it, Alex." She rolled onto her back and punched me in the arm.

"Okay, I'm glad you're awake. I can't figure out why Sandy would kill Pito, but I know she did. Everything else surrounding his death is too much of a coincidence. And, why did she and Glenn think they needed to silence Cherry and Tom?"

She'd settled in again. Her eyes were closed, but I knew she was listening when she mumbled, "Who's Glenn?"

"Victoria's husband."

"Which one's Victoria?"

"The vet tech who let Glenn into the vet's office to get stitched up after the door had been locked. So why would Sandy and Glenn want to silence Cherry and Tom?

Megan sighed, semi-sat up and plopped her chin on her fist. "You don't know if they did."

"Everything points that way. Ruthanne said Glenn had a stitched-up knife wound in his belly. There were boot prints at the camper that matched the pattern on Glenn's boots and shoe prints about the size of Sandy's feet."

She shrugged. "Well, maybe they thought Tom and Cherry had seen them dump the body. You said they were the first ones to find it, right?"

"Yeah, but that still doesn't connect them to Pito. And why was Pito wearing the old man's coat? And why did I find Gia's prize bottle of Scotch in his apartment?" I pushed out of the chair, checked to make sure Casey and Kate were both okay, and then headed out to the nurse's station.

"Hey, wait up. Where are we going?" Megan came padding out after me in her stocking feet.

"Sandy's on this floor somewhere. I want to go see her."

"I thought the priest used Jesus to bash her head in."

"He didn't use Jesus. He used one of the thieves."

Megan shrugged "Whatever." She walked up to one of the night shift nurses and said, "Excuse me. Do you know where the baby burner is?"

The nurse raised her brows and I saw the wall coming up. With a decidedly cold tone, she asked, "Are you family?"

Before Megan could shut down the woman's help button even more, I pulled out my badge. "I'm one of the officers on the case. Casey Bowman, in room 234, is my partner."

The woman turned suspicious eyes on Megan. "And you are?"

Megan jabbed a thumb in my direction. "I'm with her."

All the nurses I've ever known have perfected the art of the narrowed eyes. They can convey suspicion, amusement, disdain, tyranny, and incredulity with that one look. I assumed they learned it in nursing school, because they all possessed that very handy skill. This one turned "the look" on Megan, who, true to form, remained blissfully unaware.

When the nurse returned her attention to me, I rolled my eyes. "She's harmless. I'll keep an eye on her."

That must have smoothed her ruffled feathers because she pointed down the hall. "Go down this hallway, turn left, go through the double doors and *Ms. Hoffelder*," she emphasized the name while glaring down at Megan, "is in room 248."

Even though Hoffelder would probably never come out of her comma, a guard had been stationed outside her door. He stood when we walked up and I saw it was Arnold Keswick, one of my friends from Team Two.

"Hey, Alex. How's Casey?"

I shrugged. "She'll be down for a while," I smiled, "but never out."

"Thank God for that."

I stepped past him and walked over to Hoffelder's bed. She'd had surgery, apparently, to relieve the swelling on her brain. A ventilator tube snaked into her mouth, and I hoped she'd wake up long enough to choke on it. "This is what monsters look like."

Megan stepped up beside me. "I guess this means she'll never really go to prison. That's too bad. I can think of all kinds of tortures I'd wish on her if she did."

I turned to look at Megan, wishing she never had to experience anything that happened in my work, but she quite often did. It had become habit, especially with my more complicated cases, to bounce things off her. Even though she seems so innocent, there's a brilliant mind behind that veneer. What I loved about her was that it wasn't a façade, her innocence.

When I chuckled, she said, "What?"

"Sometimes I wonder if you're schizophrenic. One person one minute, and the complete opposite the next." I glanced around the room to see what items Sandy came in with. "Hey, Arnold. Where's her personal stuff?"

He stuck his head around the door. "In the closet. The homicide dicks said they already went through her stuff and took everything they needed. Everything else can stay with her."

The closet was on the other side of the bed, so I stepped around the heart monitor and ventilator and opened the door. The space was only about two feet wide, but it stretched from floor-to-ceiling. They'd put her belongings into a brown paper bag, which I pulled out and emptied onto the long bed table.

There wasn't much. Homicide had taken all her clothing. They'd left the book she'd been reading the first time we'd met. I pulled it out and read the blurb, "In this twisted psychological thriller, prolific writer Joyce Carol Oates has crafted yet another story where the evils of paranoia and the people we surround ourselves with are more terrifying than any creature that goes bump in the night."

Something bulged between the pages, but before I could see what it was, Megan moved to look over my shoulder. "What book's that? Sounds like it could have been written about this whack job." When she took it from me and turned it over to see the title, a black, beaded bookmark fell onto the floor. "Oops, sorry."

She bent down to retrieve it and, probably a little too loudly, I shouted, "Leave it!"

She whipped her hand back like she'd been burned.

"Fuck." I ran my hand through my hair, irritated that only Megan could testify that I hadn't slipped the bookmark into Hoffelder's things, and nobody would trust her to be impartial when it came to anything to do with me.

Arnold, who'd apparently been standing in the doorway, walked over to us. "What's the matter?"

My heart leapt when I realized I might have a more credible witness than Megan. "What did you just see happen?"

He blinked and pointed to the beads. "That fell out of the book."

"No, start from when you first looked in the room. What did you see?"

"Well, you went to the bed, then you pulled the bag out of the closet and then you reached in and..."

"Was I holding anything when I reached into the bag?"

He shook his head, "No. You pulled out the book and read the back. Your friend here took it from you and those fell out."

I breathed a sigh of relief. "I need you to write a report detailing everything you just told me. Put it under the case number for Agapito Mancini's murder."

He nodded. Writing reports was something patrol officers did many times over the course of the day and I knew he didn't think it unusual that I'd told him to document our visit. "Leave the beads there for right now, okay?"

"Sure thing."

I left the beads on the floor and stepped out into the hallway to call Sergeant Logan. I knew they had several scenes to process and even though it was coming on midnight, he'd still be on awake and on duty. When he answered, I said, "Sarge, this is Alex Wolfe. Has Kate kept you up to date on Pito's case?"

"Yeah, why?"

"Do you know about the black beads we found in the dumpster and in Tom Handy's camper?"

"Yes."

"Do your people know about them?"

"What's this about, Alex?"

"Can you tell me who went through Sandy Hoffelder's belongings?"

"Dempsey. Why?"

"Why? I'm still trying to connect the dots between Sandy Hoffelder and Pito's murder. I'm at the hospital with Casey, so while I'm here I thought I'd come over to check on Hoffelder. Do you know what I found in the belongings that Dempsey sent with her to the hospital? The ones Arnold Keswick was told she'd be allowed to keep?"

His silence gave me a pretty good idea he knew what I was going to say. "Inside a book that I saw her with when I first met her at the homeless camp was a black, beaded bookmark. One that would be impossible to miss."

He blew out his breath. "What are you saying, Alex?"

"I'm not saying anything. Arnold Keswick was watching me the whole time I've been in the room. I'm having him write up what he saw me do so no one—"

He sounded both resigned and irritated. "I got it, Alex. So, no one like Dempsey can say you planted them."

"Yup."

"Where are they now?"

"I left them on the floor where they dropped out of the book."

"Put Keswick on the phone."

I handed Arnold my cell and listened to him "Uh huh," and "Yes, Sir," and "You got it," before giving me back the phone and digging the keys to his patrol car out of his pocket. "Is there any chance you could run down to my car and bring me an evidence bag and a property sheet? It's in the police parking on level two in the covered garage."

On the way to Keswick's car, I thought about Dempsey concealing the fact that those beads were in the book. They weren't a silver bullet or anything. They didn't conclusively link Sandy to Pito in the dumpster. They did link her to Tom Handy, who'd taken the beads from the scene, however. They were one more piece of the puzzle that Dempsey should have collected. That is, if he wanted the truth about what really happened to Pito to come out. The beads were an inconvenient piece to the puzzle he was trying to construct out of thin air, pinning Pito's murder on Gia.

I grabbed the stuff Arnold wanted, brought it back to the room and then left him to collect the evidence. Properly this time.

Megan and I headed back to Casey's room where I was finally able to get to sleep knowing the pieces were finally going to start falling into place. It was just the way things worked in my life once the picture inside the puzzle began taking shape.

CHAPTER 9

Casey woke up the next morning not having a clue how she got to the hospital. She remembered the priest, but that was about it. We ate breakfast with her and then Megan had to get to work.

Kate's silence when I filled her in on the beads didn't bode well for Dempsey. It would be nearly impossible to prove he'd concealed evidence on purpose, but nobody wants to be in Kate's line of sight, particularly when she's pissed. Nobody. Kate left for the office, and I told her I wanted to go thank Kelly for all her help and I'd meet her there after I'd finished.

When I left, I met Father Riggers at the elevators on his way to visit Casey. We talked for a bit and then I drove to the main library downtown. A young man at the front desk told me Kelly was on the second floor helping a woman find a book.

She saw me and waved and then held up a finger, asking me to wait.

There were some private study rooms near the stairs and I went inside and waited for her to finish up.

"Hi, Alex. Did that information help?" Her bright yellow slacks seemed to enter the room before she did and I hid a smile at her usual, vibrant wardrobe.

The enormity of what she'd discovered hit me, and I said quietly,

"You literally saved my partner's life, Kelly." My throat closed and without warning, the tears came. I was barely able to tamp my emotions back down before Kelly saw them.

Apparently, I hadn't done such a great job because Kelly pulled a tissue out of her pocket and handed it to me. In some kind of sympathetic reaction, she became emotional too and I couldn't help but laugh at the absurdity of us sitting in a library study room wiping away our tears.

When we both had ourselves under control again, Kelly said, "Tell me what happened."

I shook my head. "It's a long story, but when we're all finished with the case, you have an open invitation to come to my house where we'll eat pizza and drink wine coolers and talk all about it. Right now, I have to somehow link Sandy Hoffelder with the first murder victim in the dumpster."

"Can I help?"

"If I think you can, I'll definitely call."

"Is there any possible connection? Did they know the same people, or have they ever lived in the same area? Sandy Hoffelder and Delores Mefisto both grew up in Evanston. For that matter, so did Sandy's sister, Veronica before she disappeared."

"No, no connection." I was embarrassed to admit I didn't have a clue where Evanston was, but since I was already grasping at straws, I swallowed my pride. "Where is Evanston, anyway?"

"It's in Illinois."

I can't say something actually clicked when she said that. It was more like a clunk, actually. But I couldn't put my finger on where the clunk had come from.

Kelly's head cocked to the side. "Where's your murder victim from?"

"Here. He lived here."

"Do you know where he grew up?"

I remember my friend, Chuck, who'd investigated organized crime for the last fifteen years, telling me a long time ago that Tancredo Angelino had left Chicago after his son was killed. I shrugged, "Maybe Chicago?"

She smiled slightly, "Maybe you should confirm that."

"Why?"

"Evanston is right outside of Chicago."

I know I blushed at my geographic ignorance as I pulled out my phone and called Gia. The answering machine picked up, which I thought strange until I remembered Kate suggesting a trip to the country might be a good idea. I flipped through my contact list and found Gabe's cell number.

Gabe picked up on the first ring. "Yeah?"

"Gabe, it's Alex. Do you know where Pito grew up?"

"Chicago."

"Right in the middle of Chicago, or..?"

"Place north, called Evanston. Why?"

"Did you grow up there, too?"

"We all did. Everybody in the same neighborhood. Kind of a family thing. Well, everybody except the boss. He lived in the swankier part of town. Why?"

"Because the person who killed him lived in Evanston, too. I'm trying to find a connection."

"Who?"

I hesitated, wanting to think things through before giving Gabe that kind of information. It wasn't like he could come into town and kill her. She was pretty much already dead. And would I really mind if he did? I gave myself a mental slap on the head and told myself, of course I'd mind. That would be a bad thing after all. Bad. "Her name is Hoffelder. Sandy Hoffelder."

"The baby burner? We went to school with her. Pito, me, everybody. She was a whack job then, too."

I let that percolate a moment.

Gabe said, "So ya think she's the one that whacked Pito?"

"I do, but she had her brains caved in by a priest with a crucifix."

He didn't say anything, and then the Italian, Catholic altar boy kicked in. "That ain't funny, Alex."

"It's true. A Roman Catholic priest saved me and Kate and Casey by caving Sandy's head in with a crucifix." I could practically hear him crossing himself.

"I need to talk to Ms. A."

"Sure, thanks for the info."

Before I could hang up, he said, "Oh, I almost forgot. I know who Pito was shackin' up with. You care? Wanna talk to him?"

I sat forward and practically yelled into the phone. "Hell, yes! When were you planning to give me this little tidbit of information?"

"I wasn't."

"So why are you?"

"Cuz Ms. A. said I should let you talk to him before...uh...before I do."

That didn't sound good. I pulled out my notebook and Kelly dug a pen out of her pocket and handed it to me. "What's his name? Do you know where I can find him?"

"Tony Giovanni. An' he's sweatin' bullets in the back of the Land Rover."

"Uh, why is he in the back of the Land Rover?"

"'Cuz of a camel colored coat and some whiskey."

Uh oh. "Where can I meet you?"

"You know the place Ms. A met you and the sarge?"

"Yeah."

"I'll be there in fifteen." He hung up.

I sat there a minute staring at Kelly, not really sure how to handle Gabe's little pronouncement.

"Well?"

I blinked back into the present. "Um, well, we definitely have a connection. Apparently they all went to school together in Evanston. You did it again, Kelly. You need to apply to become an investigator. You're a better detective than a lot of the jamokes on the department."

She beamed with pleasure. "I'm definitely going to hold you to that pizza night, Alex. Pepperoni, onions, the whole works. And beer. Stella Artois. Or Guinness. Or both! I can hardly wait."

I left her with a silly grin plastered across her face and drove to a dead-end road on the west side of Tucson. When I crested the hill, I saw Gabe leaning against the Land Rover, arms crossed and waiting. I pulled up next to him and got out. "I hope you haven't done anything to him. He might be the best witness I have to prove Gia didn't order the hit on Pito."

A dimple appeared in his cheek and he slowly shook his head as he stepped to the back door and pulled it open. He hadn't been kidding when he said the guy was sweating bullets. And, lo and behold, it turned out to be our burglar from Pito's apartment.

"Well, well, well. Look who we have here. Mr. Giovanni, is it?"

He shot Gabe a terrified look, and then obediently nodded.

I stepped back and motioned to my car. "We need to chat."

He hustled out of the back seat and practically ran to my car.

When he opened the front passenger door, I stopped him. "Uh uh. Back seat."

He nodded and quickly switched to the back.

I turned to Gabe. "You're not getting him back tonight. He's both a witness and a burglary suspect. But thanks for giving him to me."

He snorted. "Thank Ms. A. If it was up to me—"

I held up my hand to shut him up. "I don't want to know."

The dimple reappeared and then he was gone.

I got into the car, flipped on my recorder, read Giovanni his rights and said, "I want to make sure you'll be giving us this information willingly and that you're not under any type of duress to give us said information. Is that correct?"

He nervously looked over his shoulder in the direction Gabe had gone. "Yeah. I just wanna get this over with and then you'll put me in jail, right?"

I drove Giovanni back to the station where I proudly paraded him in front of Kate's cubicle on the way to the interview rooms in the back of the bullpens.

Without me having to say a word, she followed and sat in on the interview.

I turned on the recorder and once again gave all the preliminary information. "Mr. Giovanni." I started in and then stopped, turning an innocent look on Kate. "Mr. Giovanni, what size shoe do you wear?"

He looked down at his oxfords. "Sixteen."

I looked triumphantly over at Kate who was rubbing her good eye with her fingers and slightly shaking her head.

I went ahead and continued the interview. "You and Agapito Mancini lived together, is that correct?"

"Yeah."

"What can you tell me about the night Mr. Mancini was murdered?"

"Me and him, we was goin' to th' Backdoor—"

"The Backdoor is a gay bar, correct?"

"Yeah. On the way there, we seen this broad. Real ugly. He stops the car, rolls down his window an' takes a good, long gander. The broad, she stares right back. Pito does one of these..." Giovanni pretends his hand is a gun, "an' when he does, she cocks her head and grins, evil like. Gave me the willies. Anyway, we drive to the Backdoor, an' Pito says, 'You know who that was?' and I says, 'nobody I wanna know,'' an' he says, 'Ever heard 'a th' baby burner?' an' I says, 'nah, she's in hole, ain't never comin' out,' and he says, 'that's her. I know it. I know her, I did her once. That's her all right.'"

When Giovanni stopped talking, Kate asked, "Did Mr. Mancini ever see her again?"

He shrugged. "That's th' thing. The guy she was with, he come in the Backdoor an' comes over and starts givin' Pito shit about how he didn't see nothin' if he knows what's good for him. Now, if you know Pito, he don't take shit from nobody. He shoved the guy an' Gus, the bartender, he makes 'em take it outside."

I interrupted, "Did you go with him?"

"Nah, Pito can take care of himself. Only... only this time, he didn't, did he? He never came back in an' I had t' take a fuckin' Uber back to the apartment." His overwhelming grief was touching.

Kate sat back. "So why did you have to break into the apartment if you and Mr. Mancini were both living there?"

"Pito drove, didn't he? He had th' fuckin' keys. Th' asshole."

"And why did you run when Detective Wolfe and I showed up?"

"'Cuz you're fuckin' cops. Whaddya think?"

CHAPTER 10

A month later, Kate, Casey, Teri, Megan and I all rose to our feet as the entire auditorium gave Kelly and Father Riggers a standing ovation. I'd never seen such a happy, proud and excited look on Kelly's face as I saw that moment as she stood on stage wearing the two medals that his honor the mayor and Chief Sepe had placed around her neck.

Apparently the good Father had received many medals during his time in the Royal Fusiliers and this wasn't quite the life affirming honor to him as it was for her.

Everyone from the library had come to honor her and Gia had anonymously paid for most of Kelly's family to fly in from various locations around the country.

I thought about Pito, and how he'd tried to make my life miserable even in death. I smiled as I watched Kelly being surrounded by her family and friends and thought, "Not this time, Agapito Asshole Mancini, not this time, and not ever again."

ABOUT THE AUTHOR

"If you don't like to read, you haven't found the right book." – J. K. Rowling

Alison, who grew up listening to her parents reading her the most wonderful books full of adventure, heroes, ducks and puppy dogs, promotes reading wherever she goes and believes literacy is the key to changing the world for the better.

In her writing, she follows Heinlein's Rules, the first rule being *You Must Write*. To that end, she writes in several genres simply because she enjoys the great variety of characters and settings her over-active fantasy life creates. There's nothing better for her then when a character looks over their shoulder, crooks a finger for her to follow and heads off on an adventure. From medieval castles to a horse farm in Virginia to the police beat in Tucson, Arizona, her characters live exciting lives and she's happy enough to follow them around and report on what she sees.

She has published nine fiction novels and one screenplay. Her first novel, The Door at the Top of the Stairs, is a psychological suspense, which she's also adapted as a screenplay. The Screenplay advanced to the Second Round of the Austin Film Festival Screenplay & Teleplay

Competition, making it to the top 15% of the 6,764 entries. The screenplay also made the quarter finalist list in the Cynosure Screenwriting awards.

Alison's previous life as a cop gave her a bizarre sense of humor, a realistic look at life, and an insatiable desire to live life to the fullest. She loves all horses & hounds and some humans...

For more information:
https://alisonholtbooks.com

ALSO BY ALISON NAOMI HOLT

Mystery

Credo's Hope - Alex Wolfe Mysteries Book 1

Credo's Legacy – Alex Wolfe Mysteries Book 2

Credo's Fire – Alex Wolfe Mysteries Book 3

Credo's Bones - Alex Wolfe Mysteries Book 4

Credo's Betrayal - Alex Wolfe Mysteries Book 5

Credo's Honor - Alex Wolfe Mysteries Book 6

Fantasy Fiction

The Spirit Child – The Seven Realms of Ar'rothi Book 1

Duchess Rising – The Seven Realms of Ar'rothi Book 2

Duchess Rampant - The Seven Realms of Ar'rothi Book 3

Spyder's Web - The Seven Realms of Ar'rothi Book 4

Mage of Merigor

Psychological Thriller

The Door at the Top of the Stairs

Credo's Betrayal Written by Alison Naomi Holt

Published by Alison Naomi Holt

Copyright © 2020 Alison Naomi Holt

All rights reserved. No part of this publication may be reproduced, stored in a retrieval system, or transmitted in any form or by any means, electronic, mechanical, recording or otherwise, without the prior written permission of the author.

This ebook is licensed for your personal enjoyment only. This ebook may not be re-sold or given away to other people.

The characters and events in this book are fictitious. Any similarity to real persons, living or dead, is coincidental and not intended by the author.

For more information about the author and her other books visit: http://www.Alisonholtbooks.com

Made in the USA
Monee, IL
05 April 2021